Wolverine Bros.
Freight & Storage

Also by Steve Ulfelder

Purgatory Chasm
The Whole Lie
Shotgun Lullaby

Wolverine Bros. Freight & Storage

STEVE ULFELDER

Minotaur Books

A Thomas Dunne Book

New York

A THOMAS DUNNE BOOK FOR MINOTAUR BOOKS.
An imprint of St. Martin's Publishing Company.

WOLVERINE BROS. FREIGHT & STORAGE. Copyright © 2014 by Steve Ulfelder. All rights reserved. Printed in the United States of America. For information, address St. Martin's Press, 175 Fifth Avenue, New York, N.Y. 10010.

www.thomasdunnebooks.com
www.minotaurbooks.com

Library of Congress Cataloging-in-Publication Data

Ulfelder, Steve.
    Wolverine Bros. freight & storage : a Conway Sax mystery / Steve Ulfelder. —
First edition.
        p. cm.
    "A Thomas Dunne book."
    ISBN 978-1-250-02810-5 (hardcover)
    ISBN 978-1-250-02811-2 (e-book)
    1. Automobile mechanics—Fiction.   2. Murder—Investigation—Fiction.
3. Kidnapping—Fiction.   4. Alcoholics—Fiction.   5. Mystery fiction.
I. Title.   II. Title: Wolverine Bros. freight and storage.
    PS3621.L435W65 2014
    813'.6—dc23
                                                                    2014003834

Minotaur books may be purchased for educational, business, or promotional use. For information on bulk purchases, please contact Macmillan Corporate and Premium Sales Department at 1-800-221-7945, extension 5442, or write specialmarkets@macmillan.com.

First Edition: May 2014

10 9 8 7 6 5 4 3 2 1

For Jenny, Dave, and Abby. Farkles forever!

ACKNOWLEDGMENTS

In writing this book, I often turned to friends for specialized knowledge. Author Tammy Kaehler offered advice on demographics and geography in Southern California. College chum and artist John S. Webster filled me in on surfing lingo. Andy Bettencourt educated me on firearms, while friends Nick Barbara and David McClanahan, both longtime federal law-enforcement agents, shared their expertise graciously. Teresa Stanton assisted me with conversational Brazilian Portuguese.

Credit for any accuracy and authenticity in these fields goes to the folks named. Blame for mistakes falls on my shoulders alone.

I'm grateful as ever to my literary agent, Janet Reid; to my editor, Anne Brewer; and to my wife, Martha Ulfelder.

Finally, I tip my cap to the late James Crumley, author of *The Last Good Kiss*. Because without an alcoholic bulldog named Fireball Roberts, there wouldn't have been greyhounds named Cha Cha Muldowney and Dandy Dick Landy.

Wolverine Bros.
Freight & Storage

CHAPTER ONE

You can't even count on a jack handle anymore.

This one came from the spare-tire well of my rented Chevy Tahoe. A two-ton SUV like that, you'd expect something stout. Something that could take or dish out a little punishment.

This handle was junk, pot metal with an outside diameter of a half inch at best. I wanted to, I could've bent it no sweat.

But it was what I had.

All I had.

And I knew that right now, Kenny Spoon was in the cinder-block building across the way. And I'd been in Los Angeles damn near a week, and it was my first taste of solid info.

So far, I wasn't too impressed with California. It'd rained three days running, which the locals said was about right for February. Things cost a fortune, even compared to Massachusetts. And the freeways were everywhere. Half the time, they cut right through neighborhoods that would've been damn nice otherwise.

This was not one of those neighborhoods.

This neighborhood—or town, or suburb, or whatever—was Van Nuys. In a place everybody called the Valley with a sneer on their lips.

The one-story building had once been painted turquoise but was now mostly graffiti covered. It was half garage and half headquarters for a lowrider crew called Los Bajamaros. To the right from my vantage point, the HQ was jammed against I-405, which the locals called *the* 405 or sometimes the San Diego Freeway.

A fenced area that tied into the building was filled with sweet old cars, everything from donor chassis to show-quality lowriders with fifteen-thousand-dollar paint jobs. They were all GMs, mostly Chevys. A few were from the fifties, a few from the seventies. The rest were Impalas and Biscaynes from the sixties.

Carwise, you had to hand it to California.

You're stalling.

Yeah. I was.

Knock it off.

Yup. I opened my Tahoe's door to confirm the *bing-bing-bing* that meant the keys were in the ignition. It had been a tough call: Pocket the keys and fumble for them while crossing the street on my way back, maybe half-dragging Kenny Spoon, maybe with a couple of pissed-off Bajamaros in pursuit? Or leave them in the ignition and risk running out to a hole where my stolen SUV used to be?

I'd gone with the *bing-bing-bing*. It was quarter of five on a Sunday morning, and the neighborhood was asleep except for freeway hum.

Quit stalling.

I breathed deep three times, regripped my pot-metal tire iron, looked both ways, trotted across the road. Got a hand on the front door handle, tugged just enough to make sure the dead bolt wasn't thrown, paused, took another pair of deep breaths, pulled hard, stepped into . . .

. . . one hell of a dark room, filled with the prettiest guitar sounds you ever heard.

Man, it was dark. I had to blink like crazy to get my eyes working, even though the morning outside was gray and new, with a three-day rain just letting up.

Feeling exposed and paranoid, I half-ducked and scanned the big room.

It was obviously a former bar. Posters for Corona Beer and bikini contests and car shows had been masking-taped across a pair of good-sized windows that ran along a side wall. That accounted for the dimness.

The bar, a squared-off U whose bottom faced me, dominated. Other than that, call it a typical dude clubhouse. Hand-me-down sofas and tables that people left behind when they moved. Overflowing black plastic ashtrays, the kind you used to see everywhere but didn't anymore. Pool table, its felt stained with who knew what, two bent cues dumped atop.

Underneath it all, thirty years' worth of stale-beer stench.

I nearly missed the man on my first scan, either because he was so still or because I was rusty. Or both.

He wasn't more than eight feet away, to my right, the last place my eyes fell during the scan. He could've shot or stabbed me while I blinked and had my look around.

Although he didn't look like the shooting or stabbing type. Looked more like he had all the shooters and stabbers he needed on speed dial.

He was a boy-sized man, and the giant armchair he sat in, mint green, made him seem even smaller. His fingernails were manicured. He wore a greased pompadour straight out of 1956 and a mustache and beard trimmed as carefully as a Chinaman's in any kung fu movie. His eyes were calm, but not in a reassuring way.

We stared at each other.

"That guitar," I finally said. "Pretty."

"More than pretty," he said with no accent I could make out. "Transcendent."

"You're Lobo Soto."

"Yes."

"Any more Bajamaros here?"

"No."

"I came for Kenny Spoon."

"Yes."

"Where is he?"

"Booth Three," the little man said, nodding at a hall just to the right of the bar, the hall you'd expect to lead to bathrooms and a pay phone.

"Stand up."

He did. Moccasins, narrow chinos, short-sleeve button-down with vertical stripes.

"Turn around."

He did. He was carrying no gun.

"Move away from the chair."

He did. I stepped to it and felt around while keeping my eyes on the little man.

There was no weapon stuffed behind the chair's cushion.

"Give me your phone," I said.

He did, then watched me boot-stomp it. His eyes never changed. They never showed any anger. They were patient eyes. They measured me.

Which worried me more than a lot of brave and useless talk would have.

I gestured at him to sit.

What else was I supposed to do? On TV, the cop slugs the bad guy just hard enough to knock him out for a few minutes. Try that in real life, you either break all your knuckles or kill a man.

One song ended and another began.

"Booth Three," the little man said. And leaned back in his giant chair and closed his eyes.

I put my back to him, not liking it.

In the hall, far from what little light the poster-covered windows allowed, it was dark as hell. I eased past reeking men's and ladies' rooms, sliding my boots to avoid tripping on the random junk that covered the floor. Old desktop computers, stacks of car magazines. Like that.

What the hell is Booth Three?

As my eyes came up to speed, I saw the hallway was longer—that is, the building was deeper—than it looked from out front.

I passed a presswood door on my left. Stick-on letters read BOOTH ONE. Then there was something that surprised me: a massive pane of reinforced glass, four feet wide by four feet tall, with an intercom about shoulder height.

I squinted through the glass, saw a mattress atop an old box spring. That's when I figured out what this place was, or used to be.

I'll never claim to be a prince. Back when I was drinking, I ended up in a lot of ugly places. Still, I can truly say I'd never been in a place like *this* before.

This was a jackoff parlor. Once upon a time, pre-Internet, men paid their money out front, then came down the hall and looked at a girl in a booth and told her what to do and did what they needed to do.

The realization made my skin contract. I all of a sudden wanted a shower.

Focus. Booth Three.

A few long strides took me past Booth Two. I stumbled over a stack of old pizza boxes—judging from the flies, they still held a few slices—and pulled up in front of Booth Three.

And looked through.

He looked back at me.

If not for the eyes, I wouldn't have recognized Kenny Spoon.

They were blue going on purple. Just like his mother's.

Like Eudora's.

She said they were the only feature of hers that ever was worth a damn, called them her Liz Taylor eyes. Said Kenny's were the same.

She'd been right. His were bloodshot and puffed mostly shut and mostly dead, but even from here, even by the light of a two-inch candle on his crappy nightstand, I could make out those blue-going-on-purple eyes.

I took in the rest of him.

"Hell," I said.

And shouldered into the room.

CHAPTER TWO

He sat on a wretched sheetless mattress, reading a comic book. Archie and Jughead.

I knew him to be nearly forty, but his blond hair was a kindergartner's bowl cut.

He was naked.

On the table, next to the candle: a three-quarters-empty bottle of White Horse Scotch.

I don't know if it was Hollywood acting chops or booze bleariness, but the only move Kenny Spoon made when I plowed through the door was to slowly set his comic book over his privates. He looked at me, a slow take, head to boots, taking his sweet time. Then he did it again, boots to cowlick.

"You look," he finally said, "like a very specific fantasy I used to have. Back when I had fantasies."

Then he laughed.

It was an ugly, soulless laugh, the laugh of a man who'd been busted up inside for a long time.

"We've got to go," I said, ignoring the way my heart had dropped in my chest, thinking practically instead. Thinking, truth be told, about the calm and tiny man up front. "Grab your gear."

He spread his arms like Jesus Christ, flipping away the comic book as he did it. "There is no gear, darling. I am just as you see me. Nudity, it turns out, is a surprisingly effective form of imprisonment."

"Let's go."

"But I *like* it here, dear heart. Booth Three is palatial compared with my former home, Booth Two. They moved me over when the cockroaches grew too fierce."

"I mean it. Come on."

His face fell into a pout. He folded skinny arms across a sunken, three-hairs chest. "By whom, exactly, am I being rescued?"

"Let's *go*, Kenny."

More pout. More crossed arms. "I demand information, O strapping one. Who exactly *are* you?"

"Conway Sax. Friend of your mother's. From AA. The Barnburners. Ring a bell?"

He squinted. "A muffled one. But then, these days they're all muffled. Swaddled, even."

I must have cut a glance at the Scotch, because he half-laughed, patted the bottle like a dog's head, and said, "Precisely. This stuff is God's own swaddler."

"We need to leave *now*."

"How do I know this isn't a frying-pan-to-fire situation? And why, for heaven's sake, did Mother send you?"

"You know why."

"Actually, I don't."

The response carried an honest vibe that made me hesitate. "She called you," I said. "She told you what's going on, why she needs you back home."

"She did not, sir." He folded his arms, and I'm damned if I didn't believe him.

But it was time to go.

I sighed. Flipped the jack handle into my left hand. Strode to the bed, got my right arm around Kenny Spoon's waist and my hand across the clammy small of his back. Bent my knees, lifted until he jackknifed over my right shoulder. Adjusted my grip to lock him against me with my arm pressed across the backs of his calves.

Tried to ignore his naked ass next to my face.

He wasn't a happy rescuee. He flailed and squealed and hit me with soft little fists. As I turned to get the hell out, I felt him put a little extra effort into the flailing.

Then he relaxed.

I giant-stepped up the hall. Cleared the bathrooms. Tensed as I neared the doorway to the big room. It was a choke point—my buddy Randall had taught me how vulnerable you were in spots like that. I had a still-slightly-squirming naked man over one shoulder, and nothing but a lightweight jack handle for a weapon.

Hell.

I took a fast step through the doorway and spun to my right so fast Kenny thumped his head on the wall behind me.

"Ow," he said as I lifted the jack handle, ready for a threat to my right.

"Sorry," I said, feeling dumb because there was nothing there.

"Bravo," Lobo Soto said, laughter in his voice.

I spun again to face him, taking care not to rap the other side of Kenny's head.

He still sat in the giant green chair.

The guitar music had ended.

"You must be so proud," Soto said. "You must feel so smug."

I said nothing.

Kenny, whose nose was pressed against my right kidney, said, "Conway Sax, you would be well advised to kill this man."

Soto and I ignored him.

"While you walked down Come Stain Alley to make your rescue," Soto said, "I passed the time thinking about how many weapons I could lay my hands on. Weapons in this room, weapons I could use to kill you before you so much as knew I'd followed you down the hall."

"Because if you fail to kill him," Kenny said to me, "he will certainly kill you."

Soto and I ignored him some more.

"For demonstration purposes only," Soto said. He slipped the toe of a moccasin beneath the skirt of his chair, twisted his foot in a way that looked awkward, and slid out a black .45. Smiling, he pushed it toward me like a geezer playing shuffleboard.

The gun stopped when it hit my boot. I guess Kenny could see it, because he said, "I rest my case."

"You're braver than you are smart," Soto said.

"Yup," I said. "And I'm not that brave."

I stooped to pick up the .45. Crammed it in my jeans pocket as best I could without dropping Kenny or the jack handle. Stepped toward the front door.

Stopped. Turned. "Why?"

The little man knew what I meant: Why was I still alive?

He held up three fingers. "One, Bajamaros don't shit where we eat." He folded away one finger. "Two, our fee for babysitting little Kenny has been received in full. We find him tiresome, as you soon will yourself. You're actually doing us a favor." He folded away another finger.

And said nothing.

"What's three?" I said.

"Three," Lobo Soto said, "is how many carloads of guys are outside."

He slipped a phone from his pocket.

A different phone.

A phone I might've found if I'd done a better job searching him.

Hell. Not much I could do about all that now.

"Watch your head," I said to Kenny Spoon, stepping outside.

CHAPTER THREE

Watch my head?" Kenny said. "Watch your ass. Lord knows you can't help but watch *mine*." He giggled at his little joke and wriggled the rear end that was rubbing my ear.

I thought about dropping him.

But reminded myself I was doing this for Eudora Spoon, not for her sad-sack son Kenny, who'd reenacted the tired play where the talented kid goes to Hollywood, makes a bundle, blows it, and dies broke in a fleabag motel.

Kenny Spoon's only original touch, far as I could see, was that he'd been getting set to die not in a fleabag but in an old jackoff parlor that was now a lowrider clubhouse.

Thinking all this as I trotted through puddles to my rental, looking left and right, not seeing any carloads of Bajamaros. That was a break: It looked like even Lobo Soto had his limits when it came to rousing thugs at five in the morning.

We neared the Tahoe. My exposed back felt like a giant bull's-eye, its center midway up my spine. If the little man stepped from the club-house with any half-decent weapon, I was dead.

And so was Kenny.

And that would mean breaking a promise to Eudora Spoon, a Barnburner.

And the Barnburners saved my life.

And I hadn't broken any promises yet.

Not to them.

So I ignored the icy bull's-eye feeling and trotted.

Would have made it clean if I'd been forty-five seconds earlier.

Tire squeal gave them away. The Bajamaros' building snugged up against an exit ramp from I-405 southbound. The exit was tree-screened, so I couldn't see them, but I sure did hear them.

The pavement had dried enough so their tires squealed on the off-ramp. The sound had purpose, urgency. It wasn't a punk kid. It was somebody headed this way, in a car with a pushrod V8.

I sprinted the final twenty yards. Opened the Tahoe's right rear door, flopped Kenny across the backseat. Wasn't gentle about it—didn't have time for gentle.

He fell on his back and giggled . . . and treated himself to a nice slug of Scotch.

Huh?

I did a double take at the Scotch.

The bottle had been on his bedside table. He must have grabbed it while I flipped him onto my shoulder.

Drunks and their priorities.

I climbed in, dropped the SUV into drive, made a fast U-turn, barrel-assed out of the dead end. Was planning to hook a quick one-eighty onto 405 South . . .

. . . but then I saw what had caused the tire squeal: a Chevy Caprice Classic, mideighties, the squared-off kind that used to be taxis and cop cars.

The Caprice was tricked out lowrider style. Its paint was flat black, a big look for hot rods that year. Its windows were blacked out, too, and the car sat ridiculously low.

How low? As the driver made half a bootlegger turn directly in front of me, his chrome bumper dipped, hit asphalt, and fired off sparks.

It was an effective turn: The Caprice spun just enough to block both lanes.

I was sixty yards away and coming hard. Needed to clear the Caprice, make the main drag—it was called Haskell Avenue—and hop on the freeway.

Both of the black car's left-side windows, the ones facing me, lowered at the same time.

Gun barrels got my attention. They looked bigger than they were. They looked big as manholes.

I didn't stop. I didn't even lift.

I aimed at the driver's door, keeping my foot in the throttle. My senses, operating at max intake the way they do when things get rough, had measured both sides of the street. The right side, at the Caprice's back end, featured an eighteen-inch concrete curb and a fire hydrant.

No dice.

The left side was a hair narrower and edged by a chain-link fence, but there was a soft dirt berm instead of a curb.

Left. That was my move.

I eye-locked the driver of the Caprice.

Four seconds earlier, after his big bumper-scraping skid, resting his handgun on the door of his lowrider, he'd felt like a hero.

With my two-ton Tahoe arrowing at him—not at his car in general, not at his rear door, but at *him personally*, the SUV looking twelve feet tall from his silly low position—he didn't feel like a hero anymore. Eyebrows popping above his shades told me so.

He never did fire his weapon.

I waited until it was too late, then waited another half a tenth of a second, then jerked the steering wheel hard left. Before the Tahoe's slow steering and mushy suspension even received the message, I jerked it right.

We cleared the Caprice. Hell, we didn't even touch the chain-link fence, though I did hear vine tendrils scrape my window.

The Tahoe was still rocking side to side on that mushy suspension when I made another hard left onto Haskell. There wasn't much grip after all the rain, and the SUV was rear-wheel-drive only, so I showboated with a little power oversteer, hanging out the back end, drifting away from the poleaxed gangbangers. One more left would put me on the San Diego Freeway, clean and clear, and I got set to treat myself to a rebel yell and a fist-pump . . .

. . . and saw, dead ahead and coming at me, another Caprice.

"Well that's damned inconvenient," Kenny said.

And held up the Scotch bottle, offering me a slug.

And I swear, if he'd been wearing a collar, I would have grabbed him by it and thrown him onto the street.

Instead, I repeated the double-jerk move with the steering wheel, but this time I slammed us right, then left, as the Caprice shot past. I was getting to know the Tahoe's habits and limits, so this time I felt its stability-control computers trying to figure out what the hell was going on.

All this happened at about forty-five miles an hour.

I used to race cars. You need to use your mirrors, but you don't get a lot of time to do it, and you learn to act fast on what you see.

A tenth-of-a-second glance in my side-view told me the second Caprice—which was charcoal colored where the other one had been dead black—was stopping in a hurry. Brake lights, a dipping nose, tire smoke because the old car had no ABS.

I didn't hesitate: jerked the wheel left, stomped the Tahoe's emergency brake with my left foot, leaned forward, used my left hand to fish for the e-brake release.

It's called a bootlegger turn because they were the ones who invented it, back when they used to round a bend in the North Carolina hills and find the road plugged by revenuers. The emergency brake locks up the rear wheels only, so a bootlegger turn gives you the quickest, tightest one-eighty-degree spin you could ask for.

It's not hard to do, either. Ask your teenaged son, if you've got one: Dollars to doughnuts he's practiced the move in your car.

Focused on the turn though I was, a corner of my head noticed Kenny Spoon's naked ass sliding across the backseat, noticed him hitting the right-side door hard, noticed a second thump when his head whiplashed against the window.

Good. Maybe that'd shut him up for a while.

The hard part of a bootlegger turn is getting out of it. Release the emergency brake too soon and your one-eighty dies an embarrassing death at a hundred degrees or so, and there you are pointed at the woods with your thumb up your ass. On the other hand, you don't want to wait too long, or you'll have to get going from a dead stop.

Considering the vehicle I was working with, I did okay. Popped the e-brake release and buried the throttle just at the tail end of the slide, got moving again, closed on the second Caprice.

The good news: The car was dead still, sitting at the intersection of Haskell and a main drag called Sherman Way. Maybe it'd stalled out and the driver was having trouble refiring, or maybe he was right where he wanted to be.

Either way was fine.

The bad news: A skinny dude had eeled from the passenger window and propped his rear end on the windowsill, and he was aiming a bazooka at me.

Maybe not a bazooka, but it was big and black and it was one hell of a shotgun. And he was resting it on the Caprice's roof, fitting his cheek to it like a man who knew what he was doing.

About the time I decided I didn't like this setup one bit, he cut loose with a round. I flinched as the Tahoe's left front corner shredded.

A tire blew, pulling me left as I buried my boot in the brake pedal and felt the ABS pulse. I steered right and kept control, but didn't like the physics of the thing: I was going to get us stopped just fine—about forty feet from the Caprice and the shotgun atop it.

Then it was going to be duck-and-pray, and I was going to find out if whatever came out of that gun would cut through the Tahoe's door skins.

All this passed through my head in tenths of a second, the world so slow now, slow enough so I noticed for the first time something new, something off, like a moving version of a what-doesn't-belong-in-this-picture game.

A car. In that ugly teal color that was big fifteen years ago. Coming south on Haskell Avenue. Moving well, moving with purpose.

Moving backward.

In reverse, that is.

It was a hell of a moment, I make no bones about it. A chase scene and shootout in a halfhearted California sunrise, dawn muscling its way in from the east—my right—as this second carload of Bajamaros fired a cannon at me. Meanwhile naked Kenny Spoon, groggy from a bootlegger turn that'd happened maybe eight seconds earlier, was trying to fetch his bottle of Scotch before it all glugged out on the Tahoe's tan carpet floor.

Now a Ford Crown Vic in that funky teal was backing—*backing*—south on Haskell, zinging past palm trees and private homes and low-rise apartments at a good clip.

Backing straight at the Caprice, whose driver had spotted the threat though its shooter hadn't.

My Tahoe, as I'd feared, was rocking and scraping and squalling to an ugly stop near the back end of the Caprice, way too close, point-blank range for the shotgun, right in that sweet spot where the shot would spread out and devastate the SUV and everything, *everyone,* in it, and in slow motion I was roll-flop-diving over the backseat, hollering at Kenny to get down, get *down* for Chrissake, falling atop him, enveloping him . . .

In spite of it all, an ancient corner of my mind felt happy, and just before I heard the wreck it all came together, and the *main* part of my mind slotted home the final piece of the puzzle: I'd seen the Crown Vic's license plate.

An Oregon plate. Weak baby blue, with a pine tree in the middle and squiggly mountains across the bottom.

I believe I said out loud, just before the Crown Vic creamed the front end of the Caprice: "McCord."

I believe I smiled as I said it.

CHAPTER FOUR

There's something extra quiet about the quiet following a big noise.

And McCord had made one hell of a big noise.

I spent thirty seconds calming Kenny. Which took some doing, especially because I was lying on top of him and he was having trouble breathing.

Even lying on naked, semihysterical Kenny in the backseat, I heard enough to paint a picture of something I couldn't see.

The shotgun had fired a second time when McCord creamed the Caprice.

Now, in the postgunfire, postwreck stillness, a door opened. Then closed. Boots crunched broken glass and plastic trim. The boots were in no hurry.

A take-no-shit state trooper's voice. I couldn't make out the words, but the tone was no more excited than if McCord had been asking for license and registration.

Which he was not.

Because two sharp thumps and a short honk told me he'd taken the back of the driver's neck and slammed his face on the steering wheel.

More unhurried boots. They stopped, checking something out.

Then they approached the Tahoe.

Then the right rear door, the one near my head, opened.

Then McCord said, "You rang."

He said it like that. No question mark.

"You cut it close," I said.

He shrugged. "Portland's a long drive. Who's your friend?"

That made me realize I still lay atop Kenny.

I climbed off and out, shaking McCord's hand as I spoke. "He's the one we're helping. Kind of."

McCord cocked his head and took a good look at fetaled-up Kenny, who had his eyes shut as if he could wish all this away. "He worth it?"

"His mother is. It's about her, not him."

We heard the sirens at the same time.

I looked at McCord's Crown Vic, its long trunk buried in the engine bay of the Caprice.

He read my mind. "It'll go," he said. "Not far. Not well. But it'll go."

"Then we'd best go." I turned. "Kenny."

Nothing.

"*Kenny*. Hop out."

Nothing.

McCord sighed and rolled his eyes and leaned in and grabbed Kenny under the armpits and pulled him from the SUV. He made it look about as hard as plucking a sleeping toddler from a car seat.

Kenny's case of the vapors got worse, not better, when he looked to his left and spotted the skinny shotgun dude from the Caprice. The dude lay twisted on his chest and face, which was bleeding onto the street.

There was a lot of blood.

The wreck had knocked the shotgun dude out of his shoes.

He might be alive.

Sirens: getting louder.

"Grab your gear, you got any," McCord said to me, and he speed-walked Kenny past the shooter, then shoved him in the Crown Vic's backseat.

I took my duffel from the Tahoe's cargo area and my rental agreement from the glove box.

As I slammed the passenger door, McCord was easing his car away from the Caprice. I stood, watching to see if his bumper cover stayed on—it did, barely—then trotted and hopped in next to him.

Then we drove away. Just like that.

I remembered Soto had promised three carloads and spent a few blocks scanning for a third Caprice before deciding we'd gotten lucky. On that third carload, anyway.

I said, "How the hell'd you find me?"

"Your voice mail said L.A."

"It's a big place."

He waved a dismissive hand.

McCord.

I shook my head.

"I owe you," I said.

"I guess so," he said. "Where we going?"

I turned and tossed my duffel on the seat next to Kenny. "Do us all a favor and grab some gym shorts out of there. And do you know a place we can go? A place the Bajamaros won't be watching?"

"With a garage," McCord said. "To stash this heap."

Kenny looked past me. Through me.

"He's shell-shocked," I said to McCord.

"Hard to blame him," McCord said.

"Kenny," I said, trying for a soft voice, "I know things were ugly back there, but we need your help. Know a place?"

Kenny frowned, blinked. "Tarzana."

"Where's that?" McCord said.

"Get on the 405 South."

McCord shook his head. "No freeway. CHP's too sharp. Best to stick with surface roads and local cops."

"Then turn around and go back to Sherman Way."

While McCord drove, I pulled my phone and made two calls. Both the 911 operator and the rental outfit asked where I'd last seen my SUV. I hemmed and hawed and coughed and said things about a late night and a gentleman's club and I couldn't remember the address and say, was there any reason my wife needed to be notified about all this?

"Not bad," McCord said when I clicked off the second time. "You're a jerk businessman from out of town. Got yourself rolled outside a strip joint at four in the morning, probably by a tranny."

"I imagine the cops here get that call often enough."

McCord moved the corner of his mouth up an eighth of an inch. That was his version of a smile. "'Bout a dozen times a night, I expect."

He drove.

After a while he said, "How's Charlene?"

"Damned if I know."

He turned and looked at me maybe three seconds, giving me a chance to say more.

I didn't.

So McCord looked ahead again and drove.

The car went quiet except for Kenny's occasional directions.

McCord was a New Hampshire state trooper when I met him. He makes me look short (I'm not) and thick-waisted (I'm not). Take Abe Lincoln, shave the beard, and add thirty pounds of chest and shoulders. That's McCord.

A while back he got tangled up in a thing I worked on. To do me a favor, McCord pointed his bosses in a certain direction. The bosses didn't like the pointer. They invited McCord to keep his mouth shut and do as he was told.

He quit instead.

Then he bought himself a pair of hiking boots, drove to Alaska, and walked around for the better part of a year. That was the way he put it: not hiking, not backpacking, not adventuring. Walking around.

I'd heard he wore out his walking boots and backtracked as far as

Oregon. Then we'd lost touch. But he was the only man I could think of out west who might be useful to me, so when I landed in L.A., I'd left voice mail.

That was it. One voice mail: *I'm in Los Angeles, call if you get a chance.*

How McCord parlayed that into being exactly where I needed him five seconds before a Bajamaro blew me open with a shotgun . . . well, I'd have to ask about that again.

Though he likely wouldn't explain. He talks even less than I do.

It's probably why we get along.

"I'm swimming in these shorts," Kenny said from the back. "And by the by, rayon mesh? Really? What year is it in that duffel of yours, 1978?"

He giggled quietly.

McCord jerked a thumb over his shoulder. "The mother, the one you're doing this for. I hope she's something special."

CHAPTER FIVE

Eudora Spoon was old, and she was dying, but she wasn't dying the way old people die.

"What on earth is that supposed to mean?" she'd said when I mentioned it. This was six days before I hauled Kenny out of Bajamaros HQ.

Eudora and I had been legging up a hill in Bryar, Massachusetts, tailing a pair of greyhounds named Cha Cha Muldowney and Dandy Dick Landy. It'd been a weird winter: seemed like every week brought a solid snowfall followed by a record-breaker of a warm-up. Freeze, thaw. Freeze, thaw. An inch of sugar-bowl stuff had fallen the previous night, and the dogs were having a ball in it.

"Well," I said, knowing I'd screwed up by speaking about old people and dying. That happens to me a lot. It's why I don't talk more.

She waved a hand, chuffing a half-laugh. "Never mind. I believe I know the scene as you envision it. The master bedroom of the ancestral manse. A kindly physician tut-tuts over his spectacles and shakes his head sadly at my offspring. Covered in quilts that go back three generations, I dispense wisdom to my rapt family. Am I right?"

"Well," I said.

Eudora stepped onto a tree stump, put two fingers in her mouth, and whistled loud enough to hurt my ears. Dandy and Cha Cha stopped and turned, tongues lolling. He was black with white patches. She was the color of a deer.

Eudora stepped from the stump, then sat on it. "People die that way in *Little House on the Prairie,* Conway. I'm dying in real life." She patted the stump, which was broad enough for both of us.

I sat.

While the dogs snuffled back to us, we said nothing and looked northwest. She owned this hill. She owned a pond I could make out through the winter-bare trees. I didn't know how many acres she owned all told, but I knew she owned plenty.

Her property spanned Route 142, a semi-main drag that wandered northwest-southeast. If you looked across that road, as we did now, you could see most of a HOLLYWOOD-style sign that read WOLVERINE BROS. FREIGHT & STORAGE. Harmon's Follywood, the locals called it. Harmon being Eudora's son. Steady guy, local cop forever. Respected.

Dull, if you asked me.

But nobody ever did.

Eudora seldom mentioned Wolverine Bros. Freight & Storage, and when she did, she mocked it. Hard to blame her.

"Dying slow is lousy," she said.

I waited.

"Aren't you going to ask why?"

"I figure you'll tell me when you're set to."

Another half-laugh. "That's your answer to most everything," Eudora said, producing a treat from a pocket of her navy blue parka and feeding it to Cha Cha. That got Dandy all hot and bothered, so she passed him a treat, too.

I said, "I'll play along. Why is dying slow lousy?"

"Thank you for asking. It's lousy because . . ." She trailed off. Clapped her hands, sending the dogs uphill again.

I waited, watching breath-vapor float away.

"You think you're going to *get it,*" she said, her voice husky.

"Get what? What 'it'?"

She made a circular motion with both arms. "The *big* it. The universe, the connections, what comes next, the . . . *secret* to the damn thing."

"But?"

"But you don't, of course. Or I don't. Haven't. Not yet." Eudora grabbed the sleeve of my coat. "Which is the problem in a nutshell, Conway. I feel so *close* sometimes. I feel as if it's all there to be arranged, to be understood. And I feel so damn close."

"Horseshoes and hand grenades."

She smiled, released my sleeve, punched my arm. I wouldn't admit it to her for a million dollars, but it stung. Even at eighty-two, even dying. Eudora Spoon could still hike a half mile down and another back each morning, and she could still sting you with a punch.

"It won't quite form up," she said. "It won't quite make sense. Sometimes, when I'm floating on the painkillers . . . yes, painkillers, and I still consider myself a sober woman, so please drop the Patented Conway Sax Disapproval Deadpan, I am *dying*, for Christ's sweet sake . . . when I'm floating, it seems I can see all the pieces arranged like a baby's mobile, the type we used to string above cribs. Do they still do that? I'm babbling. How unlike me."

She set a hand across her eyes.

I put one hand on Eudora's white brush cut. She'd worn her hair that way as long as I'd known her. "Why did you call?"

She took the hand in both of hers, moved it from her head, held it. "That's the stuff. Right to the point. I've done my simpering for the day."

I said nothing, left my hand in hers.

Eudora thumb-rubbed my calluses without knowing she was doing it.

She turned to look uphill, where Dandy and Cha Cha had nearly made it back to the house. To get there, they'd run a gauntlet of signs stuck in the ground, the types politicians jam in everybody's front yards. These signs, set up to be visible from Route 142 below, had started out bright pink but were now the color of Pepto-Bismol. They all said the same thing:

NO ON 2!

Question 2, a ballot proposal on whether the town should allow legalized gambling, had been Bryar's big hairy deal for the better part of a year.

Hungry for tax bucks, Massachusetts had laid out the welcome mat for casinos. The casino operators had settled on the Blackstone Valley—Bryar and surrounding towns—as the place to build.

Then every town had held a referendum: Yes to casinos, welcoming the revenue and the jobs and the undeniable baggage that came with them? Or no to casinos, keeping the town pristine but also keeping it dirt poor?

Eudora had spearheaded Bryar's No-on-2 movement, which surprised a lot of folks because her property seemed like a great place to build. Maybe it was, but once she got the bit between her teeth she'd been unstoppable. I swear, if Bryar had a town square, she would've stood on a soapbox there.

The previous November, Bryar had voted down Question 2, thus telling casinos they'd best set up shop elsewhere.

"What I've decided to do," Eudora was saying, "is gather more pieces. Maybe, if I have enough of them, they'll all slot in. They'll all make sense."

"Pieces?"

"One very important piece, to be specific. My son. Not Harmon. My other son."

"Kenny Spoon."

She nodded. "I want you to go to California and bring him to me."

"You sure took the long way around to *that* punch line," I said.

Eudora cut loose with the first honest, unguarded laugh I'd heard out of her in three months. She slapped my thigh—hard—and rose. "Let's go up and feed the dogs and I'll tell you about it."

Her L-shaped ranch was stuffy even in the summer, the way old people's homes are. Now, with me warmed by our hike and the wood stove cranking, the place was just about unbearable.

I'd suggested the stove a few years back, following a rough winter that found Eudora griping about her oil bill. Then I'd installed it for her, laying the redbrick footing and running the chimney up and out. It was a funny thing, as she had all the money you could ask for, but something about that heating bill got under her skin.

She made coffee for me and tea for her. I stripped off my boots, pea coat, and flannel shirt. In T-shirt and jeans, I headed for the overfurnished living room and looked for a casement window that wasn't stuck.

Didn't find one.

I sighed, sat on the sofa the greyhounds hadn't claimed, looked at Dandy, and shrugged. If Dandy minded the heat, he wasn't showing it.

Soon Eudora brought in a tray. "I forget what I told whom when," she said, setting it down and sitting in a blue corduroy armchair. "So refresh my memory. How much do you know about my late husbands?"

"I figured there were two because your sons have different last names," I said. "But you only ever talk about one. Andy, the developer."

"I left Andy for Hans Kollar in 1968. Hans and I were together until he died fifteen years ago."

She smiled and looked at nothing. I sat and took it in, surprised but not really. I thought I knew Eudora pretty well, but I was damned if I recalled her talking about any Hans. Andy, sure—she talked about that one like he was down at the job site and might be home any minute.

She'd never mentioned Hans.

In AA, you think you get to know people.

And you do.

But you also think everybody's baring their soul.

And they do.

But they don't.

Nobody bares it all. Everybody holds something back.

You've got to.

I wanted more info. I could see Eudora was remembering times with Andy. From her unfocused eyes and screwball smile, they must've been quite a couple.

She had a good face. You noticed her Liz Taylor eyes first—how could you not?—but any glamour promised by the eyes was undercut by the snow-white buzz cut and the outdoors-a-lot-and-not-ashamed-of-it skin. She'd had crow's-feet around the eyes forever. Now, truly *looking* at her for the first time in a long time, I noticed the crow's-feet had deepened and had been joined by brackets around her mouth.

A good face. An honest face.

Time passed. One greyhound farted and both sighed.

I needed to jog Eudora, get her talking again. I said, "Two husbands, eh?"

"Yes!" Embarrassed that I'd caught her woolgathering, she put too much into it, slapping her thigh hard enough so that Cha Cha cocked an ear. "Kenny is, as you know, Andy's son."

"So he and Harmon are really half brothers."

Harmon Kollar had been on the Bryar Police Department forever. Was now acting chief, and everybody assumed the Board of Selectmen was going through the motions with token job interviews before dumping the "acting." In his thirties, solid citizen. Married, no kids, a damn good son to Eudora. Almost *too* good—you wondered what Harmon's wife, Tricia, thought about all the time he spent with his mother.

I thought of something. "How come you never changed your name from Spoon?"

"They say a woman's first husband resembles her father, often to a shocking extent," Eudora said, ignoring the question. "Physically, emotionally, even in speech patterns. Did you know this?"

I shook my head.

"As to the second husband, they say, the rule is simple: He must be everything the first, and therefore the father, was not." She looked me dead in the eye. "I am Exhibit A, a clichéd example. Andy was a builder"—smiling, she exaggerated the New England pronunciation, saying BIL-dah—"a glad-hander, a man for whom friendships and useful contacts were one and the same. He was the only man I've met who loved both drag racing and golf. He used to brag that he'd golfed with every mayor, selectman, and zoning commissioner in every town in Worcester County."

I'd heard the story before. "He did okay that way."

"Goodness yes! I'm not complaining. Rather, I'm setting up the contrast between Andy and Hans Kollar."

"On name alone, I'm not seeing Hans as a golfer and a backslapper."

Eudora laughed. "As I said, the point of the second husband is to differ from the first. Hans came straight out of the Black Forest and the University of Heidelberg. Stiff as a Presbyterian's best collar. He could go days without speaking a word of his own volition. Outside of work, that is, where lecturing was a necessity—an evil one, in Hans's opinion."

"What was his job?"

"He was a humanities professor who eventually found his place at Boston College. He took forever to achieve tenure because he declined to play the brown-nose game."

"Why are you telling me this?"

She blinked. "I suppose I'm just filling in blanks. Kenneth is eight years older than Harmon. Between that and the half-brothers status, their relationship was always cockeyed. I do believe Harmon grew sick of hearing about Kenneth's talent."

"Maybe that's why sports became his thing," I said. "Gave Harmon something of his own. Something he did better than Kenny."

"That is absolutely true. Harmon seemed to find the attention Ken-

neth received . . . unearned might be the word. Unearned and unde-
served. Harmon was always bringing home these awful football-coach
clichés and spouting them at dinner, mostly, I believe, because he knew
they made both Hans's and Kenny's blood boil."

"There's no 'I' in 'team,'" I said. We laughed a little.

I was sweating. Nobody cared about Eudora more than me, but I
had to get out of this overheated, overfurnished, overcanined house
pretty soon.

"Have you tried the direct route?" I asked. "Called Kenny, told him
about your cancer, asked him back home?"

"Of course I have."

Her eyes darted as she said it, and she decided the sugar bowl needed
to be pushed half an inch.

Huh.

She wasn't giving me the full story. I sighed. "Where's Kenny, and
what kind of trouble is he in?"

"He's in Hollywood, of course. Or thereabouts."

"Still? Glutton for punishment?"

"They say the place has quite an allure."

"He still a mess?" I made the glug-glug drinking gesture as I said it.

"Of course. Drugs are involved as well."

"Of course."

Eudora tried to smile. Didn't quite pull it off. "Can you help an old
pal? An old Barnburner?"

It was the magic word, and she knew it.

I thought things through.

Eudora must have read this as hesitation, because she pressed. "I
know things have . . . changed for you lately," she said. "I thought you
might have the time and the inclination to do something a bit different."

I didn't like hearing it, didn't like the way she put it.

But she had a point.

Four months earlier, things had been strong and solid for me. I'd
moved in with my girlfriend, Charlene Bollinger. That had been working

out for the two of us plus Sophie, her younger daughter. Thanks to Charlene's cosigning power, I'd launched an independent shop that worked mostly on Japanese cars. Had one full-time and one part-time employee. Business was good. Life was good.

Then it wasn't.

I'd tried helping a junkie who swore he wanted to clean up. Everything had gone to hell. A punk had firebombed my shop, and I'd put Sophie in a bad, bad place. A place no thirteen-year-old deserved to be.

It'd been too much for Charlene. She'd cut me loose.

I didn't blame her.

Since then, I'd been shambling around. Doing some of this, some of that, always for cash under the table.

I'd begun spending more time here in Bryar, twenty minutes southwest of Framingham, because Eudora needed help. Shopping, getting to doctor appointments. Like that.

So yeah, things had changed for me.

On the other hand, they hadn't. Not really. I'd had a taste of a nice life, a stable life.

I'd pissed it away.

As usual.

"An all-expenses-paid trip to sunny Southern California," Eudora was saying. "In February."

Now she really had a point. I could use a change of scenery. "You got an address?"

"Heavens no."

"Where should I start, then?"

Eudora steepled her hands and looked me in the eye. "The gutter, I would imagine."

CHAPTER SIX

In the backseat, Kenny was having a private little breakdown. I didn't blame him. Not everybody was used to daybreak chases that ended with intentional wrecks and gangbangers knocked out of their shoes.

He alternated between calling turns for McCord and making fun of the clothes he'd found in my duffel. "Now let's kick back in our rayon shorts," he said in a DJ voice, "and enjoy a little number from the Captain and Tennille."

McCord and I ignored him. It wasn't hard.

You've heard Kenny Spoon's story a hundred times. He was way too talented for Bryar, Massachusetts. The regional high school had never seen anything like him. He starred in every play, dominated every talent show. Earned some sort of drama scholarship to the University of Michigan. A real prize, to hear Eudora tell it even all these years later—apparently the school had a couple thousand applicants each year and three slots to fill.

Not even that was a match for Kenny Spoon's talent and hunger. He lasted three semesters at Michigan, starring in everything but bombing all his classes, before heading west to Hollywood with a half-dozen screenplays and a half-million ideas.

Once in Hollywood, he'd done what kids off the bus do out there: wait tables, narrate bus tours, audition, try to make connections.

His screenplays went nowhere as feature films, but a friend of a friend thought one had potential as a TV series. It was about a sensitive teen, just trying to get by in high school, whose mother is both the principal and half a zombie. Or something like that—I'd never been able to sit through the show myself.

The show got bought. The show was a hit. No, more than a hit: a phenomenon. Watercooler talk, special editions of teenybopper magazines, a spin-off lip-sync concert. Like that.

In addition to credits as creator and executive producer, Kenny had a small role in the series as the wispy, bowl-cut friend who was always ready with the perfect comeback. Something about the character—his skinniness, his violet eyes, the way he almost lisped but not quite—made him a hit with teenybopper girls. People who'd known Kenny all his life said he began to play the character whether the camera was rolling or not.

For two-plus years, Kenny made more money than you've ever seen.

Then the friend of a friend who'd hooked him up in the first place, and had become his agent and manager, screwed Kenny but good. It turned out he'd signed contracts that were either moronic or criminal, depending on your point of view.

The friend-agent-manager fleeced him.

The downhill slide was fast and total: booze, pills, homes foreclosed, cars repo'd, more booze, more pills, DUI mug shots picked up by *The Smoking Gun*.

Like I said, you've heard it all before.

Soon we reached the address in Tarzana.

It was a ranch house in a neighborhood of ranch houses on tiny lots. The homes had started as clones of one another, assembly-line tract boxes, but additions and improvements and clever landscaping had made them pop and flourish.

Kenny was at the house's front door before McCord and I even stepped onto the concrete driveway. Out of habit, Kenny fumbled for keys in the pocket of a pair of pants he was no longer wearing. He caught himself, rang the bell, then pounded on the hand-carved oak door.

I was behind him by the time it opened. Boy, did Kenny Spoon reek.

I guess I'd been expecting a man, truth be told. So when the door opened—all of a sudden, like the person on the other side had looked through the peephole and been pleasantly surprised—and somebody dove into Kenny's arms, it took me a moment to realize it was a woman.

From where I stood, directly behind Kenny, all I could tell was that she had brown hair and was an inch taller than him, which still left her short.

"Oh my God oh my God oh my *God,*" she said. "Where? How?" Her voice was husky. Fifteen years ago, you would've called it a smoker's voice. Did people in California smoke anymore?

She said again, "Oh my God oh my God oh my *God.* By the way, you stink to high heaven. And who are these men? Oh my *God.*"

As they broke the hug, Kenny turned and extended his arm like a game-show host. "Erin Barnes, I present Conway Sax and . . . I do apologize, sir."

McCord said his name.

"Conway Sax and No First Name McCord, darling. They are either my liberators or my new captors, and I'll be gobsmacked if I can say which. Erin, gentlemen, is a former flame and a dear friend forever."

I said nothing.

McCord, too.

"They appear to be surprised," Erin said. "Dumbfounded, even."

"And why shouldn't they be?" Kenny said. "My heterosexuality . . ."

"Is Hollywood's best-kept secret," Erin said.

They giggled at their little comedy routine.

Goddamn California.

* * *

Erin Barnes was smart and quick and in charge. Once we were inside, she pinched her nose and made a face, telling Kenny to grab a shower *right now*. He smiled and walked down a hall.

Before McCord was a full sentence into his request for the garage, Erin nodded once and tossed him a BMW key fob. As he left, making a circular gesture at me to indicate he would walk a perimeter of the house, she steered me to a light gray sofa that was so comfortable I nearly fell asleep while she made coffee.

It was a small house, with kitchen, living room, and dining area all in one space. Erin didn't have to raise her voice in the kitchen to talk with me on the sofa. What were likely walls originally had been turned into Spanish-style archways.

With my eyes drooping, she made all the conversation. She was from Seattle originally, had met Kenny when she was senior associate producer, "the one who makes it all go," for his TV show.

Comfy, comfy sofa. I tried to remember when I'd last slept well. Felt my head sag forward. Erin wasn't helping: The talk was vapid and upbeat. Bird chatter.

Until the shower began to run.

When it did, Erin tiptoed halfway down the hall and cocked her head. That woke me up. It seemed she was making sure Kenny hadn't started the water as a decoy, then put his ear to the door.

Huh.

Former flame and giggly best buddies, but she doesn't trust him as far as she can throw him.

He's a junkie and a drunk. How could *you trust him?*

She returned to the kitchen, then toted to the living room a blond-wood tray of coffee stuff, set it down, sat in a chair that matched the sofa, and crossed her legs. "What the *hell* is going on?"

I poured and sipped. "I'm taking Kenny back to Massachusetts."

Half-beat pause, then a finger snap. "Just like that."

"Just like that."

"At whose behest?"

"His mother's," I said.

"So this Massachusetts mother—Eldora, is it?—has some sort of magical jurisdiction here? A license to kidnap?"

"Her name is Eudora. She's my friend. And she's dying. And she wants to see her kid. And her jurisdiction is me."

Erin looked at me for maybe twenty seconds. I looked back. Boy, was she pretty. The brown hair was short, the brown eyes unafraid. She had a tan that was no big deal in California but that folks back home would kill for. The very short sleeves of her black T-shirt showed she was fit even if she was thin.

She said, "I take it you're a detective?"

"I'm a mechanic."

"You're a mechanic."

I said nothing.

I sipped.

The coffee was good. Strong.

"You do realize," Erin said, "I can torpedo your plan with a simple phone call."

"Well." I slipped from my shirt pocket a cell phone, holding it at shoulder height until she realized it was hers.

"Hey," she said, twisting to glance at her pocketbook, which rested on a bar-style chair near the kitchen island. Then she cut her eyes to the landline on a low shelf near the front door.

"McCord'll have sliced the cord at the box outside," I said. "You'll want to put in a service request on that. Sorry, but we need to know what we're dealing with. My plan got snafu'd, and we had to ask Kenny for a fallback. I don't trust him. Judging from your little listen at the bathroom door, neither do you."

"I," she said.

"You can't," she said, pounding tiny fists on blue-jean thighs.

"You can't . . . *do* this!" she said.

I said nothing. I understood. She'd been dealt a rough hand that she couldn't have seen coming.

"This is my *house*! Are you . . . *gang*sters? *Kid*nappers?"

"I'm a mechanic. McCord used to be a cop. Not sure what you'd call him now."

"Mechanic my ass. Cop my ass. You know this will all come out, don't you?"

"You care about Kenny," I said.

"More than you could possibly grasp."

"He live here?"

"He has been. Had been. Platonic City, splitting the mortgage."

"How long's he been gone? How many days since he was in touch?" I knew it was at least seven. Wanted to see if she lied.

She didn't. Instead, she went red in the face. "He went off on a toot. We've . . . he's got irons in the fire. Things are being pitched. Which brings pressure. When the pressure rises, Kenny flees on a toot. He's been doing it since season two, which was more than ten years ago. To those of us who know Kenny Spoon, *truly* know him, it's an honored tradition."

"I found him naked and shitfaced. He was being held prisoner by a lowrider gang in Van Nuys."

The suntan drained from Erin's face.

"Some toot," I said.

CHAPTER SEVEN

Her lower lip shook.

"How'd he end up there, Erin?"

She said nothing.

"You said you care about him. I believe you. How'd he end up like that?"

Nothing. It seemed she wanted to say something more but couldn't quite.

Or maybe I imagined that.

The shower stopped, snapping whatever vibe I'd set up. I knew I'd lost her even before she rose, breathed a *puh* sound, ran a hand through her hair, and took the coffee tray to the kitchen.

I tried not to look at the back of her jeans. Failed. As usual. When she moved, they were loose and tight both. The way the best jeans are.

"Come to Massachusetts with us," I said.

"You're joking."

In the bathroom, Kenny sang that he just flew in from the windy city. You could picture him toweling off as he sang it.

Erin and I laughed. Couldn't help it.

"Pretty good voice," I said.

"Don't tell *him* that, for the love of God. His head's big enough already."

"When he gets back," I said, "Kenny's in for a shock. You're good for him. I haven't seen much, but I can see that. You could be a big help."

"Do you have any idea what this town's been like?" she asked, bustling more than she needed to, putting things away. "I was out of work two and a half years. Three months ago, a game show"—she sneered as she said it—"hired me as an associate, no 'senior.' Tell my new boss I'm sashaying off to Massachusetts for an unspecified duration? No thank you."

"What game show?"

She waved a disgusted hand. "*Syn*dicated."

I didn't know what that meant. I let it slide.

Kenny sang that the windy city was mighty pretty.

"He paints his mother as a big tub-thumping AA type," Erin said. "Is that what you're all about? Is this essentially an intervention?"

"It's how I know his mother. But it's not what I hired on for."

"Oh."

"Disappointed?"

"I worry. All his friends do."

"But you let him go. On what you call toots."

"Am I my brother's keeper?" She couldn't look me in the eye as she spoke. Shame showed through.

"You ought to meet his mother. She's something, believe me."

"He doesn't fly, you know."

"Tomorrow he will."

"You'll force him? And *you're* supposed to be the compassionate one, killing me with guilt? Did you see the two-parter we did in Hawaii?"

It took me a few seconds to realize she was talking about the TV show. "Hell no."

"They . . . we had to dump Scotch and Vicodin down his gullet, practically with a funnel, to get him on the flight."

"With friends like you," I said.

"I'm not proud of it. The point is, good luck crowbarring him onto an airplane."

The truth was, I'd been worried about that. Had struggled with it.

On the one hand, my job wasn't to get Kenny Spoon sober. My job was to get him home. If I had to lubricate him to do it, well, there you were. I've talked with guys who haul drunks and junkies to rehabs, and while nobody will admit it publicly, the idea is the same: Look the other way and let the creep do what he needs to do to get where he's going. The help starts once he's there.

That's what I'd been telling myself this past week in California.

But I hadn't liked it. Not one bit.

Had toyed with another plan.

A dumb plan, most likely. One that'd make Sophie, Charlene's smart-as-a-whip daughter, roll her eyes and call me the last romantic.

I'd thought maybe, just maybe, I could start sobering up Kenny Spoon.

I knew a place. I'd connected with a group my first night here.

I said, "Do you know his stash spaces?"

"Pardon?"

"Kenny's stashes. He'll have half a dozen. And since he's a pill-head, they'll be small."

"He has eight. No, nine if you count my golf bag in the garage, where he keeps a liter of vodka." She met my gaze. "I *do* care about him."

"If I sit on him for a few hours, can you dump everything?"

"Seriously?"

I said nothing.

Erin Barnes leaned on a Spanish arch, put a fist on a hip, and made a slow smile.

It was one hell of a smile.

"It would be my great and sincere pleasure," she said.

Kenny burst from the bathroom with a brown towel cinched at his waist, raised both arms toward the ceiling, and belted out the big finish.

He seemed puzzled when Erin and I paid him no mind.

CHAPTER EIGHT

Not to be a rube," McCord said that evening as we tooled up North Detroit Street, "but you sure this is Hollywood?"

"Not what you expected?"

"Not quite."

I cut into a three-quarters-empty parking lot fronting a windowless metal building. Above the building's only door was riveted a sign:

SHAKY PETE'S NOT QUITE PRECISION ENGINEERING

Kenny moaned.

He'd done a lot of that on the ride over. We ignored him.

We'd stuck him in the backseat of Erin's ice blue BMW 320i. Six thousand miles on the odometer. Nice car. To me, though, it felt like driving a computer. Am I old-school? I guess. I like machines that feel like machines.

Bet you a hundred dollars she leased it the minute her game-show job came through.

As we'd backed down her driveway, Erin had rushed from her house with a plastic trash can, opened Kenny's door, and thrust the can into his clammy arms in case he needed to puke.

"Last time I'll mention it," McCord had said to Erin, "but I ought to stay here with you."

"Absolutely not," she'd said. "I'll lock everything and not answer anything. Besides, if they wanted to come here, they would have by now."

McCord had made a suit-yourself shrug as she shut Kenny's door, but I could tell he hadn't liked it.

Me neither, but what could you do?

As for that wastebasket: Kenny'd been in rough shape ever since his big "I Just Flew in from the Windy City" finale, when I'd ordered him, as he stood dripping, to plant his ass on the couch while Erin cleared out his booze and pills.

Until then, he'd been sailing along on something or other. True junkie that he was, though, he couldn't enjoy *this* high unless he knew where the *next* one was coming from. So the color had drained from his face while Erin did her thing.

Kenny had sat quiet for a while.

But as Erin had begun riffling one stash after another, he panicked and went to work on me, using every tool in the junkie toolbox.

He tried charm.

He tried calm argument.

He tried medical necessity.

He cried.

He cussed out me and Erin both, in language that would get you tossed from a whorehouse full of bikers.

He cried some more.

In the middle of all this, McCord reentered the house. I guess he'd decided we were Bajamaro-free. Or maybe the cussing intrigued him.

When Erin, humming, made for the garage and Kenny's liter of vodka, Kenny howled like a coyote and McCord moved the corner of his mouth an eighth of an inch.

That is, he smiled.

The rest of the afternoon was babysitting time, beginnings-of-withdrawal time.

An ugly time. Always is.

The master bedroom was pulled together in a quiet way, like the house's public areas. Not-quite-pink walls, queen-sized bed, hand-painted vintage dresser and mirror, area rug. I'd spent three hours sitting in a club chair in the corner of that room, watching Kenny thrash and listening to him moan and squeal and curse.

Sometimes I looked at Web sites on my phone. Mostly, though, I looked at Kenny and wondered why I was doing this—and hoped it was the right move.

Eudora hadn't said a word about getting him straight. She had no illusions about where he stood sobriety-wise. She wasn't one of those clueless mommies who thought her jerk son was an angel.

She wanted to connect with Kenny, jerk or no. That was all.

She wanted me to track him down and lug him home. That was all.

I'd done the first part. McCord, armed with Eudora's credit-card info, was out in the living room right now reserving a flight. So we had the second part covered.

But it's not enough for you. You want style points. You want to make the job harder. Maybe too hard.

"Nah," I said out loud, the first sound I'd made in an hour.

"Fuck you!" Kenny said, torquing in sweat-soaked sheets.

If you were a damn pole vaulter and you saw you were going to make your jump, you'd stop in midair and jack up the bar an inch. Just to make it interesting.

"Nah," I said.

"Blow me!" Kenny said.

I sighed and checked my watch and counted minutes until we could leave for Shaky Pete's.

Jeez, had Van Nuys in the rain really happened *this morning*?

Busy day.

I was thinking this as we crossed Shaky Pete's parking lot and watched the sun begin to set. We passed full-custom Harleys worth a hundred grand apiece and a Deuce highboy roadster that must have cost three times that to build.

By now, Kenny was acting like a cross between a surly fifteen-year-old and a cripple. He sweated and shuffled and said not one word, and I swear he would've fallen over if we hadn't each taken an arm.

"I'll bite," McCord said. "What's the draw here?"

"Meeting," I said.

"Your AA tribe? Doesn't look like any church basement I ever saw."

I laughed some, pressed a doorbell.

Shaky Pete answered, peered through plate glass, checked his watch, opened up, shook my hand, and waved us in.

We stood in a typical machine-shop office: old beige PC on a left-over desk, dorm-sized fridge and microwave in a corner, mismatched filing cabinets, Snap-On calendar. Hanging over it all: machine-shop perfume, a blend of fine oil and metal shavings and this grit that you never quite see but that works its way into your knuckles.

"You're late," Pete said.

I looked at my own watch, a warhorse Seiko 6309-7049 that's been with me through thick and thin. "Thirty seconds late."

"Late's late." He ran the heel of a hand across the bottom of his nose, cut glances at McCord and Kenny. "All aboard?"

"What do you mean?"

"It's a closed discussion meeting."

I apologized. From the way Barnburners back home had talked about Shaky Pete's, I'd assumed it was an open meeting, one at which everybody was welcome whether they were a drunk or not.

Here's the way it works: AA is one big network with lots of subnet-works. For the most part, those networks are regional, but there's a tight little group of Barnburner-style outfits that don't exactly do things by the book. Hardcore outfits.

Groups like the Barnburners and Shaky Pete's have our own jungle drums. We're AA, but we're more than that.

Or less. Depending on who you ask. I've heard some uptight AA types call us vigilantes. That's too dramatic. We just like to help our members, and by the time they become members, they've got some ugly problems.

Groups like ours know about each other whether we're in Massachusetts, Los Angeles, Laramie, Amarillo, or Palermo, Italy.

I'm serious about Palermo. The stories I've heard out of there would curl your hair.

Back home, when I'd told a few Barnburners where I was headed and why, every last one of them had pointed me at Shaky Pete's. They said he knew everything worth knowing in L.A. Sure enough, he'd listened to my story about Kenny Spoon, a washed-up celebrity currently residing in parts unknown, and said he'd look into it.

Then Pete, a Samoan who didn't shake one bit as far as I could tell, had said he'd heard about me.

That was a surprise. "What do you hear?"

"I hear you're pretty good in a jam."

I said nothing.

"I hear you done state time back east."

I said nothing.

"I hear that state time was Barnburner related. I hear you kept your mouth shut and did a bit you maybe didn't have to do."

I said nothing.

That was good enough for Shaky Pete. He'd put out feelers on Kenny's whereabouts. I'll never know how he got the info, but thirty-six hours later Pete had called my cell, told me to come by his shop, and slid me a business card with an address: Los Bajamaros, just off Haskell in Van Nuys.

I said thanks.

"You want to thank me?" he'd said. "Bring this half a TV star to our Sunday night meeting. We'll put the fear of God in him. Making celebrities pee their pants is sort of a house specialty."

So here we were. Feeling stupid again for hauling McCord over—we should have told Erin he was babysitting her and that was that—I turned to him.

"You ready to declare to the world you're an alcoholic?"

"Not today."

"A drug addict?"

"Not yet."

"Then you can't come in the back room with us. My mistake."

McCord said nothing. Just fell into a yard-sale armchair and opened a copy of *Rat Rod* magazine.

CHAPTER NINE

Shaky Pete knew how to create drama.

I'd had a tour of his machine shop when I first came by. Of course he had a CNC operation, a bedroom-sized machine that could shape any chunk of metal into anything once the operator pushed a few buttons—the CNC is for "computer numerical control."

But the CNC was an afterthought here. Pete's specialty was tools half a century old or more, some of them dating to World War II and scavenged from West Coast shipyards. A Van Norman crankshaft grinder, a Warner & Swasey No. 3 lathe, a Bridgeport milling machine, a band saw stamped J&R JORDAN—MILWAUKEE. Hell, Shaky Pete had one tool twelve feet long that was built to balance crankshafts for the diesel engines on Liberty Ships. I'd asked what use he put it to here. "None yet," he'd said. "But it's a hell of a thing, ain't it?"

It *was* a hell of a thing.

Tools built with pride. Tools built to last. Tools no computer could run, but with which a man could work little miracles.

The right man, that is.

Tools like these, and the people who used them to turn out little miracles, reminded me of a line in a song I like: "The fingertips know what the brain does not."

Pete led the way, threading a path among the tools while I guided invalid Kenny through the dark.

The dark. The drama.

Pete had killed all the lights but one bulb in a low-hanging sheet metal dome that hung in the center of the space. The dome lit a circle with a twelve-foot diameter. Spaced around the circle were folding chairs, more than a dozen but fewer than twenty, all occupied.

As we neared, the talk stopped and every eye turned on us, the people not bothering to be polite.

The unofficial Barnburners motto is *Serious AA for serious people.*

It looked like the motto fit Shaky Pete's, too.

Pete stepped into the dark for three seconds, returned with a chair beneath each arm, made room, and set them down.

Kenny and I sat.

"Introductions," Pete said.

"We fucking did that already," said a tiny woman in a big pea coat and a Yankees cap. "They're late."

"They're guests," Pete said.

"They're fucking *late.*"

Something about her voice.

I looked close.

She was an actress, been in movies, some of them big. If I said her name, you'd recognize it.

She was also staring at me.

"Late's late," she said. "What kept you, big boy? What makes your time so much more ever-fucking important than mine?"

I took a deep breath. Then another. Then made eye contact with everyone in the circle, ending with the actress. "Sorry we're late," I said. "I'm Conway. I'm a drug addict and an alcoholic out of Framingham, Massachusetts. Grateful to be here, grateful to be sober today."

You could feel the tension drain, though the tiny angry actress muttered something I didn't catch.

Then we went around the circle. It was a pretty typical crew. Heavy on bikers, maybe, but upscale bikers—clothes and nails and hair-cuts and the cars in the lot told me there was plenty of money in the room.

When it was finally his turn, Kenny, seated to my right, did his best to screw everything up. With all eyes on him—knowing it, liking the attention—he stared at his sneakers and crossed and uncrossed his arms.

And said nothing.

"You're up, partner," Pete finally said. "Sooner you say it, sooner we can move along."

Kenny said nothing.

"Waste of my fucking—" It was the tiny actress, stage-whispering, but boy did she hush up when Pete shot her a look.

Sitting there turning red, embarrassed at having gummed up some-body else's meeting, I decided I was good and sick of Kenny Spoon. I was no fan of the foulmouthed movie star, but she was right: I'd wasted nearly ten minutes of another group's time babying Kenny, who sat there doing his drama-queen bit. His act had worn very, very thin. If he thought his status as a guy who used to be on TV was going to impress the gang at Shaky Pete's, he had another think coming. I straightened in my chair, got set to apologize and quick-step the little snot out to the car, cut a glance his way . . .

. . . and froze.

He was trying.

His mouth was moving.

No words came out. Nothing but a croak, at first. But he kept trying.

"I'm Kenny Spoon," he finally said, "and I'm a damn *drug addict*."

The room was so quiet.

"I'm a *drug addict*. I'm an *alcoholic*. My life is hell be*cause* of it."

So quiet. Most everybody in this circle of light was an AA veteran. We knew what drama queens sounded like.

We also knew the sound of a man tipping, a man breaking.

We knew Kenny Spoon was breaking.

He said, "Oh-fucking-*kay*?"

"Bet your ass okay." It was the actress. She rose, stepped across the light, crouched before Kenny, took his hand in both hers.

That's when he finished breaking.

He sobbed.

He sobbed until you could feel his chest ripping. I've heard it more times than I wish I had. It's bittersweet, the scariest moment of a drunk's life. The last girder gives out and his chest rips and he tumbles into helplessness. He's never been there before, so he free-falls.

Where the free-fall ends, *if* it ends, nobody knows at this point.

That's what makes it scary.

The Shaky Pete's crew was there to help. Strangers to Kenny ten minutes before, they now surrounded him and murmured to him and rubbed his shoulders. A biker who had to be six-six, wearing a walrus mustache and gang colors I didn't recognize, planted a sloppy kiss on his cheek.

In the midst of all this, Pete caught my eye, nodded, rose, left the light.

Seemed like an odd time to vamoose, but it was his joint, and he'd helped me a lot without much cause to. So I followed.

Joined him in the corner by the giant crankshaft balancer, where the only light dribbled from the AA circle forty feet away and a red EXIT sign above.

I waited.

"You think it's for real?" he asked, jerking a thumb. "You think *he's* for real?"

I took my time answering.

"I think so, but it's hard to tell," I finally said. "Sometimes they just want their big moment. They get caught up in it. Don't even realize themselves they're bullshitting."

He nodded. "And for some of 'em, the big moment becomes the new addiction. They need it again and again. They shop for new groups that ain't seen their act yet. We see it all the time from industry types. You known any junkies like that?"

"A hundred."

We were quiet. We looked at the circle, where people were still flooding Kenny with feel-good. The tiny actress had set her Yankees cap cockeyed on his head.

"But we keep pushing that rock," Pete said. To himself, really. A near-whisper.

"Because sometimes they're not bullshitting," I said. "Sometimes they're really breaking. Really getting somewhere."

"Keeps you going, don't it?"

"Yes." Long pause. "You got something else to tell me?"

"I'm stuck with this guilty feeling," Pete said, still looking at the circle of light. "Don't know if it was a good idea to point you at Los Bajamaros. They're serious men."

"Now you tell me."

He ignored that. "See, they're strictly a for-profit outfit. Do work for the old-school mob, the cartels down south, the Russians, the Cambodians. Even did a few hits for some crazy IRA spin-off, if half what you hear is true."

"That makes sense," I said. "When I said I was leaving with Kenny, they handled it like a cost-of-doing-business problem. Like when a FedEx goes missing."

Pete was shaking his head before I finished. "Yeah. No, I mean. It *is* a cost of doing business. But it needs to be made right. And Los Bajamaros only know one way to make things right. Anything less is a sign of weakness to the people they contract with."

"I figured that out, too," I said, thinking about the carloads and their bazookas. Thinking how calmly Lobo Soto had told me I was dead. "They came after me like zombies in a video game."

"The young pups do whatever Soto says. *Anything.* Got nothing to lose, most of 'em. It's half a gang and half a cult."

I nodded. "I can see it. That Soto, he's got something. He's a born leader."

Pete's head swiveled. "You met Soto?"

"I took Kenny away from him."

"In *person,* though? Face-to-*face* you met him?"

"That's what I said."

"Hell, Sax. Now I *really* feel guilty."

"It makes you feel any better, we're out of here tomorrow morning. LAX, wheels up at five forty. Be in Boston before the afternoon rush hour."

"Boston," Shaky Pete said, half-snorting it. "Not far enough."

CHAPTER TEN

The drive back to Tarzana was strange. Kenny thrummed in the backseat, reliving his moment, fondling his new Yankees cap. Up front, I tried to fill in McCord—quietly, so as not to scare hell out of Kenny.

McCord: skeptical. The link between the Barnburners and Shaky Pete didn't impress him. He was a former state cop, with a cop view of the world. The way he saw it, a machinist I'd known less than a week had told me scary bedtime stories about punk gangbangers. Big deal.

He grew less skeptical when we returned to Erin's place.

First, she didn't answer her door. Kenny had to let us in with his key, then punch a code into the control pad of an alarm system.

Erin didn't answer when we hollered for her.

Searching the small house took two minutes.

Kenny found her in the garage.

It was an oddball size, one and a half cars, really. Erin was on the far side of McCord's big Crown Vic. We had to squeeze between its front bumper and a pair of plastic trash cans to see her.

She'd been hogtied with long black zipties. Belly down, cheek on stained concrete, wrists and feet joined at the small of her back by the plastic strips.

The seat of her jeans showed she'd peed herself.

I thought she was dead. My heart dropped an inch in my chest.

Then Kenny pulled a strip of duct tape from her mouth, and Erin inhaled like she wanted all the oxygen the garage had to offer.

Then she was trying to sob and talk and breathe all at once, not doing too good a job at any of it. Kenny sat in an awkward cross-legged pose, cradling her head, while McCord found a utility knife on a shelf and began to cut her free.

Once he did, Erin threw her arms around Kenny, still sobbing, still babbling. I got my first good look at her face.

She was a wreck. Her left eye had puffed shut. It would be black tomorrow, and the white of the eye would be stop-sign red. Makeup, black and pale blue, leaked down her cheeks from both eyes, running with tears. Her nose wasn't much better than her eye—blood from one nostril coated her lips and chin.

That was the scariest thing. People, even bad guys, learn everything they think they know from cop shows on TV, where a strip of tape's the perfect way to hush somebody.

Bullshit. A hunk of tape across the mouth is either useless—the vic slobbers it off with his tongue in five minutes—or deadly. All you leave for breathing is two little nostrils. Vics panic. Vics hyperventilate. Vics fill their throats with puke. Vics suffocate.

We got Erin into the house, onto the sofa. McCord disappeared down the hall for a few seconds. He reappeared with a beach towel for Erin to wrap around her middle.

In my head, anger fought pain fought guilt at the way we'd left her alone.

The look in McCord's eyes told me he was fighting the same battle.

She wept and bubbled and burbled and lisped. It was hard to square this woman with the Erin Barnes who'd been messing with her iPad when we left a few hours ago, fit and smart and self-sufficient.

I nodded McCord away, giving Erin and Kenny some space. I found a bag of frozen peas in the freezer and tossed them to Kenny. He had Erin press the peas to her eye.

Soon Erin walked down the hall, clutching peas in one hand and the beach towel in the other. Kenny mouthed *She wants a bath*. I nodded.

Once the tub was running, I turned to McCord. Like me, he was leaning on the granite bar that split kitchen and living room.

"I'm staying here," he said before I could speak. "Obviously."

I nodded. "Obviously. There's a .45 under your car's seat. I took it out of Van Nuys."

He nodded. "Got a couple of my own. A 1911 I've always favored, and a dumb-ass Dirty Harry wheel gun I came across outside a bar."

I wondered exactly how he came across it. But didn't ask.

"Turns out your machinist spoke the truth," McCord said. "Guess there's something to this underground-AA-railroad bit."

"Guess so," I said. "Are you up for this? Not much doubt anymore. Los Bajamaros mean business."

"Me too."

Erin stayed in the tub forty-five minutes, with Kenny coming and going, bringing her things.

She returned to the living room in a billowy flannel nightgown, off-white with tiny roses, something you'd see on *The Waltons*. Washed and makeup-free, her face looked worse. She sat in an armchair that was oversized enough that Kenny squeezed in next to her, trying to look fierce.

"I'm sorry as hell," McCord said.

"As you fucking well should be," Kenny said.

Erin shushed him.

I said, "What happened?"

"An idiot happened," she said. "They said they were here to fix the phone. And the idiot, who would be me, didn't check her e-mail to see if AT&T had responded to her request. I just assumed. You know?"

I looked at McCord. "That means they saw you cut the line when we got here."

His face went red. "And I didn't *see* them see me."

I said nothing for a while. Finally, "Then what?"

"They grabbed me and . . . sort of muscled me around. Mo . . . molesting me but not really, if you know what I mean, just proving they were in control."

"What did they want to know?"

"Who you were. Where you'd taken Kenny. Were you coming back."

"What did you say?"

"I didn't get a chance," Erin said with a rising laugh that didn't sound healthy. "Not because I'm some kind of Noble Nellie, but because the one began slapping me a little too hard, according to his partner, and before I knew it I was knocked silly and I *couldn't* say anything." She began to cry. She put her face against Kenny's shoulder. "I suppose the overenthusiastic one must be a thug in training. This will surely go on his puh . . . puh . . . permanent record."

Then she cried for a good long time.

It hurt my heart.

It hurt McCord's, too. I saw that.

Nobody spoke.

We listened to Erin cry her way out of it, and I watched McCord breathe.

After what seemed like a long time and a lot of tissues, when she'd mostly pulled herself together, he locked eyes with her. "If I could change it I would," he said. "I can't. But what I can do is stay here. I will protect you."

"Sure, *now*," Kenny said.

I thought about slugging him.

The look Erin shot him likely hurt more.

Then she looked at McCord again.

"I will protect you," he said.

A tear slipped from Erin's good eye.

"I will protect you," McCord said. "My vow."

He leaned across the space and extended his massive hand. When she shook the hand with her tiny one, he made a bow that reminded me of a horse dropping its neck.

CHAPTER ELEVEN

Y ou can't go home again," Kenny Spoon said eighteen hours later.
"And yet here I am."

Here he was. After displaying guts I hadn't expected by climbing on a 737-800 stone cold sober. From the time we'd left Erin's house for LAX to the time he stepped from the Logan jetway, Kenny hadn't said a half-dozen words. His face had been the color of prison peas, and he must've sweated off five pounds he couldn't afford to lose.

But he'd done it.

So here we were.

Bryar.

Where the sun had mostly dropped away, February style. During our drive from the airport, news radio had said our whipsaw winter was up to no good again. During my week in Los Angeles, we'd apparently had a deep freeze, eight inches of snow, and a flash-flood-producing thaw.

Fine by me. All other things being equal, I'll take warm.

As we cleared the long drive's final bend, Eudora came into view. She wore her dark blue parka—intended for a man, judging from the way it hung on her—unzipped. No hat, no gloves.

I stopped fifteen feet away from her.

Behind Eudora, the front door of her house opened.

My headlights lit Harmon as he stepped out, stood beside his mother, and tried to put an arm around her.

She shrugged it away.

"Little bro," Kenny said, staring through the windshield at the man who was a head taller than he was and twice as wide.

Harmon hadn't always been that wide.

If a man can be hard and soft at the same time, he was. Fleshiness was beginning, now that he was solidly into his thirties, to creep into his face—jowls where there didn't use to be any. His eyes were small to begin with, and puffy weight had narrowed them more.

It was the eyes that kept him hard. Cop eyes. They told you from the get-go you were never going to be friends with Harmon Kollar.

He'd been a three-sport star at the regional high school, with football his favorite, but he never got the local-celebrity treatment most boys in his shoes would have. That was partly because Eudora didn't give a damn about sports herself, and partly because around the time Harmon should have been the talk of Bryar, his older brother was first making, then blowing a fortune in Hollywood.

Harmon had found his own way out of Bryar, and it was nearly as rare as Kenny's hit TV show: Harmon sifted through a hundred offers and accepted a football scholarship to the University of Michigan.

Yup, the same school where Kenny had spent a few semesters before moving on to show business. It was one of those coincidences a shrink would say wasn't truly a coincidence. Sure, plenty of little brothers end up going where big brother goes—but keep in mind that Harmon was much younger than Kenny, that the family had no other ties to the U of M, and that Harmon could have just as easily ended up at USC or Texas or Florida State.

Keep all that in mind, and make of the Michigan decision what you will.

His sophomore year, he'd worked his way off the bench, looking pretty decent as a strong safety/outside linebacker hybrid.

Then, starting for the first time in the Wisconsin game, he'd injured himself in a big ugly way. Covering a tight end, running downfield at a dead sprint, Harmon had gotten his legs tangled and managed to kick his own right calf with his left foot. Result: an awful compound fracture that millions of goombahs watched over and over that weekend on *SportsCenter*.

The coaching staff made all the right noises about what a great kid he was, about how he would come back stronger than ever, about all the maize-and-blue glory in his future.

Right.

The truth: His coaches forgot his name the instant they saw the jagged end of a tibia poking a hole in his football pants.

Harmon Kollar's career as a Michigan Wolverine was over.

Eighteen months later, he was back in Bryar with a limp, taking the exam to get on the cops and on with the rest of his life.

Here's the funny part, though, the part that makes you scratch your head: Years later, when he got a chance to open his dream business, he named it after his handshake with glory. The lettering on the WOLVERINE BROS. FREIGHT & STORAGE sign was maize and blue.

Michigan colors.

Go figure.

"Well," I said.

"Well," Kenny said.

I killed the truck. We climbed out. I unbungee'd his suitcase from my bed, passed the handle to him, and watched him cross to his mother.

The drag bag's plastic wheels made little tracks in what remained of the snow.

Eudora and Kenny stood eighteen inches apart and looked at each other.

Then she stepped to him and they hugged.

They hugged a long time.

After a while, Harmon reached over and patted Kenny on the shoulder, the way you'd pat a neighbor's dog that you didn't like.

Then Harmon went back in the house while the hug lengthened.

"Well," I said out loud, turning to leave.

"Don't you dare, Conway Sax," Eudora said. "You come and join us."

Greyhounds don't bark much, but Dandy and Cha Cha whurfled at Kenny a few times to show how brave they were. Then they skittered to the back of the house.

The place was hot and stuffy as ever, and by the time we were all inside, Harmon had spread himself out in such a way that he took up most of the couch. He wore his khaki uniform but no belt or gun.

I stood. Kenny flopped into the blue corduroy chair and heel-rubbed his eyes. "Well, *that* was awful," he said to his half brother. "My first sober flight in twenty years. Cross-country, no less, and with only Silent Sam for company." Jerking a thumb at me. "It was like spending five hours with Mount Rushmore."

Harmon said nothing.

Me too.

One of the things I didn't say to Kenny during the flight was that Los Bajamaros scared me—and ought to scare him. I kept thinking back to Shaky Pete's comment when I said we were flying three thousand miles due east: "Not far enough."

I'd spent time at Walpole. Massachusetts Correctional Institution–Cedar Junction, they like to call it now. You learn something about gangs there whether you want to or not. I'd learned all the major gangs were now nationwide, even international, with chapters everywhere and reciprocal deals with other gangs in cities where their presence was light.

McCord knew all this, too, of course, though from the cop's perspective rather than the con's. Before we left Erin's house, I'd asked him to call around about Los Bajamaros. Wanted to see how heavy the threat truly was.

For the next few days at least, I was going to keep a hell of a close eye on Kenny and his mother's place.

Eudora bustled in with a can of ginger ale. Watching Kenny twist it in his hands, she dry-washed her own. "Canada Dry," she said, trying to smile. "Your favorite."

"It's diet," Kenny said, setting it on the table unopened.

Eudora's face fell.

Man, that was new. I'd never seen her this way.

"It's diet," Harmon said.

Two words only, but they shut down the room.

"It's *diet*?" he said again, leaning forward. "After everything she did? Getting your latest SOS, dropping everything—in her state—to haul your scrawny ass back here . . . and you bitch about *diet soda*?"

"I sent no SOS, I assure you," Kenny said. "I was fully prepared to sleep in the bed I'd made, as Conway will attest. Got that, little brother?"

"*Half* brother," Harmon said.

"Boys," Eudora said.

"Cool it," I said.

But Kenny pressed. He stared down Harmon, looking like a man with a hole card. "I was a mere pawn in the game my captors were playing," he said. "And I do believe *you*, bro, were the king. Or, at the very least, a strategically placed rook. Oh, we don't like hearing that? Oh, we're storming off now? Ta ta, *bro*."

The front door slammed behind Harmon.

Eudora put her face in her hands. "I knew it," she said, beginning to cry.

"What the hell," I said to Kenny, "was that all about?"

"Ask him." Kenny nodded toward the front door. Outside, a truck started.

"I hoped for better," Eudora said. "I hoped Harmon had grown up. But I'm a fool. Deep down, I knew this would happen."

I stepped over and put an arm around her shoulders.

She let me.

CHAPTER TWELVE

I damn near left the Barnburners for Eudora Spoon. That's something you need to know. About me. About her. About where she fits.

AA's full of suggestions. That's a big word around the halls. They *suggest* you work your way through the twelve steps. They *suggest* you hit your knees and say thanks every morning and every night.

There's an undercurrent, though, a hum beneath it all, like the hum beneath vinyl record.

In AA, a suggestion's not really a suggestion.

It's an order.

The undercurrent, the LP hum, goes like this: *You got here because you spent a lifetime doing things your way—and screwing up royally. If you've got the sense God gave a goat, and we're not sure you do, you'll work things exactly as we say—as we* suggest—*and then, amigo, and only* then, *might you make something of your thus-far-miserable life.*

If I had to name a top reason AA's not for everybody, I'd say it's this LP hum, these suggestions that aren't suggestions. To truly accept the program, you have to set aside your will.

Hard to do?

Yes.

Especially hard for addicts?

Hell yes.

Me, I'd managed it. I didn't question why. Still don't, really. I did what people told me to do. They had sobriety, *good* sobriety, not the white-knuckle, sweaty-sheet type I was used to. I wanted what they had. So whenever a suggestion that wasn't really a suggestion made me grind my teeth, I ground them, and said yessir while I did it.

Until they told me Eudora Spoon couldn't be my sponsor.

That just about drove me away.

Backstory: I never was any good as a sponsee.

I've been told that's not a real word. But in AA, you can bet your ass it is.

I'm no good at it. Never have been. Don't talk enough. Don't pick up the phone. Would rather sit in my room and work things through on my own.

AA *suggests* everybody have a sponsor.

I ran through a dozen in my first year. They all quit on me because I wouldn't talk to them, wouldn't reach out. One guy, and I'm not proud to admit it, boxed me in after a meeting, reminded me I'd been his sponsee for three weeks, and asked if I knew his name.

I didn't.

I'm still friends with a bunch of those guys. I was just lousy as a sponsee.

It all changed the night I stepped on Eudora's foot at the weekly Barnburners meeting. She was a regular, that much I knew. But I didn't realize she was a major-league Barnburner, a Meeting After the Meeting vet who'd declared a few years previous that she was too old and too jaded to do it anymore.

That night, trying to cross the premeeting room in a hurry, I stepped on her ankle. Paused, said I was sorry, asked was she okay.

"Better than Big Vig Vukovich," she said, keeping her eyes on her knitting. "You paid him a visit last week and stepped on his *knee*. Until it broke. Or was I misinformed?"

My mouth made an O. How had this old lady, with her white brush cut and her purple eyes and her pink yarn, heard about *that*?

"Fear not, secret's safe," she said, finally looking up at me with laughing eyes. "Nobody likes a loan shark. Especially one like Big Vig, who lures new clients outside the methadone clinic."

Me: poleaxed. I paid attention to nothing during the meeting, then hit Butch Feeley afterward for a download on the knitting lady.

Butch had laughed and laughed. Had clapped me on the shoulder, had said there was a lot more to Eudora Spoon—it was the first time I heard the name—than knitting.

That's how that started. Once we connected, I found myself spilling like an eighth-grade girl. Whether we were riding in my truck to a meeting—this was more than ten years ago, but Eudora'd already thrown in the towel on driving after dark—or walking her dogs or playing board games, I talked and talked and let her in on things I'd never before said out loud.

And never will again.

Why Eudora Spoon?

Damned if I know.

I just know it worked for me.

I guess it did for her, too, because one summer evening on her back porch, after rolling double sixes to skunk me at backgammon, she said, real casual, "It seems to me we ought to formalize this relationship. What say you?"

It took me a few seconds to get it. "You mean sponsor-sponsee?"

"That's exactly what I mean."

"That's, ah, not suggested." Men sponsor men. Women sponsor women. That's the way it is. It's *suggested* by AA, always has been, and everybody knows it.

"I've told you a dozen times I'm too old to give a rat's red ass about their suggestions," she said, looking at me over her glasses. "If you'll pardon my French."

She reached across the table to shake my hand.

And there it was. Me, with an AA sponsor I could blab to, a sponsor I trusted.

A sponsor whose name I could remember.

Because say what you will about Eudora Spoon, and it turned out quite a few Barnburners had quite a lot to say about her, she was memorable.

Sponsor-sponsee deals come and go. It's all informal. There's no master list in a vault, no Secretary of Sponsors keeping track. So Eudora and I could have gone on forever, quietly, and everything would have been just fine.

Eudora had other plans.

For reasons I didn't understand then and still don't fully, she needed to make a big show of it. So at the Barnburner meeting following our summer backgammon game, during the call for new business that nobody ever paid attention to, she rose and cleared her throat and announced she was thrilled to now be sponsoring Conway. May he continue to enjoy one-day-at-a-time sobriety and be an asset to the group, et cetera, blah blah blah.

The world stopped.

The silence piled up.

I'd been in the jury box at the time, and I felt lucky that eyeballs couldn't fire laser beams.

I don't know if anybody else says "jury box," so I'll explain it.

Saint Anne's has an odd bump-out on its northern wall. In addition to the usual army of folding chairs facing the podium, there's space for another dozen or so arranged kitty-corner. The old-timers and leaders gravitate to these chairs, which give you a view of the whole room. They—we—use them to keep an eye on the scene. People who sneak out for a smoke, or palaver with their neighbor, or fall asleep, or send text messages, get a talking-to. People who do it again get tossed by Pablo and Skinny Dennis.

Serious AA for serious people.

The jury box is where Barnburner leaders sit. It's informal but it's not, just as AA suggestions aren't really suggestions at all. Those of us who take those jury-box seats hold a little thing called the Meeting After the Meeting, where we talk about which members need a hand and who's going to offer it.

After Eudora's big announcement that night years ago, Meeting After the Meeting types had strafed me one by one. Who did I think I was? Didn't I know men sponsored men and women sponsored women? Didn't I pay any attention to the suggestions? Wasn't sixty years of AA wisdom enough to persuade me? Hadn't ten-plus years on the bum, in hobo jungles and county jails, convinced me that doing things my way wasn't such a hot idea?

It took me by surprise. The firestorm showed me, for the first time, cracks in the all-for-one front presented by AA. By the Barnburners. Especially by Meeting After the Meeting insiders. There was something personal and ugly about the way they turned when Eudora made her announcement.

I was ready to fight. I was ready to go down in flames. I was ready to stand with Eudora and tell the world to go shit in its fist.

Who talked me out of that?

Eudora Spoon.

Of course.

"So you rise," she said one night as the two of us drove to a meeting. "You rise, and you make your *Mr. Smith Goes to Washington* speech. Fifes, snare drums, righteousness, et cetera. For a big finish, you tell AA and the Barnburners they can all kiss your sturdy rear end. What happens after that, Conway? Have you thought it through that far?"

"Well," I said.

"What happens," Eudora said, "is they go right back to making their suggestions that aren't suggestions. And you, my dear, go out and get drunk."

"Like hell I do."

"Not that night," she said, setting a hand on my wrist. "Not for a week, a month, a year. But yes. Eventually, you get drunk. Imagine yourself without the Barnburners and tell me if I'm wrong."

I imagined it.

She was right.

I said nothing.

I wondered why *she'd* gone public with the announcement, then told *me* not to make waves.

I didn't ask.

CHAPTER THIRTEEN

With Harmon gone, the feel of Eudora's house changed all at once. She stepped behind Kenny's chair and set both hands on his shoulders. It hit me: She'd invited me in to referee when both sons were around. Now she didn't need or want me there.

That was okay by me. I had somewhere to go. I said quick good-byes and left.

At the end of Eudora's driveway, getting set to take a right and head for I-495, I eased past a pair of stone pillars and looked both ways.

And caught a glimpse of Harmon's taillights.

I knew they were his—we both drive F-250s, and when we're forced to talk with each other, trucks are one of the few things that come up.

Harmon, headed west.

It was odd. His house was right across the road—I was looking up his driveway right now. He'd worked a long day. The nearest restaurants, takeout joints, and convenience stores were all to the right. Besides, Harmon was a creature of habit, as anybody in Bryar could tell you. In Eudora's house, he'd worn no Sam Browne belt. That was a dead giveaway that he was in for the night, done with official duties.

Huh.

Snap decision: I hooked a left and followed him.

Before long, he made another left onto a little spur road connecting 142 to 140, a shortcut to Milford and Mendon.

It's an oddball road with oddball zoning that's made for oddball neighbors. You've got Bryar's old cemetery, which ran out of space a hundred years ago. Then Saginaw Fence, a dirt-lot outfit that rents chain link and Jersey barriers and security to construction sites.

Saginaw Fence wasn't doing so hot lately, but that's another story.

Then the Golden Dragon, a Chinese restaurant that squats on a half acre of tarmac as if a helicopter dropped it there.

By the time I came up, Harmon was idling in an empty corner of the Dragon's lot.

He wasn't alone. Had rolled up to another truck, a Dodge Ram, window to window. Was talking with its driver.

I couldn't swear to it, but I thought something was tossed or handed from Harmon's truck into the Ram.

Huh.

Just like that, the meet was over. Harmon made a quick one-eighty, spitting gravel in a miniburnout that was more temper tantrum than anything else, and headed back the way he'd come.

I let him build a lead, then followed again.

The Dragon was mostly a bar catering to the Saginaw Fence guys, contractors, roofers, electricians—that crowd.

I'd eaten there. Once.

Nobody eats at the Dragon more than once.

The joint was run by a good guy named Willy. I'd never seen anybody else behind that bar. He slept there, for all I knew.

I eased east on 142, pretty sure Harmon was headed home now, not wanting to ride his bumper.

Sure enough, he cut the hard left into his own uphill driveway.

Lots to think about.

But not now.

Because I was late for my dinner date.

I may have smiled as I hit the gas.

* * *

Got there early. A mall in Marlborough. Good place to meet my date because it's midway between Framingham and Shrewsbury.

Funny thing about malls: I like them a lot, always have. I know I'm supposed to think they're plastic and generic, but I get a nice feeling when I'm inside one. My friend Randall once said I like malls because they let me be around people while remaining alone. I never thought it through that far, but Randall's a smart guy.

I wound up at the second-floor food court with a cup of coffee. Sat, sipped, scanned the foot traffic for my date.

Behind me was a coin-operated arcade and play land. Its rinky-dink music fought with bubblegum pop piped from the ceiling. The play-land music made me smile. I'd been bringing Sophie here most of her life, and that damn music hadn't changed one note. There was a time I could blow five bucks in quarters putting her on the cheesy merry-go-round.

I didn't recognize her, not at first. Not until she was two feet away and smiling.

Because Sophie Bollinger looked so damn grown up.

She was with a friend, which was unusual—Sophie's a loner, always has been. The friend was much taller, but the pair of them were dressed like twins: suede boots, skinny jeans tucked into the boots, long-sleeve tops, makeup that made my heart sing and break at the same time because it was so ladylike but so amateurish.

"What college you girls go to?" I said, feeling a big dumb smile on my face.

"I *told* you," Sophie said to her friend. Then to me, "This is Lily."

The tall girl made a pretty, self-conscious smile. "I'm Lily. And I'm leaving. I'm Leaving Lily. Okay, bye."

She walked away, stifling giggles.

Thirteen-year-old girls. You know?

I'd assumed Sophie would want Burger King—that was our tradition—but she led me instead to the Thai place and asked a bunch of questions about what was grilled and what was fried. She wound up with mostly vegetables.

"Sit rep," I said once we found a table. "Give it to me."

She smiled. She can't get enough military jargon. Sophie bugs Randall, who's ex-army, for fresh terms every time she sees him.

Charlene had booted me out, and I understood that. Respected it. Deserved it. But Sophie and I had shared something from the get-go, something Charlene only half grasped and—maybe because she only half grasped it—resented.

Sophie and I needed to stay in touch. *Needed* to. She means that much to me, and I guess I mean something to her.

So it was calls and texts and emails . . . and, whenever we could swing it, dinner in the food court.

It was better than nothing.

She talked about one of my cats, Davey, who was staying with her on a sort of extended loan and loving it.

"How about you?" I asked. "How are those genius classes, the PA stuff?"

She laughed. "Advanced Placement. *AP,* not PA. They're fine. They're fun."

"How about the classmates? Any better?"

Sophie's a stone genius. In her freshman year at Shrewsbury High, she was taking AP—not PA—English and chemistry. She was a thirteen-year-old in college classes, practically. Which was pretty cool.

Except most of the seniors in the classes had decided to be jerks. They froze her out. Sabotaged her projects. Like that.

I'd wanted to do something about it. Sophie had to beg me not to visit the jerks in the parking lot.

"The classmates are fine," she said. The way her eyes flicked told me she was lying.

Anger flared. I tamped it. She'd made it clear I was to butt out.

"And you've got Leaving Lily," I said.

"I've got Leaving Lily. Her wicked stepmother is picking us up in"—she looked at her white plastic watch—"forty minutes."

We ate.

From the play land, the merry-go-round tune played for the tenth time since I'd sat. I set my fork in pad Thai remnants. "Ring a bell?"

Sophie knew I meant the music. She smiled and speared a green bean. "It always will."

I watched her nibble the bean. "Any word from Jessie?" I asked.

"She called from New Orleans. She wanted money. For art school, she said."

"Yeah, right."

"Yeah, right. Mom shot her down hard."

Jessie is Charlene's older daughter. Got her share of problems. Maybe more than her share. Put it this way: The *best* move she ever made was to run off to Boulder, Colorado, with my son, Roy, when they were fresh out of high school.

He kept her semisober for a while.

Jessie dumped him for being too straight, came back east, found a half-dozen flavors of trouble, split again. Every once in a while, she popped up and tried to squeeze dough out of her mother for whatever habit she was into.

She didn't have much luck with that. Not for lack of money—Charlene has plenty, owns a transcription-and-translation business. Unfortunately for Jessie, though, Charlene's a recovering junkie and completely unbullshitable.

"How's your mother?" I tried to keep it neutral.

"Business has slowed down for the first time ever," Sophie said. "The states and towns are broke. The Feds can't go broke because they just keep printing money, but they've raised the slow-pay to an art form."

I smiled. "You're quoting her."

"But of course."

"Just the two of you around the house. How is that?"

She shrugged. Did not meet my gaze. "You know Mom. Life is good when business is good."

"And right now, business is bad."

"Lily sleeps over a lot. It helps. I think Mom likes having a third party around as much as I do."

"Just not this third party in particular." I bumped my thumb to my chest and tried to smile. Not sure I pulled it off.

"The fault, dear Brutus, lies not in the stars."

"Huh?"

"Never mind." She sipped water through a straw. "Okay, it's your turn under the hot lights. Sit rep, amigo. How was California?"

I told it. It took a while.

She was quiet when I finished, latched on to an idea. I know the look.

"How well do you know Eudora?" she finally said.

"She's a Barnburner. A Meeting After the Meeting type from way back. I've told her things . . . I've told her things I haven't told God."

"Yeah yeah yeah"—did she roll her eyes some?—"you'd lay down your life for her, walk through fire, et cetera. But how well do you *know* her? How much has she shared with you?"

"She's shared goddamn plenty." I felt my face go hot as I spoke, not liking Sophie's tone. That's the trouble with smart kids. They're smart.

If she sensed my anger, she ignored it. "Here's why I ask. Her rationale, the whole MacGuffin here, is thin. Don't you think?"

"What's a MacGuffin?"

"It's a cinematic . . . never mind. All Eudora said to set off this chain of events was that she wanted to see her son. But her *reason* for wanting to see him, as you've related it to me . . . it's flimsy at best. Wouldn't you say?"

"Well."

"Missing pieces? The secret to the universe? Spare me."

"People really do think about things differently when they get close to the end," I said. "It's one area, maybe the *only* area, I know more about than you, punk."

Sophie half-smiled. "Noted. But does it jibe? Does the sudden longing for the ne'er-do-well son mesh with Eudora's personality?"

"Maybe more than you think. She seems to . . . *like* him more than she likes Harmon, the one who stuck by her all these years. Does that seem weird to you?"

"Familiarity breeds contempt. Absence makes the heart grow fonder. Any cliché in a storm."

We were quiet for a minute. Leaving Lily circled like the world's most timid shark. It looked to me like Sophie had something on her mind.

"I told Mom," she finally said, "that I was worried about you being on your own. She said not to worry. She said all good men are alone anyway."

I said nothing.

A smile fluttered on Sophie's lips. "Then she added, in a big transparent rush, that all *bad* men are alone, too. And do you know what I said?"

"What?"

"I asked, 'What about the ones in the middle?'"

"What did she say to that?"

"She said, 'Why would anybody ever mess with them?'"

Then Sophie rose, came around the table, set a hand on my shoulder, and kissed my cheek. "Think about Eudora, okay? Just this once, don't take everything at face value."

She walked off with her friend.

I did as she'd asked. I sat in the near-empty food court and thought about Eudora Spoon and listened to the cheesy merry-go-round music and remembered the weight of Sophie's hand on my shoulder.

CHAPTER FOURTEEN

I rolled east toward Framingham, where I was staying in Floriano Mendes's basement.

Yup. At my age. Living in the semifinished basement of a buddy.

More than a buddy, really. A blood brother who'd helped me in ways I didn't deserve.

About ten years ago, Floriano and his wife, Maria, bought a massive Victorian near Framingham's downtown. The place was in rough shape, but we went through it system by system, then room by room. Now it was the nicest home in the neighborhood.

Which wasn't saying an awful lot. Framingham, Massachusetts, doesn't know what it is or wants to be. North of Route 9, the east-west main drag, it's a commuter suburb for folks who work in Boston. Route 9 itself is one of those Miracle Mile roads, strip malls that everybody hates but everybody uses.

Down here, south of 9, Framingham's a little city, and not a good one. You know the recipe: manufacturing out, immigrants in, old-timers who don't like the tax hikes pushed by the powers that be. Soup kitchens, a big Salvation Army, methadone clinics, halfway houses. If it weren't for a state college, a solid hospital, and a swarm of Brazilians who work their asses off and aren't in a position to ask for much in return—a lot of them are illegals—Framingham would collapse on itself, like a Leominster or a Fall River.

I parked. The house was dark inside except for a light in the bedroom of Dozen, the youngest son. Kid was always doing homework, looked to be the first Mendes headed for college.

Maria must be in bed, and Floriano was part of a night-time janitorial crew.

Fine by me. I didn't feel like talking.

What had Eudora said to me, that day she shanghaied me into rounding up Kenny? *I know things have changed for you . . . I thought you might have the time and the inclination to do something a bit different.*

And how. I sighed, locked my truck, toted my duffel up the walk and front steps, then let myself in through the oak door.

Inclination to do something a bit different? Why the hell not? I had no girlfriend. I had no job—was living on the insurance payout from a shop of mine that'd been torched by a creep. It'd been a good shop, too, booked up from the get-go. I was looking around for a new site. Although if you want the truth, I wasn't looking as hard as I ought to.

These days, I didn't have many Barnburner responsibilities, either. I'd made some mistakes. Barnburners had suffered. In our world, deeds meant everything and words meant shit. My mistakes had caused the Barnburners to rely on me less.

It had to be that way.

But it hurt.

The Barnburner freeze-out was a big part of the reason I'd been spending so much time in Bryar lately.

All I know how to do, all I *want* to do, is be useful.

I hadn't turned out to be very useful to Charlene.

Same went for the Barnburners.

The torched shop meant that for a while anyway, until I regrouped and rebuilt, I wasn't even useful as a mechanic.

So I'd flowed to the first person who could keep me busy.

Eudora, when she told me she had cancer.

I'd come to know her needs, her rhythms. Not to mention her family and even her town.

It struck me once while watching the National Geographic Channel at two in the morning that I was a certain kind of pilot fish.

You know pilot fish. They're parasites—they swim alongside sharks, waiting for a kill, surviving on fallen morsels.

Me? I find need. I attach myself, swim alongside.

I try to tell myself I'm the *opposite* of a parasite. After all, I don't wait for a kill and snap up morsels. I ease the need. I bring something to the table.

It's the attaching that bothers me. What would I be, I sometimes wonder, what would I *do* if I was purely on my own?

Lesson: When insomnia hits, watch something other than the National Geographic Channel.

Inside, I stepped quietly through the foyer, past the dining room with its dual portraits of Jesus Christ and Ayrton Senna, down a hall, through the door to the basement.

Dale, my easygoing cat, was happy to see me. He chirped. He rubbed his head on my hand. He followed me around, flipping his tail.

I gave Dale a good rubdown, changed his litter box, and recharged his food and water. Then I washed up and stripped and hit my knees and prayed and went to bed, knowing that in the morning I would pilot-fish my way out to Bryar and attach myself to Eudora's family problems.

Dale jumped onto the cot and marched around on me until I splayed my legs. Then he curled up between them and went to sleep.

He's a good cat.

It's an early house. Dozen's school bus comes at quarter to seven, and Floriano, Maria, and the miscellaneous cousins that come and go— I'm pretty sure there's no blood relation, that Floriano provides beds for new-in-country illegals, but he calls them cousins, and what do I care?—all begin their first jobs around then.

So the next morning, I made it to Eudora's in time, I thought, for her morning walk with the greys. Snow had moved in overnight, a little nor'easter that had veered inland later than it was supposed to.

The house was freezing, the dog beds empty.

"Sheesh, old lady," I said out loud, smiling. "Try sleeping in one day of your life."

I got the wood stove cranking and put coffee on. I would join the hike, then have a talk with Eudora.

Out the door, zipping jacket, pulling on hat and gloves, taking a left.

When I got around front, facing the road, I squinted against snow that fell at a forty-five-degree angle. Spotted movement, looked ahead. Saw Eudora's hand-knit hat on the other side of a small rise that partially blocked my view of 142.

She reappeared gradually. Hat, then pink face, then blue parka. Walking well, walking strong. The dogs reappeared, too, wearing their coats. The first time I'd seen the coats, I'd rolled my eyes and mumbled something about spoiled hounds and Zsa Zsa Gabor. "Look at them," Eudora had said. "They've got very little fur and next to no fat. When we're cold, they're cold. Ignorance is not pretty, Conway."

She could put you in your place when the spirit moved her.

Coats or no coats, the dogs weren't one bit happy with the blowing snow. Dandy especially pranced and stamped and turned his head toward Eudora, pleading for mercy.

When Eudora made it to the top of the rise, she stopped and grinned down at me. Feet spread at shoulder width, fists on hips.

She was proud of her stunt. Proud to be hiking her property with her greyhounds on her terms. Age be damned. Blizzard be damned. Small-cell carcinoma be damned.

In that moment, I loved Eudora Spoon more than ever.

I cupped my gloved hands. "How is cancer supposed to kill you," I said, hollering to be heard above the wind, "if you freeze to death in a snowdrift?"

Her smile grew bigger. "That's the point!" she said and began to take a step.

She didn't finish it.

Instead, she whiplashed. It looked like an invisible football player had put his shoulder pad in the small of her spine: shoulders and head snapped back, then forward toward me. She rose on the toes of her boots. Her mouth made an O, and I swear she looked me in the eye.

I swear she did.

Then Eudora fell on her face.

She slid a foot and a half.

Then she stopped.

I've been asked a hundred times if I heard the shot, and all I can say is I don't know. The wind was blowing in my direction, so you'd think I would have.

But context is king. And what's more out of context than a rifle shot when you're joking around with your friend in a snowstorm?

Add to that the way everything blended and merged and tilted once I saw Eudora whiplash and fall and slide.

Honest answer: I don't know if I heard the shot.

I know I scrambled to her, thinking only that she'd fallen—but that it'd been a nasty fall, a heart-attack fall.

At that point, the dogs knew more than I did. They knew something was not just wrong, but *big-time* wrong. They froze, the both of them. Just stood there, shivers their only movement.

I scrambled. The rise was no big deal in good weather, but it was slick as hell now. I slipped twice, wound up scrabbling the last ten yards on hands and knees.

She was facedown. I didn't notice the entrance puncture in her parka. Wasn't looking for one. Was still thinking of a faint. A heart attack, a stroke. Low blood pressure, maybe. Or something related to her meds.

I said her name.

She said nothing.

I slapped my shirt pocket through my jacket, realized I'd left my cell in the truck. Cursed.

I rolled her over. They always say you shouldn't, but what else was I going to do?

Eudora's nose was scraped raw from the fall and slide.

Her eyes were closed.

Her face was white. So white. Too white.

The snow beneath her was a pretty red.

Blood spurted as I shifted her. The exit wound was near her breastbone.

Something made a noise like a crow.

I guess it was me.

CHAPTER FIFTEEN

The second shot I definitely heard. Like I said, context is king: Just before I heard it, there on my knees, cradling Eudora, pressing a palm over her breastbone, watching my glove turn the same pretty red as the snow beneath us, the ground beside my right knee puffed.

Instinct pulled my head in the direction of Harmon's home, but farther left: the no-man's-land between the house itself and Wolverine Bros. Freight & Storage.

It wasn't until then, really, that things snapped into place.

Somebody had shot Eudora Spoon. Shot her in the back.

Now he was shooting at me.

The ground puffed again, in nearly the exact spot as before—maybe eight inches from my right knee—and finally, for the first goddamn time all morning, I did something useful.

I flipped backward, lunging from my knees, hanging on to Eudora as I did it.

The lunge plus the slickness propelled me like a toboggan with Eudora riding me.

I watched her mouth move like a fish's in the bottom of your boat.

Then I watched her eyes open.

She was speaking. Or trying to.

"Save it," I said. "Just breathe."

Her eyes fluttered shut, but her mouth kept moving. So weak.

Warm cheeks told me I was crying as we reached the bottom of our little toboggan run.

"Just *breathe*, Eudora."

She didn't listen to me. As usual. The eyes fluttered open.

"I don't want the bastards to have it," she said. "And know what the funny part is?"

I shushed her.

"The funny part," she said, ignoring me for the last time, "is that I don't even remember *why* I don't want them to have it. It's all so . . . unimportant."

I shushed her again. Held her to me, heart on heart. Thinking, if I was thinking anything, that pressing hard on the exit wound might help.

Blood pulsed against my jacket.

I bet she'd have some toboggan stories to tell. Growing up around here, a hell of a hilly place, all those years ago. When kids knew how to get outside and have fun.

I bet Eudora Spoon could tell you stories of sledding parties and toboggan rides all day.

But not now.

Because she died then.

I could tell. We lay there, heart on heart, snow falling on my eyelashes.

Everything just left her. There was . . . *less* to her.

Cha Cha came over and snuffled at Eudora's hair, at her neck.

Dandy followed.

The pair of them snuffled and pawed and stamped.

I remembered Eudora telling me greyhounds have giant hearts.

She would know.

What do you do?

What would *you* do?

One thing I knew: You don't lie there in the snow and wait to get shot.

I rolled Eudora on her back. I knelt, hunching without realizing it, pulling into myself like a turtle, making myself a smaller target. Craned my head to the right, scanning, and relaxed some: that last bit of hill, the one we'd just tobogganed down, blocked my view of Harmon's property.

If I couldn't see the shooter, he couldn't see me.

So get to work.

Charlene says I compartmentalize. She says it like it's a bad thing.

Not when you do what I do. Compartments are just what you need. They get you through.

Eudora Spoon—friend, Barnburner, back-shot from her son's yard—went in one compartment.

I slammed a lid on it.

A new compartment lid opened: *Don't get killed. Catch the shooter.*

I was about to run for my cell when I spotted a flat bulge in the right front pocket of Eudora's dungarees.

Phone?

Yes.

I fished it out.

I called 911.

I ran while I punched the numbers, ran in an instinctive hunch because once I stood, the shooter across the road regained his line-of-sight connection.

Just before I reached the front porch, the greyhounds passed me. The damn things run forty miles an hour. It's hard to believe until you see it.

They pawed at the door. I let them in as the emergency operator finally picked up.

"Shooting," I said. "Bryar, Route 142."

A man's voice said, "Is that West Upton Road, sir?"

"It's . . . I dunno, it's 142 to me. Yeah, West Upton Road. I guess. It's Eudora Spoon. Harmon's mom."

"She's the one been *shot*?"

"Yeah."

It was a regional system, and I had no idea who was on the other end of the line, but these are small towns, and law is always friends with law. The man I was talking with knew Harmon. Had to.

"Jesus Christ," he said. "I'll send 'em all."

"She's dead. Shot from across the way. A long gun."

"Jesus Christ."

"Yeah." I clicked off, saw the dogs had already lain on the floor on their blankets, back to back for warmth. That seemed good enough, so I flew out the door and to my truck. Forearm-brushed snow from the driver's side of the windshield, hopped in, fired it, took off.

As I drove down Eudora's driveway toward 142, I goosed the throttle a few times to gauge how much traction I was working with.

Answer: not much, but more than none. It was a good thing I'd mounted my snow tires, that was for sure. The flakes were fat and wet and blowing from the northeast. Enough had fallen in a hurry so that even with my snows on, I worried about getting up Harmon's long drive.

Who the hell shot her?

I shook my head to chase the question away. Needed all the focus I could pull together. Focus and compartmentalization.

Find the shooter.

Catch the shooter.

Questions were for later.

Grieving, too.

When I reached the road, a glance told me I didn't have to worry about making it up Harmon's driveway. Fresh tracks led from there to 142. A car had come down too fast, cranked its front tires full right, locked everything up—not easy with ABS, but not impossible on snow or ice—plowed into the road, recovered, and taken off.

West.

I turned left and headed that way.

Picked up speed, reminding myself to drive smart. Smooth is smart. In snow or rain, that goes double. Every push of the throttle, every nudge of the steering wheel, should be slow slow slow. A road-racing buddy with a rep for being unbeatable in the rain once told me if you did all your braking and steering at half speed in the wet, you were doing it too fast—try quarter speed.

It was good advice. Works in the rain, and it was working for me in heavy snow.

Route 142 runs along the bottom of what was a river valley a million years ago. So the road's never straight and never flat. Blind curves, off-camber turns. Dangerous as hell—even in dry weather. There are a couple of head-ons here every year. The newspapers write editorials. Then the state does studies on the cost of blasting through granite to flatten out the road, and after looking at the price tag, everybody decides a few more warning signs will do.

Once I got my momentum up, I clipped right along. Between its rear-wheel drive and its light back end, the F-250's bed wanted to come around every time I gentled my foot from the throttle. That's called being loose.

The good news: Loose is fast.

The bad news: Loose is loose.

I figured it out. I dealt with it.

I heard snow-muffled sirens. Squeezed right, watched an ambulance and fire truck marked GRAFTON FIRE & RESCUE rip past me, headed east.

Headed for Eudora.

Compartmentalize.

To take my mind off her, I ran figures in my head, wondering how many minutes' head start the shooter had, how long it would take to catch him, where that would happen.

I drove hard, following the only set of westbound tire tracks.

After maybe five minutes that seemed a lot longer, I saw it.

Something tall and black, an SUV.

It vanished around a hilly corner.

I drove harder. Felt my back end step out as I cleared a turn, saved it, kept my foot in the gas. With all senses in max-intake mode, as they'd been the morning I found Kenny Spoon in Van Nuys, a corner of my head noticed the twelve-foot rooster tail of snow my rear tires were spitting.

It was a strange chase. The snow ate up most of the sound, and after the fire truck I never saw another vehicle or human being. Everybody was playing it smart, staying inside for the duration.

Except the man who shot Eudora Spoon.

And me.

The quiet made everything seem more desperate somehow.

I was closing.

The SUV was a Ford Excursion. Huge, looked like a two-story shed on wheels. I smelled diesel fuel—the diesel always was the engine to have in those trucks. My ears got in on the act: Clickity-clickity told me the Excursion wore studded snow tires.

Maybe I imagined it, but I thought the driver did a double take when he noticed I was gaining. I believe he glanced in the mirror, spotted me, glanced again, and thought *What the hell?* He lifted without knowing it, got just a little bit sideways, then clenched his teeth and rolled back into the gas to straighten himself out.

Now, as 142 merged with Route 140 and we ripped northwest through Grafton, I was in his head. He had four-wheel drive and studded snows. I had an ass-light two-wheel-drive pickup truck with a torquey V8, a true bitch to drive in the snow, and I sure didn't have studded tires.

I wasn't supposed to catch him.

Or so someone had told him.

He'd been misinformed.

CHAPTER SIXTEEN

How fast were we going? That's what people always ask.

I saw sixty-five-plus on my speedometer around the time I drew close enough to the Excursion's back end so that the world grew even quieter. I was in his draft, unbuffeted by air now.

Sixty-five doesn't sound so fast? The speed limit fluctuated between thirty-five and forty. That was considered safe when the road was dry.

So try going sixty-five on that road, in a snowstorm, in a rear-drive truck.

Then tell me if it feels fast.

I stared at the back end of the SUV, waited for him to make a mistake.

In my Busch Grand National days, I had a spotter who used to say the same thing over and over when I closed on a car: "Get in his mirrors. Show him your nose. Fuck with him."

It works. Even with pros. Stay in a guy's mirrors long enough and he'll either make a mistake or half-consciously let you by just to be rid of you.

I showed the Excursion my nose. I fucked with him.

Popped into his left mirror, then his right, then drove along six inches from his back bumper.

He was good, dumb, desperate, or all three, because other than the bobble when he first spotted me, he didn't make a mistake.

Then things got worse. I heard a pop-pop-pop. It was quiet, snow-muffled, innocent-sounding.

I moved to the right a few feet to check it out.

Saw a handgun sticking out the truck's passenger window.

Pointed at me.

Pop-pop-pop.

Self-preservation instinct took over and I tapped the brakes, knowing in an instant I'd screwed up. My back end slewed left.

I steered left.

My back end slewed right.

I steered right.

My back end slewed left again.

It's called a tank-slapper, and the problem is that the pendulum swings try to get bigger and bigger until you're backward.

The other problem, *my* other problem, was that the Excursion was driving away from me.

I kept steering into the pendulum swings, adding a little throttle—gentle gentle gentle, too much would cause a snap-spin—when I could.

After ten seconds that felt like ten years, I had the F-250 gathered up and I began closing again.

You can be damn sure I now shaded my truck to the left, making it impossible for anyone in the passenger seat to crank more rounds at me.

We hummed up a long hill, nearing Grafton's old-fashioned town common. I closed the final few feet to the SUV. All I could see now was its giant back doors. If the passenger/shooter kicked out a window on one of those doors, his gun's muzzle would be four feet from my face. I was ready to tap the brakes again, but I didn't want to.

I wanted to end it.

I said out loud, in the weird no-turbulence quiet, "I wonder if he likes bump-drafting."

Bump-drafting is a fancy term in NASCAR for nailing a guy's rear bumper with your front. Back when I raced, we just called it ramming a guy. But now it's a big strategy for going fast at Talladega and Daytona.

I bump-drafted the Excursion.

It didn't feel any different than ramming him.

But if today's ten-million-dollar-a-year NASCAR hotshoes need a fancy name for it, that's okay by me.

I tried to hit the Excursion square on its bumper, but I was off an inch, and so we both got sideways. I lost half a truck-length chasing my own back end, but then made it up—I believe I'd finally rattled the driver—and rammed him again.

He slid dead sideways past an auto-body shop and a Chinese restaurant. The buildings reminded me we were close, very close, to Grafton Center.

Which gave me an idea. The place to wrap this thing up was dead ahead.

I thought through and refined the idea in the two seconds the Excursion slid sideways in front of me.

Had to hand it to the driver: He knew when to lift and when to nudge the throttle and which way to steer when, and I'll be damned if we weren't both back up to sixty-five when we passed a Cumberland Farms gas station on our left.

The Cumberland Farms was the first landmark I'd been looking for. Not far beyond it was a train-track crossing with a nice hump. A few hundred yards past that, the road ended in a tee at the town common.

The curb ringing the common was a real New England special, eighteen inches tall and granite.

The driver of the Excursion knew what he was doing, but my gut told me he didn't know this area. If he did, he would've taken a left, not a right, out of Harmon's driveway. Would've hit I-495 in ten minutes, and I'd never have seen him again. No, he'd taken a right because that's what drivers do when they're in doubt.

Now he was doing sixty-five—no, make it seventy—in blinding snow, in a truck that weighed three tons, a quarter mile from a dead end.

I rammed him as we hit the train-track hump.

Or maybe I bump-drafted him. You tell me.

I'd timed it right, hitting the Excursion as its front end unweighted over the tracks.

I spun that truck. I spun it good.

The driver tried to save it, but when he left my field of vision he was out of shape a half-dozen ways. The giant SUV was sliding, dead perpendicular to the road—I got my first real look at the man in the passenger seat—rocking back and forth on its shocks, both right-side tires locking and unlocking as the overworked traction-control computer wondered what was going on.

No doubt in my mind: The Excursion was going to slide into the town common's eighteen-inch curb, was going to hit square with both left-side tires at an honest forty miles an hour. Was going to barrel-roll at least once, more likely one and a half or even two times.

It would have to do all that without me as a witness.

Because the instant I rammed the Excursion, I got very busy. The impact, plus the near-zero traction, plus the short flight over the tracks, knocked my F-250 into its own spin.

As I'd known it would.

When my truck's back end came around, I didn't fight it. I let it happen.

The old-school advice on what to do when you're out of control: *In a spin? Both feet in.* The "both feet" means clutch (which I didn't have, my truck being an automatic) and brakes. The idea is to lock up all four tires *right now,* before you get yourself in even worse trouble. That way, you just keep sliding in whatever direction you're already headed until you stop.

Or hit something.

It's good advice.

For amateurs.

But when you're getting ten million a year to sell deodorant or breakfast cereal, it's not enough to bury your foot in the brakes and hope for best. Your job is to stay off the wall. To get yourself four fresh tires, get back on track, and claw for all available points.

Watch a NASCAR spin in super-slow motion sometime. Sure, those guys lock the brakes when the car starts to come around—but as soon as the ass end is pointed at anything made of concrete, they get off the brakes and into the throttle *hard*, trying to avoid the impact or mini-mize it.

I'm not a pro driver anymore, and I made something under ten million last year.

Still, I didn't want to hit that granite curb any harder than I had to, and I didn't want to be tangled up with that Excursion when *it* hit the curb and flipped.

That eerie snow-muffled quiet. Those empty roads. The slow motion that took over in my head, the way it does.

I let my truck spin until its tailgate faced the common. I shifted my right foot from brake to gas, punched it, looked through my windshield—train tracks and Cumberland Farms receding, fast but slow—then in my rearview mirror, where the Excursion was still slid-ing sideways, the man in the passenger seat taking forever to reach for the grab handle above his door.

Sixty yards from the curb and still moving fast. Too fast.

I worked the steering wheel to keep my truck moving straight, back-ward but straight, and tried to feel what the spinning rear snow tires were doing.

They were doing okay. Much better than the Excursion, which grew farther away as I slowed and it didn't.

Forty yards from the curb.

New motion, new color, caught my eye. I looked through the wind-shield again and saw a black Crown Vic police car, with angry strob-ing red and blue lights, barrel-assing toward me. I guess it's wrong to read emotion into a machine, but with its squirrely back end and the snow-spittle flying from the chains on its rear tires and its flashing headlights and the red-blue strobing, that Crown Vic looked *pissed* at what was happening in its town during a nor'easter.

I was slowing. Had the throttle buried now, felt the rear tires biting. Maybe Grafton had sanded the roads here at the common before the snow began. I hoped so. Needed all the traction I could get.

Twenty yards. Slowing like crazy.

Instinct pulled my eyes to the rearview.

One thing surprised me—motion, something unexpected—but with so much happening, I wouldn't take time to make sense of that until later.

Otherwise, things played out so much the way I'd pictured—what, fifteen seconds earlier, at seventy miles an hour?—that the wreck itself was nearly déjà vu. Nearly anticlimactic, if you can believe that.

I'd gotten one thing wrong: hadn't anticipated this much sand on the road surrounding the common. That made for a burst of traction as the Excursion slid the final fifteen yards, and *that* gave the SUV a head start on its first barrel roll before it even hit the curb.

Everything else I'd gotten just right.

The way the Excursion's sidewalls caught the curb.

The first barrel roll, the truck smashing onto its left flank, still carrying speed, missing the town's prized bandstand by maybe a foot.

The wobbling flip as the truck showed its underside: leaf springs and undercoating and one hell of a long exhaust system.

My F-250 coming to a perfect stop, rear tires smoking as they bit through snow and spun on tarmac. I popped my boot from the throttle and put the transmission in park and watched my mirror some more.

The Excursion started its second full roll, and I spotted something so strange it took me three seconds to process it.

Man, those three seconds cost me.

But I didn't know that yet.

Because I wasn't paying enough attention to the pissed-off Crown Vic, the new player on the scene.

Here's what I saw in my mirror as the giant black SUV began its second roll: When its right side faced skyward, something launched from the passenger window.

No, not something.

Some*one*.

He truly did launch. He didn't come out like a sack of laundry, the way the dimwits do on those shocking-video TV shows. No, he'd had the smarts to hold himself in place during the first, most violent, flip, then time it just right and . . . *propel* himself from his open window during the second roll.

You had to hand it to the man.

To Lobo Soto.

It had to be him. I knew it even as his arms flailed in midair and he turned his cannonball shot into a semigraceful flip, landing a full thirty feet beyond the still-tumbling Excursion.

He landed flat on his back. In three, maybe four inches of snow.

Four inches of snow is no featherbed, but it's a lot softer than February New England earth.

He lay there, likely with the wind knocked out of him, for a second or so while I stared at all this in my mirror.

Then he rose and ran. Ran dead west, putting distance between himself and me, the snow making him hard to spot already. He ran in moccasins and loose chinos and a useless canvas jacket that only a man from Los Angeles would wear in the winter.

He looked like he could run all day.

Then—finally, boy do I wish I could get those three seconds back—I was out of my truck and running hard, chasing Lobo Soto.

Everything else was gone: Eudora bleeding against my chest, the car chase, the town common that now looked like a wrecking yard, the groaning Excursion on its roof, the pair of moveless arms extending from its shattered driver's window.

Everything was gone but adrenaline and a black-red-black pulse in my head and Lobo Soto's canvas jacket, running from me, running with ease and confidence.

Would I have caught him?

He was ten years younger than me, a hundred pounds lighter.

On the other hand, I sure wasn't going to lose his trail. Not in this snow.

I'll never know.

Because blue-white pain exploded everywhere, and I went down heavy.

And a voice behind me said, "Sir, stop or I will deploy my Taser."

And as I blacked out I noticed the cop had tased me before warning me.

And I didn't blame him one bit.

CHAPTER SEVENTEEN

When a Grafton sergeant led me from a holding cell to an interview room that looked just like every police-station interview room you ever saw on TV, I knew it meant a state cop was coming. In Massachusetts, small-town PDs turn over their murder and wrongful-death cases to the staties as fast as they can dial the phone.

I guess I expected, without putting much thought into it, someone in a suit, because I was surprised to see a *uniformed* state trooper step into the room. Air force gray pants and shirt with blue accents, Sam Browne belt, Smokey the Bear hat, the works.

She sat opposite me, pulled in her chair, set her hat flat on the table to her left, turned on a tablet computer, and placed it on the table before her.

"I'm Venezia," she said. "Lead investigator on the murder of Eudora Spoon. You found the body?"

Find the body?

That was one way to put it.

Everything felt heavy. Had since I came to with a pair of Grafton cops, the one who'd tased me and another, lifting me into a cruiser and asking did I want medical assistance.

Heavy and slow and gray, and I couldn't get a good breath. That was how I felt, how the world looked.

I said, "You guys catch him?" My voice sounded odd. I realized I hadn't spoken since the 911 call.

"He wasn't hard to catch," Venezia said. "His left arm was just about amputated when the truck rolled. He bled out before they could extract him."

"Not him."

She ignored me, scrolling through her tablet, then reading. "Rivera, Reinaldo. Twenty-two years old, ex-army, now a gangbanger in L.A."

I was getting a bad feeling. "His gang is Los Bajamaros out of Van Nuys. And I'm going to guess that in the army he was a sniper, or at least a hell of a marksman."

She hid any surprise she felt, the way cops do. Typed a note on her tablet.

"What about Soto?" I asked, already knowing the answer. "You get him?"

"Soto who?"

"Lobo Soto, for Chrissake. The Bajamaros' boss. He was riding shotgun in the truck. He jumped when it rolled." I explained the way he'd ejected.

It sounded sketchy even to me, and I'd watched it happen.

Venezia looked at me maybe thirty seconds. She was a redhead. Judging from the braided ponytail pinned up in a bun, the hair was long. It was hard getting a straight-on look at her. I got the feeling she'd busted her nose somewhere along the line and did makeup tricks to mask it.

Her eyes were green.

"The Grafton officer on scene didn't mention a passenger," she finally said.

"He wouldn't've noticed, and you can't blame him. That cop was young. He was *pissed*. He was focused on me." I leaned forward, feeling some energy now. "Rivera's going to be your shooter, but Lobo

Soto's *el jefe*. This was a pure-D hit. Professional all the way, organized to the hilt. They set up across the road, on Eudora's son's property. I bet you'll find the Excursion was stolen early this morning."

"And you just happened to be prancing around with the victim at
six in the morning. During a snowstorm."

I said nothing.

"And then the mastermind, this Soto, did a circus trick to jump out
of a flipping truck. And he landed safely. And sprinted off to parts
unknown."

Hell. When you put it that way.

I said, "Has it been snowing out there since they brought me in?"

"Yes. Slowing some now. Finally."

"Then it's too late. You won't find Soto's tracks."

"Pretty convenient for you."

I stared, leaned, tapped the table. "Eudora Spoon was a friend of
mine for a long time. We were tight in a way you've never been tight
with anyone in your life. I squeezed her, bear-hugged her, trying to
keep the blood inside her. But I . . ."

I stopped. The room was going blurry.

Then Venezia did something she wasn't supposed to do, not according to any Massachusetts State Police Suspect Interview Hand-
book.

She reached across the table and patted my hand.

Once. Twice.

Then she pulled back.

The feel of her hand lingered.

I blinked until I could focus. I looked at her face.

Her expression hadn't changed.

"Tell me what happened," she said.

I did. I edited along the way, though, leaving a lot unsaid.

Why?

Because I wanted to settle with Eudora's killer my own damn self.

Even with the edits, my story took a while.

"We'll look at it," Venezia said when I finished. "All of it, Soto included."

Then it was quiet in the gray interview room.

"They're holding you," Venezia finally said, "on Driving to Endanger. It's a criminal charge."

"It's a misdemeanor."

"I'll see what I can do."

She rose and set her hat on her head and left the room.

CHAPTER EIGHTEEN

I'd wondered about turnout for the funeral. Especially because Eudora's will called for burial the day after she died, and the state cops didn't want to release the body. Fortunately for Eudora, her lifetime of AA connections included a couple of high-ranking staties who called in favors to make it happen. There was a time you would have called Eudora Spoon the queen of the Barnburners, the group's most beloved member.

But in the past few years, she'd changed. Her gung ho had eroded. She'd gone cynical, many thought. She'd pulled stunts like sponsoring me and bragging about it.

Had Eudora stepped on too many toes, wandered too far off the reservation, pissed off too many Barnburners with her recent spurts of independent thinking?

Nope.

I shouldn't have worried. I'd underestimated the Barnburners and drunks in general. They had long memories, in a good way, and they had a lot of love in their hearts.

Love for Eudora.

Saint Anne's overflowed. The sanctuary filled an hour before the service, which was held at ten the morning after Venezia interviewed me. The room downstairs that we used for Barnburner meetings, rigged with closed-circuit TV, filled soon after. Drunks from all over New England, some of them sober half a century, sat or stood on the church steps, on the sidewalk, in a Brazilian bakery across the road.

Eudora Spoon had lived one hell of a life.

TV news was there, of course. When a beloved octogenarian is cut down by a sniper in a military-style hit, that's news. When the same octogenarian is the mother of a TV star, even a former TV star, and it turns out the son returned home just before the hit . . . that's *big-ass* news.

They made space for me and Charlene in the front pew, with family and a handful of Meeting After the Meeting Barnburners.

Charlene looked pretty in a black dress.

I didn't sit next to her. Instead, I moved around, scanning the space as the organ music built and the priest stepped in.

I imagine everyone thought I was too broken up about Eudora to sit through the service.

That wasn't it.

I was worried about Kenny.

Worried as hell.

I didn't know exactly why Los Bajamaros had snatched him—neither he nor Eudora had given me the straight scoop, which was something I planned to deal with. Maybe Kenny was no longer important now that his mother was gone. But I had to assume he was. Had to assume Lobo Soto and his crew would be back for more.

I'd enlisted Pablo and Skinny Dennis, the Barnburners' self-appointed sergeants at arms, to help me out.

"What we looking for?" Pablo had asked.

"Anybody we don't know," I'd said. "Especially Mexicans. Gang types."

If that offended Pablo, who cheerfully told people he was the son of a Mexico City whore, he didn't let on.

The three of us stood well behind the preacher, near separate doors, scanning the crowd.

I made eye contact with Skinny Dennis. We swapped nods that meant everything looked okay in here. Then, as a blessing began in Latin—Eudora had requested an old-school mass—I slipped through my door, down a set of stairs, into an alley that ran alongside the red-brick church, and up the alley to Jenkins Street.

Which was a nuthouse.

Jenkins is a dead end that feeds into Framingham's downtown.

Thanks to a rotary, two main roads, and a heavily used set of train tracks, traffic was always ugly down here. Right now, though, it was more chaotic than I'd ever seen it. I counted four news vans, their crews spread out for live shots of the church. There was the hearse, one of those black Chrysler minivans that didn't seem right for the job no matter how they dressed it up, with a pair of Town Cars behind for the run out to Bryar, where Eudora would be buried alongside her second husband. There were a couple dozen Harleys, all occupied by members of Pablo's and Skinny Dennis's Milford crew.

And there were people . . . everywhere. Hundreds, just standing on sidewalks, spilling into the street. I knew Mary Giarusso of the Barn-burners had hired a detail of Framingham cops, anticipating the turn-out. Clearly they'd dropped the ball—I saw just one cop, standing near the junction of Concord Street and Union Avenue, talking on his shoulder radio, probably begging for help.

Somebody had linked the church-service audio to a pair of speakers on the sidewalk. Preacher Latin and hymns and prayers blared. It was hard to think out here.

A sharp whistle caught my ear. I looked left, across the church, and spotted Pablo. He made an exaggerated shrug that said, *What the hell do we do now?*

I pointed at my eyes with two fingers, just like the guys in war movies. Then I pointed at the sky. Message: *Get to high ground and look.*

He nodded and disappeared.

I continued to scan. The crush of people made it hard to do much of anything, but I got lucky: Not six feet away was parked a beat-to-hell Dodge conversion van. It had a ladder bolted to its hind end. Even better, it wore a half-dozen bumper stickers: LET GO LET GOD, I AM A PERSONAL FRIEND OF BILL'S, SERENITY NOW. Like that. It belonged to a drunk, and most likely one I knew.

So I climbed.

Up top, I had a hell of a view. Saw a couple of cruisers, lights on, coming to help the overmatched solo cop.

The mob, or mourners, or both, extended just half a block in all directions. From up here, things didn't look so crazy.

That was the good news. The bad: When I looked up at potential sniper hidey-holes, the number of windows and rooftops overwhelmed me in three seconds.

If Lobo Soto had another shooter set up hereabouts, he was going to have an easy shot.

I'd tried to tell the family to use a side door when they moved from Saint Anne's to their limo.

They'd looked at me like I was nuts.

You should have fought harder.

"Why in God's name would anybody shoot at me?" Kenny had asked, fussing with his necktie.

"Same reason they kidnapped you," I'd said. "Same reason they killed Eudora."

"Which is *what,* exactly?"

"I don't *know*!" I'd said, shaking, barely staying beneath a roar. "That's what I need to find *out,* for Chrissake!"

Kenny had stared at me. From another room, Harmon had said, "The hell's going on in there?"

I had breathed myself calm.

It wasn't easy.

Eudora Spoon. Bleeding out, bleeding into my winter jacket, the two of us falling, tobogganing down the little hill in her yard.

Black-red-black.

The red-mist pulse in my head. The revenge gene, Sophie had once called it.

Ugly things happened when things went black-red-black in my head.

Kenny's refusal, or inability, to see that he was in danger hadn't helped.

The whole family had been that way: Kenny, Harmon, Tricia. In spite of the kidnapping, the murder, Lobo Soto on the loose. They reminded me of rabbits, sitting in a field, declaring that since a wolf had just eaten one of them, the rest were safe.

Or maybe—I hated to look at it this way, but I had to—they knew somehow that with Eudora gone, the danger was over.

I was going to look into that.

I was going to raise holy hell for everybody who had anything to do with her murder.

My vow.

Black-red-black.

CHAPTER NINETEEN

When the family followed the pallbearers—none of them younger than sixty-five, and I worried about a dropped casket as they wobbled down Saint Anne's bluestone steps, but they made it—for the ride to the cemetery, I was still atop the conversion van scanning rooftops. Pablo, who'd managed to climb atop the roof of a deli half a block north, was doing the same. I didn't know where Skinny Dennis was, but I'd bet a paycheck he was making himself useful somewhere.

Nobody shot at Kenny.

I admit I felt foolish making my way down the van's ladder.

Things cooled out during the trip to Bryar. I guess the news vans had what they needed, because they peeled off. So did most of Eudora's casual AA friends. Only family and the Meeting After the Meeting inner circle headed west to Bryar's overfull cemetery. The place turned weedy in the summer—the town didn't have much budget for landscaping—but it was pretty enough today, with a fresh coat of snow and a sky the color of your favorite jeans.

Eudora would be buried beside her second husband, Hans Kollar, with a plain, shortish headstone that matched his.

The machinery of modern winter burials was there, tucked away as much as possible. The priest who'd run the show at Saint Anne's spoke for fifteen minutes, and he impressed me. Young guy, Hispanic. I'd never met him or heard Eudora speak of him, but it was clear he'd known her personally, and that he was taking her death hard.

I sat kitty-corner to Kenny, Harmon, and Tricia.

A smart man once told me you should never read too much into grieving. People grieve the way they grieve, the smart man said, and it's a sucker's game to analyze it. Still, I couldn't help but compare the half brothers.

Kenny hammed it up. There's no other way to put it. You would've thought the news cameras were still aimed at him, that he was auditioning for a part. From the get-go, he cut loose with big wah-wah weeping. Or weeping *noises,* anyway—not sure I saw any actual tears. There was a handkerchief. There were shaking shoulders. There was a lot of loud "Why? Why? Oh, God, *why?*"

Harmon was different. Stolid. Steady Eddie, especially compared with drama queen Kenny.

Until the priest spoke softly about what made Eudora special, about what he would miss most. Then Harmon's chest began to heave. Slightly at first, Harmon working hard to control it, but then more and faster.

As the preacher fired off a final burst of Latin and crossed himself, Harmon's face collapsed.

He wept.

He wept concussive tears.

They racked his torso.

They drew attention.

They were the tears of a broken heart.

Everybody noticed. You couldn't not. Kenny's woo-hoo-hooing stopped as if he were put to shame by the real deal.

Tricia, seated beside her husband, hovered a hand for a few seconds, then patted Harmon's sleeve. Eudora and others had hinted to me that the marriage was bad and getting worse. After witnessing the pat, I believed it.

Then it was over. They didn't put Eudora in the ground—would do that after we left. The two dozen or so of us left the grave site and filtered across rock-salted walks toward our cars.

Charlene was twenty feet ahead. Part of me wanted to increase my pace and catch her. Part of me wondered why. Habit, I guess.

Scrabbling and slipping behind told me somebody was trying to catch *me*. I stopped and turned.

And drew a blank. Because I knew the man, I *knew* I knew him, but he was out of context and I didn't recognize him. Short. Late fifties or early sixties. A white-hair comb-over, a white walrus mustache. He was huffing from the effort he'd put in.

"Damn shame," the man said and hitched up the pants of his gray suit.

Then I knew who he was: Russ Budde, a longtime Bryar cop. I'd heard he was Harmon Kollar's competition for the acting chief job, but twenty-five years as a lousy cop, rousting teenagers for beer and cruiser-sleeping in church parking lots, had caught up with him: He was passed over for the younger man.

I nodded. "Damn shame."

He fell in beside me, trying to catch his breath as we walked. "I hear the statie running the investigation's a broad."

"Venezia. She's okay."

"And a *trooper,* they say. Not even a detective." Budde shook his head. "Different world."

"She's okay. Smart." I lengthened my stride, but Budde did, too. I wondered what he wanted.

"Well, good luck to her," he said, panting at the pace. "Her work's cut out. Lotsa closets, lotsa skeletons."

I stopped short. "The hell's that supposed to mean?"

The sly, ugly smile beneath Budde's mustache told me he was finally getting to it. "I just hope this Vesuvius, who's not even a detective and a broad to boot—"

"Venezia."

"Whatever. You say she's smart. I hope she's smart enough to dig deep. To look past her nose, to look at what they call institutional memory."

"What does that mean, Budde? Say what you want to say."

"I ain't no statie flatfoot investigating a big-time murder," he said. "Hell, I can't even get myself appointed acting chief in a shit-ass town like Bryar. But it was me, I'd want to have a chat with Ruthie Luciani over at Town Hall."

"About what?"

"About Eudora Spoon's property, for starters. Eudora's land and Question 2."

Russ Budde cackled off to his truck.

I stood still for a while.

It was a short drive to Harmon's place. I made it a slow one, thinking along the way. I tried to persuade myself to drop the whole thing, to let Venezia do her job.

But I didn't try hard.

I know who I am.

I know what I do.

Eudora had died pumping blood onto my chest.

Everybody who'd played a role was going to pay big.

So call that settled, and work on the who and the how.

Start with this Ruthie Luciani, courtesy of the jerk Russ Budde.

Had he been manipulating me? Did he have an ax to grind with Harmon?

Of course, but I was happy to be manipulated if it pointed me in the right direction. I needed something, anything, to hang my hat on. Right now I needed to visit the family. Pay respects, dig some to see if Harmon had any fresh info on the murder.

Ruthie Luciani at Town Hall would be my first stop tomorrow.

Running through the to-dos reminded me to call McCord, see what he'd dug up on Los Bajamaros.

"All quiet on the western front," he said when he picked up. "And I'll say it again: I'm sorry as hell about Ms. Eudora. Sounds like she was really something."

"She was. I'm on my way to her son's place now."

"One of those after-funeral receptions? I hate those things."

"Nah, the family decided to skip that. Eudora was a Barnburner. We Barnburners have our own style of send-off."

"If you say so."

"Erin okay?"

"Tough kid," McCord said. "She piled on the makeup, went to work, told 'em a BS story about falling against a towel bar."

"They buy it?"

"Not exactly. But the alternative in their minds was that Kenny beat her up. She said they found that harder to believe. Kid's got a sense of humor."

"Any Bajamaros trouble?"

"No drive-bys, nobody followed her to work, no weird phone calls." He hesitated.

"There's a 'but,' " I said.

"I did my homework. Los Bajamaros are badass pros, and Lobo Soto is one smart cat. They say he could be mayor of L.A., and they're only half joking. His gang's trying to go legit, funding city programs and all that."

"But?"

"But old habits die hard. Meth and crack are still their mother's milk."

"Any presence around here?"

"Not as far as anybody knows. But I hear they have reciprocal agreements with Brazilian gangs in all the cities back east."

"All the big gangs do. That's how it works these days." I thought a few seconds. "Something doesn't add up. Soto himself came three thousand miles to kill Eudora."

"I was thinking the same. For an operator like him to take such a risk, it must've been important as hell."

"Makes me think Kenny's not out of the woods. You should've seen the funeral. It was a zoo. I about went crazy looking for shooters."

"Watch him. Watch yourself, too."

"Copy that."

I clicked off and swung into Harmon Kollar's driveway.

CHAPTER TWENTY

Harmon wasn't home.
 Tricia was.
 She invited me in.
 "They're making you work?" I asked, nodding at her Bed Bath &
Beyond name board. She'd swapped her funeral dress for black slacks
and a copper-colored blouse. The blouse made her hair, which was a
color Charlene called Whatever Brown, look nearly red. Which worked
with my favorite thing about Tricia's looks: a strip of freckles across
her nose.
 In fact, I thought, following her into the kitchen and watching her
rinse a plate and glass, she looked damn nice overall. I seldom saw
her with fresh makeup and a pretty outfit. We'd bumped into each
other at a few cookouts and softball games since I started hanging
around Bryar. Or maybe I'd see her after a BJ's Wholesale Club run
when she dropped things off at Eudora's. That was about it.
 You almost never saw Tricia and Harmon together.
 She was a cheerleader at Michigan when she met him, she'd told me
at a softball game. An "ironic cheerleader" was how she put it. I wasn't
sure what that meant, but it seemed important to her.
 They became an item, the way football studs and cheerleaders do.

When Harmon destroyed his leg and his career and his shot at the NFL, Tricia vowed to stand by her man.

And you know what? She did. Quit the U of M after her sophomore year, pulled up stakes—she was a local, an Ann Arbor girl—and moved east with Harmon.

You got the feeling they wanted kids. Or had. I never asked.

I'd always liked her, in case you didn't guess that yet. There was something about her way, open and confident and not taking herself too seriously.

We clicked. We gravitated to one another at events. I knew she and Harmon were on the rocks, and it may have been my imagination, but Tricia sure seemed to find out in a hurry when Charlene and I were over.

"Didn't you know?" she asked, still at the sink. "They made me manager. And I've got a new gal to train on the front end, and I'm closing." she sponged the countertop. "I don't mind. It's something to do."

I leaned on a stainless-steel refrigerator that cost more than a lot of trucks I've owned. Harmon and Tricia hadn't skimped when they built this house, one of those modern ones that look like interconnected boxes. It nestled into the valley wall, seeming to hang over Route 142. The whole place was organized around sunsets: Every west-facing wall featured as much glass as possible. Looking over Tricia's shoulder as she cleaned, I had a hell of a view of Eudora's house and the Blackstone Valley beyond.

From what I heard, Harmon and Tricia had raised eyebrows when they brought in a hotshot architect from Great Barrington. Around here, when you build a nice house, you build a straight Colonial, period. Me, I'd thought the place looked silly.

Until I sat on the deck one evening and watched a sunset.

"I assume you came to see Harmon," Tricia said. "He's long gone. He changed out of his suit and split."

"It's none of my business, but I'm half surprised he came back here at all."

She smiled. "Don't you just love a small town? Everybody knows everything. Sometimes he's here, sometimes he isn't. It's a big house."

"He's taking it hard. Not that he shouldn't, but . . . I guess he's taking it harder than I expected."

Tricia made a brisk shrug. "I don't know any more about that than you do. Look . . ."

She stood at the counter with her back to me.

I waited.

"Look," she said, still not facing me. "We were *this* close to a divorce. Wow, I've never said it out loud. It actually feels okay. Let the small-town jungle drums commence."

"You said 'were.'"

"I have to wonder how Eudora's death will affect things. It would be pretty icy of me to hustle him straight from his mother's funeral to the divorce lawyer." She spun, finally, and looked at me. "Wouldn't it?"

I said nothing.

"Pardon me all to hell for saying it, but I envy you and Charlene. No muss, no fuss. You packed your bag and you moved out."

"No muss," I said. "No fuss."

There was a long pause.

"I'm sorry," Tricia said. "That came out sounding awful. I just meant . . ."

"Look," I said, wanting to point the conversation in another direction, "Eudora had me haul Kenny back here so she could connect with him before the cancer got her. I guess she didn't want to die with a son who wouldn't talk to her."

"I see."

"But I got the feeling," I said, "that there was something else. That she had some kind of big family powwow in mind. Harmon wasn't making it easy. You know anything about all this?"

"I heard Harmon's end of a phone conversation, so yes, I know a showstopper of an announcement was afoot. And I know Harmon was being a pain in the ass about it. I was shocked, *shocked*." Smiling as she said that last part.

"What's he got against Kenny?"

"I'd tell you if you had an hour to spare. How does Kenny look? Is he healthy?"

"He looked lousy when I found him. But I dragged him to a couple of meetings, and with him it might take."

"I understand you found him like a needle in a Los Angeles haystack, liberated him somehow, and persuaded him to climb aboard an airplane. That's amazing, Conway."

Those pretty brown eyes. Those freckles.

Tricia Kollar was something.

I shrugged. "It's what I do."

"Hollywood to Bryar. Quite an adjustment. Did you ever watch Kenny's show?"

"I tried."

She smiled. "I remember now. We've discussed this. You watch those shows about dams and tunnels and ships. If they made a mini-series about digging a hole in the ground, you'd be glued to your set."

She had me there. I guess I smiled, too.

"I still watch Kenny's show," Tricia said, soft-focus-gazing at nothing. "I got a secret Netflix account to do it, because Harmon flipped out when he caught me DVRing it. *That,* Conway, is how much he hates that show. What do you think of a man who checks up on his wife's ever-loving TV habits?"

I said nothing.

"Noncommittal," she said, smiling again, the smile pretty and tired and sad. "I don't blame you. It's a wise approach." As she spoke, she dug through a pocketbook and pulled from it a phone. Thumb-typed on the phone a few seconds. "You came here looking for Acting Chief Kollar. Well, I'll tell you his precise location. Himself is at . . . waiting, waiting, waiting . . . right this moment, he's at the cop shop."

"What's that app all about?"

She turned her phone so I could read its screen. Then she waggled her eyebrows. "It lets you track any phone on your family account. They market it as a way to keep an eye on your kids, but everybody calls it the Cheater Beater. Dear God, I can't believe I'm telling you all this. Do casual acquaintances often whiz in your ear this way?"

I said nothing. I'd come here to talk with Harmon about his ideas on who killed Eudora. Instead I found myself playing third-rate therapist to an unhappy woman.

Quite a woman . . . but still.

"People *do* whiz in your ear, don't they? There's something . . . *absorbent* about you. I feel as if my words will go in here"—she put a small hand square on my chest—"and stay there. Forever."

My face went red. I wanted out *now*.

"Sorry I busted in," I said. "I, ah. Sorry."

I ran out of words.

Sorry you can't watch a TV show without a secret account?

Sorry your marriage tanked and you're spying on your husband?

Sorry you spilled your guts to a casual friend who wandered by at the wrong time?

I made for the front door. Tricia followed, heels clicking on the poured-concrete floor, regret pushing ahead of her like a pressure wave.

I had a hand on the doorknob when she grabbed my upper arm. "Let me help you."

"You probably ought to get to work," I said.

She let go my arm.

But it took her a while.

"I probably ought to get to work," Tricia said.

By the time I got to the police department, Harmon was gone. The only cop in sight said there was a tanker-truck rollover on an I-495 off-ramp in Hopkinton, one of those all-hands-on-deck calls, and God knew when Harmon would be finished with that.

Then Floriano texted, reminding me of a promise to help him cut, split, and stack wood from a tree that'd fallen in his neighbor's yard.

It all added up to a sign that much as I might want to, I wasn't going to learn anything today from Harmon Kollar.

I tried to tell myself it was for the best. No man should be pumped for info on the day of his mom's funeral.

Still, time was pressing down.

The sooner I learned why Eudora had died, the sooner I could make them all pay.

CHAPTER TWENTY-ONE

At 9:05 the next morning, I pulled into a parking lot and looked up at a steeple.

See, most of Bryar's town offices, along with its police HQ and the school administration, were in an old Presbyterian church.

Eudora had filled me in on why.

Bryar was like a lot of dying burgs in the Blackstone Valley. The oldsters stuck around in homes not worth selling, but most kids left town before the ink dried on their high-school diplomas. A few nice cul-de-sacs had sprung up here and there, billed as executive housing for folks who commuted to the big data-storage company over in Hopkinton, but Bryar's schools weren't strong enough to really attract that crowd.

For the better part of a decade, the town had limped along with mucho state aid. Bryar'd even managed to build a swank new headquarters for the fire department—a redbrick palace everybody now called the Garage Mahal.

Then the bottom had dropped out in 2008, and there just wasn't any more money. The state and the Feds were as broke as the town.

It was rotten timing for the cops: *Their* sweet new building had been penciled into the town's fiscal '10 budget. Just in time, too—the old HQ was slipping into the river it'd been built near. Slipping at an accelerating pace. A pace that got it condemned.

Bottom line: Just when Harmon Kollar earned what should've been the biggest promotion of his life, to acting chief with the full-on chief title to follow, his headquarters was deemed unsafe to inhabit. The desperate Board of Selectmen took a church Bryar had been given in lieu of back taxes, drywalled in some half-assed office suites, and moved most of the town government there.

I hate to say it, but this was the story of Harmon Kollar's life. You could almost understand why he named his storage company to celebrate something that happened when he was nineteen—he hadn't done much to brag about since.

Thinking all this as I stood smiling at Ruthie Luciani in a window-less basement room. It had to be her: The plaque on the counter bore her name. She seemed to be town clerk, tax collector, registrar of deeds, and a notary public.

She was barely five feet tall. Her hair was thin and orange-red. Her eyes looked tired as hell, but the eyes smiled even when the mouth didn't.

"I'd sure appreciate a look at a piece of property," I said. "Out on 142, belongs, or belonged I guess, to—"

Ruthie didn't need to hear any more. She sighed, disappeared into a big closet, and emerged with a blue-bound book—huge, nearly the size of an unfolded road map. She flopped it on the counter, turned it to face me, and found the page I needed.

I said, "Guess I'm not the first to ask about this, huh?"

"Nor the last, sweetie." A little smile, an eye-crinkle really. Then she headed for a desktop PC.

The smile. The eye-crinkle. The way every movement started with a sigh. It all reminded me of someone. My mother.

"How many jobs do you do?" I asked. "Half a dozen?"

"If so, I'm still waiting on five paychecks."

"Keep waiting."

"Oh, sweetie," she said. "I'm good at waiting."

I leaned on the counter, took a few minutes to figure out the map and orient myself.

Wow.

The lots, one on each side of Route 142, were in the name of Eudora Anne Spoon.

The one that held Eudora's house was a tidy eleven acres. Nice piece of land.

The other lot, the one Harmon's home and business sat on, was more than nice.

If you were building a casino resort, it would look a *lot* more than nice. It would look just about perfect.

The eighty-six acres consisted mostly of high ground—no wetlands for the tree-huggers to block development with. There'd be mostly ledge under the thin New England topsoil, but that wouldn't slow the builders much.

The roads, though, were the thing. The access.

The lot was no more than three miles west of I-495 and about the same distance south of the Mass Pike. Route 142 was right there, of course. Not far west was Route 146, a state road that was just begging to be turned into a big-time highway.

Eudora Spoon had been sitting on a gold mine.

Eudora Spoon had been stubborn as hell, too. Loved her regular hike with her dogs. Loved her land, loved her view.

Loved telling the world to pound sand.

Hated the idea of a casino on her property.

Huh.

Did her death change anything, casino-wise? Who benefited? Harmon? If I was right and Russ Budde had it in for him, you'd think so. Harmon had never expressed much opinion one way or the other on the casino question, though. Had ducked behind his badge when the topic came up, saying he would uphold the law no matter what happened.

Then there was his chest-racking grief at Eudora's funeral. That hadn't been fake, no way no how.

Another big question: How the hell did Lobo Soto fit in?

"Best watch out, sweetie," Ruthie said, jolting me. "Selectmen see you standing there they're liable to gin up a fee for wearing out the carpet. Lord knows they got fees on everything else."

I said, "Who else has been looking at this map lately?"

"My lips are sealed."

"Developers? Indian tribes? Vegas people?"

"*Sealed*, sweetie." She grabbed the book's covers, gave me a half second to move my elbows, and slapped it shut.

I needed a different tack. "Bryar voted no on casinos already. So it's a done deal anyway. Right?"

Ruthie smirked. "Sure thing, sweetie. Because billion-dollar businesses and their lawyers bow to the will of the people, and they love taking no for an answer."

"So what's up? Tell me a little more. Give a guy a break."

She almost did, too. I could feel it. Ruthie Luciani was lonesome, and I was here, and she just about spilled.

Just about.

Somebody walked past in the hallway. I didn't bother turning to see who it was, but Ruthie's eyes flickered.

Then her face went cloudy, and she shook her head a little.

I knew I'd lost her. For now, anyway.

She looked both ways, exaggerating the move like a silent-movie actress, and leaned across the counter and whispered. "I'm doing four people's jobs for twenty-two thousand a year, and the pension went away last year, and word on the street is health care's going away next year. And you know what? I'm one of the lucky ones. Can't risk that twenty-two a year. Sorry."

I made a surrender gesture out of respect. "You never know," I said. "Might be plenty of good jobs right around the corner."

She made a tiny smile and sighed that sigh. "Yes on 2, sweetie. Yes on 2. It ain't over till it's over."

I wasn't done with Ruthie Luciani yet. Spending all day alone in that dumpy office, watching the town take back everything it'd promised her. All that knowledge—what had Russ Budde called it, institutional memory?—and nobody to share it with.

She wanted to talk to somebody, anybody. All she needed was a breather and a little motivation.

So five minutes later, I stood inside Dunkin' Donuts and waited and thought and planned.

Had plenty of time to do it, too. Everybody's worst nightmare had slipped into line just ahead of me: a kid, twenty maybe, in work boots and a Carhartt jacket, clutching a back-of-an-envelope list. The new kid on a construction crew, sent on the morning coffee run.

It was a long list.

What I knew—

Kenny Spoon: kidnapped by Los Bajamaros.

Eudora Spoon: killed by Los Bajamaros.

Russ Budde: a lousy cop with an ax to grind about Harmon Kollar. Everything I knew about Harmon, including the way he'd broken at Eudora's funeral, said he was no killer . . . but I couldn't afford to ignore Budde's pointer to Ruthie, keeper of Bryar lore.

Correction: That wasn't *all* I knew about Harmon. I knew his wife didn't trust him, and he'd been involved in a sketchy transaction in the Golden Dragon parking lot just before Eudora was killed. That was something to look at.

Los Bajamaros: Pros, work-for-hire criminals, now trying to go legit.

If they wanted to go straight so bad—and that had come from McCord, which made it solid—what the hell was boss man Lobo Soto doing hands-on in a Massachusetts hit?

Possible answers: either a payday too big to turn down, or personal involvement at some level.

The construction kid ahead of me was almost finished, thank God. For me, two priorities.

One, go back to Ruthie with an offering no office worker ever turned down.

Two, look harder at Los Bajamaros. Venezia had to be digging. She'd played it cool when she interviewed me, but she'd promised to look at Soto, and she struck me as a smart cop.

I finally stepped to the counter. "A dozen Munchkins," I said. "Mix 'em up, but no plain."

CHAPTER TWENTY-TWO

No plain?" Ruthie said. She was so short she had to stand on tiptoe to peer into the Munchkin box on her counter. "I knew I liked you. What's your name?"

I told her. Next to the Munchkins I set a medium black, three little cream containers, a fistful of sugars and Splendas, a stirrer, and two napkins.

For me: a medium regular, the usual.

She tried to hold a deadpan, but the corners of her eyes crinkled. "If you thought I was that cheap a date, sweetie."

"Can't a guy buy a lady a cup of coffee?"

"Don't interrupt. I was *going* to say if you thought I was that cheap a date, you were right." She plucked a jelly Munchkin from the box and popped it in her mouth.

We sipped and said nothing for a while.

"It came to me after you left," Ruthie finally said. "The big snowstorm chase after Eudora was shot. That was you. You half-destroyed Grafton Common. You got arrested."

"Held overnight. Not arrested."

She selected a glazed Munchkin. "Whyn't you let the cops take care of all this?"

"I am," I said. "They are. They do things their way, I do things my way. Eudora was a friend."

"Must have been a *hell* of a friend."

"Yes."

"So are you. But I still can't tell you who's been looking at the maps and the books. I read once that you shouldn't take yourself seriously, but you'd damn well better take your job seriously. I do, and it's worked out okay for me. Comparatively speaking. Last man standing, you know?"

"I'm not asking about the maps and the books anymore."

"You're not?" She frowned.

"How long you worked here?"

"Now I'm gonna date myself. You're a little young to remember the Blizzard of '78, but that was my first day on the job. Twenty-three years old, fresh out of Katie Gibbs."

"That a college?"

"A secretarial school, but I'm sure they call it something else now. Administrative assistant school, maybe." Ruthie sipped, looked at nothing, shook her head. "It's a funny world. On the one hand, you can say *anything*. They drop F-bombs on TV, you know? And the pop songs on my eight-year-old granddaughter's iPod would make you blush."

"But you can't call a secretary a secretary."

"Exactly!" She raised her cup, and we touched rims. "You can say anything, but you can't say nothing."

I wasn't going to get a better opening than that. "So say nothing," I said, "about who's been looking at those books. Those maps."

Her gray eyebrows made a question.

"Tell me stories," I said. "Thirty-plus years' worth of stories."

"I get it." She smiled. It was a nice smile, though you half-expected rust to fall to the counter when she made it. "Oh, I could tell you stories."

"So tell," I said. "My favorite stories are about Eudora Spoon.

About her boys, especially Harmon. About all that property out on 142."

Ruthie flinched and glanced down the hall when I mentioned Harmon. "Sounds like you heard some stories already. You're not a cop. Are you some kind of private eye?"

"I'm a mechanic."

"I could tell you stories, Conway."

I sipped.

"Did you know Andy Spoon, Eudora's first husband?"

"No," I said. "Didn't know the second one either."

"The second one was a shadow. Never met him. But Andy Spoon . . . I could tell you stories."

I sipped.

Then Ruthie told me a story.

I'd only ever heard about Andy Spoon through Eudora. To hear her tell it, he golfed and glad-handed his way around until he hit it big on some high-end developments. In her version he came across as kind of a jamoke, everybody's pal, building his business mostly through luck and connections.

Not according to Ruthie.

Andy Spoon, Ruthie said, was mean and hard. Bought most of his land by combing public records for people who weren't paying their property taxes, then pouncing.

I said, "What public records?"

"Residents can come before the Board of Selectmen and petition for a penalty-free extension. It's a town bylaw, goes back two hundred years. Selectmen don't *have* to grant the extension, but they almost always do. The petition becomes part of the public record. But it's a small town, and it was even smaller back then. It wasn't hard to keep public information private."

"You buried it."

She nodded. "We all did. With help from the editor of the *Bryar Clarion*."

It was a nice small-town setup, sparing residents the embarrassment of admitting they couldn't afford land that'd been in their families six generations. Most everybody caught up on their taxes sooner or later, quietly arranging to pay what they could. Since the town didn't really need the money, everybody went with the flow.

Except Andy Spoon.

The only thing he liked better than buying land for a dime on the dollar was buying it for a nickel on the dollar. So he taught himself to formulate public-records requests that Ruthie couldn't dodge or bury.

Andy Spoon knew how deeply land-rich, cash-poor Yankees feared shame.

Which became his weapon of choice.

Whenever his latest subdivision neared completion, with the finish carpenters and countertop guys doing their work, Andy would pay a visit to Ruthie. He would leave her seething, having scoped out the slow-pays with buildable parcels.

Then he would stop by a slow-pay's home for a chat.

His pitch was simple: Sell me your land at my price. Your tax problem goes away. Sure, your land goes away, too—but you'll never see your face on a flyer stapled to a telephone pole downtown, over the headline DELINQUENT and an exact figure. And you'll never see your face blown up even larger on that billboard towering over 142 where Bryar meets Upton.

"Come on," I said. "You're making that up."

"I wish I was," Ruthie said. "He actually ran that stunt once, on poor old Denny Doonan, whose family owned ninety acres on the Mendon border. Denny had two sons, an autistic one and a check bouncer, and he didn't have two nickels to rub together. Andy wanted Denny's ninety acres real bad. There was a nice stream down there, and Andy pictured high-end homes built around a nine-hole golf course. But the Doonans were pigheaded the way those French-Canadians are. Denny Doonan ran Andy off his property three times, the last time with an over-and-under shotgun. A week later, guess whose photo was twenty feet tall on a billboard?"

"Jesus."

"Nope. Denny Doonan's. Jesus had nothing to do with it, though a bunch of us sure wished a good smiting on Andy Spoon. After that, most everybody folded and paid his price and slunk out of town. What a lot of folks don't know—hey, you asked for a story, and you're getting a doozy—is that's when Bryar really went south. The writing was on the wall already, I guess, but . . . so many fine folks moved out in the space of a few years. Andy Spoon screwed this town but good."

"I'm guessing," I said, "you're getting around to when Andy bought that split property on 142."

"You guessed right."

"Swindled a Yankee for it? Maybe, hold on to your hat, 'nother guess coming . . . maybe a relative of Russ Budde?"

"Now you guessed wrong. Smart, but wrong. *Most* of the folks Andy Spoon bamboozled were Yankees. But not *all* of them."

I waited.

"One of them," she said, "was a Brazilian. Name of Paulo Monteiro."

She looked at me like the name should mean something.

It didn't.

So I said nothing.

"Paulo Monteiro was a big-time gangster," Ruthie said. "Dead what, five years now? And the name still scares the snot out of a lot of folks."

"You sure Spooner shook him down? I know my share of Brazilians, and I've heard a lot about Brazilian bad guys. Way I hear it, ripping one off is a good way to get killed."

"I've heard the same," Ruthie said, nibbling as she spoke, "and I've wondered about it. Keep in mind this was a long time ago. Brazilians were rare around here back then, and nobody knew Monteiro was a crook. I'm not sure he even *was* a crook yet."

"Probably was. Probably a crook from ten generations of crooks back home. That's how it works down there."

Ruthie shrugged. "Maybe so, but around here, he wasn't strong. He hadn't built any kind of reputation. Whatever he was or wasn't, he had no choice but to accept Andy Spoon's offer."

Huh. "Still doesn't seem right," I said. "Ever seen a Brazilian miss a payment?"

"Ain't that the truth. Sunup to sundown those people work. Then they work a night shift just to rub it in."

"So how'd Monteiro fall far enough behind to give Andy Spoon an opening?"

"Sheesh, honey, you can't expect a girl to know *everything* that goes on in town."

"Not most girls, maybe. But so far, if the town is Bryar and the girl is Ruthie, I've had good luck."

"Flattery works," she said, batting her eyes, making a joke of it. "Flattery and Munchkins. I do remember rumors around that time that Monteiro got himself in some kind of shit-fight, pardon the French, down in Providence and Pawtucket."

That made sense. The Mob—the real Mob, the Italians—had always been strong down there.

"So he was overextended," I said. "Local taxes took a backseat because they had to. He got behind."

Ruthie nodded. "You're pretty quick for a guy looks like he came to pump out the septic. Andy Spoon was a lot of things, but dumb wasn't one of them. He would've made it his business to know Monteiro was in trouble."

"He looked at your map, saw potential in Monteiro's land, and licked his chops."

"And paid Monteiro a visit."

"And?" I said after waiting.

"And no offense," Ruthie said, tossing wax paper in the trash basket and dusting her hands, "but there aren't enough Munchkins in

Worcester County to get me talking about those Monteiros. I shouldn't've started, but you got that way about you. Coffee and those bullfighter eyes and that . . . stillness. It all makes a girl want to fill the space, and you know it."

"Paulo Monteiro's dead, Ruthie. Dead five years, you just said so."

"He's not the Monteiro that worries me. You want to play detective? You want to be Sherlock Freakin' Holmes? Look up *Rose* Monteiro, Paulo's widow. And that's the last I'm gonna say about it."

Then Ruthie Luciani turned her back and got to work. Pretended I wasn't there until I wasn't.

CHAPTER TWENTY-THREE

I was in the parking lot, set to grab lunch and google the hell out of Rose Monteiro, when I heard my name.

I turned to see Harmon Kollar. Black shoes, full khaki uniform, no hat. The uniform shirt spread out some in the belly, with gaps between buttons showing a gray T-shirt beneath. Harmon hadn't yet admitted to his weight gain, hadn't started buying baggy shirts.

He said, "You looking for me?"

"Not now. Was yesterday."

"What for?"

"Tell you how sorry I was about your mother."

He knew there'd been more to it than that. I watched him decide whether to ask what the hell I was doing at the town building *today* if I wasn't looking for him. Watched him decide against. Instead he said, "Where you headed?"

It was a weird standoff. Far as I was concerned, Harmon might be the brains behind his mother's death.

Meanwhile, you could see how he might think *I* was.

When in doubt, play it close to the vest. No way was I going to tell Harmon I wanted to check out Rose Monteiro.

So I shrugged. "No place in particular."

"I hear it's nice there," he said, surprising the hell out of me. "I'll ride along." And he strode to my F-250.

I'll admit the way Harmon talked—everything a statement, never a question or a request—made me grind my teeth. When I'd mentioned it once to Randall, he'd pointed out that was just a cop thing, needing to be in charge even when they weren't. On the street, an uncertain cop is a cop in trouble.

So I let it slide.

Besides, I was curious. Harmon Kollar had never expressed any interest in me at all. He must have a reason for the ride.

"Where to?" I said.

"You're the driver. You decide. That a new exhaust I hear?"

I had to smile at that. Like I said, Harmon had a truck exactly like mine but for the color. Same year and everything. So when we got thrown together to talk, we talked trucks.

If it wasn't trucks, it was watches—we also had identical Seiko 6309 divers. They've been out of production twenty-five years, but you can't kill the damn things. I wore mine all the way through my bad years, somehow never pawning it or getting rolled for it.

Harmon was proud as hell of his watch. A few years back, he sent it out to some craftsman in California who cleaned it, serviced it, and freshened up the luminous dots so they glowed like new. Glowed *better* than new. Harmon would bore you to death by holding his wrist beneath a lamp, then killing the light and oohing and aahing at the watch's glow.

Trucks and watches. That was about all Harmon and I had in common.

Without exactly meaning to I took us over to 142, then west, driving beneath the WOLVERINE BROS. FREIGHT & STORAGE sign. Neither of us spoke. Harmon's cop eyes constantly scanned and never looked surprised.

"You're not invisible," he finally said.

I said nothing.

"Every PD from Framingham to Worcester knows about this odd-ball Barnburners crew. About Conway Sax."

I said nothing.

"To most cops, you're a joke. You're one of these guys dresses up like a superhero and runs around at night. Me, I know a little more about you courtesy of Eudora. I know you get some results. Long as you stay off my radar, I don't care what you do."

I said nothing.

"Point being," Harmon said, "I know you're playing Captain Crime-fighter around my mother's death, and it's no skin off my ass." Long pause. "Hell, maybe I even admire you for it, in some way I haven't figured out."

"What are you trying to say, Harmon? What are you *really* trying to say?"

"You're not invisible in more ways than one," he said. "The night before my mother got shot, you tailed me out of her driveway. You followed me over to the Dragon. If you thought I didn't spot you, you thought wrong."

I shrugged. "You made what looked like a payoff to a guy in a crew-cab Dodge."

"That's why we're here."

"That's why *you're* here."

He stared dead ahead maybe half a minute, working his Adam's apple, not liking what I'd said, not accustomed to being the perp.

Then he nodded, once, sharply, making the transition.

The funny thing is, I liked him more after that single sharp nod.

"Okay, that's why *I'm* here," he said. "You got me dead to rights. I'm in debt up to my eyeballs to Big Joe Redmond. And I'm here to tell you that had nothing to do with my mother's murder. If you want to catch a killer, that's something you've got to know."

Big Joe Redmond was a contractor. I had no idea why Harmon Kollar or anybody else would be in debt to him.

But I was damned if I was going to say so.

"Talk to me," I said. "Convince me."

"It doesn't happen like in the gangster movies," Harmon said twenty minutes later. "Wait, that's not right. At *first,* it's not like a gangster movie. And then it is. Then it's just like every dumb-ass gangster movie you ever sat through."

We were riding west on 140 toward Grafton, following the same route as the chase from the other day. An odd choice, I know. I just wanted to roll around on roads that were familiar to Harmon. Relax him, get him talking.

Boy, was he talking.

He sat in the passenger seat, twisted to half-face me, and he spilled. It probably felt good to pull the cork.

After months.

No, years.

"Four years?" he was saying as I tuned in again. "Almost five. Yeah, five. That's when Big Joe Redmond came in. You know Big Joe?"

"Never met him, but I hear the name around. Contractor."

"Contractor my ass. But everybody thinks so. He walks it and talks it. Makes for a good cover story."

"Big Joe's not a contractor?"

Harmon made a *pffft* noise with his lips. "Big Joe lights his cigars with contractors. Big Joe has contractors wiping his ass. See, when the banks stopped lending to small business in '08, Big Joe *started* lending."

"Got it."

"To builders. Most of these guys, they live project to project, development to development. Even the good ones aren't financial-planning geniuses, you know? They're always scrambling for the down payment on their next parcel."

"So Big Joe's a loan shark."

"And a smart one. No, not smart exactly, but . . . clever, in an in-

stinctive way. Sponsors a Little League team, drives a pickup instead
of a Cadillac. No pinkie ring, no gold Daytona on his wrist."

We came to the stop sign at Grafton Common. I looked left, turned
right, barely glanced at the spot where I'd flipped Lobo Soto's Excursion two days before. Harmon was so into his story, so happy to be
telling it, he didn't notice.

"I'm guessing Big Joe loaned you money," I said, "but I can't picture
what for. You built your house and your business before he showed up
in these parts."

"Well."

I raised eyebrows, shot him a tell-me-more look as we rolled past
ponds and strip malls.

"You know it was Kenny who staked me when we built WBFS,"
Harmon said. "Everybody knows. Or thinks they do. But the truth is,
not all of that dough went where my brother thought it went."

I noticed he'd promoted Kenny from half brother. Didn't say it out
loud, though. Instead I said, "Where *did* it go?"

"It's embarrassing."

"I go to at least two AA meetings a week," I said. "No offense, but
I hear your story a hundred times a year. You won't shock me. Booze,
drugs, some crazy sex thing, or gambling. That's about all there is."

Harmon said nothing.

I remembered Tricia's Cheater Beater app.

"Sex," I said. "A gal on the side."

Nothing.

"Or a dude. Like I said, you're not gonna shock me."

"Football," Harmon said.

"Gambling," I said.

"You bet," he said.

"Shit," I said.

CHAPTER TWENTY-FOUR

Yeah," Harmon said. "Shit."

He told it as I made a slow clockwise loop, extending the drive to let him get the whole thing off his chest. Grafton into Shrewsbury into West Boylston and Boylston, running the southeastern side of the Wachusett Reservoir. Driving the invisible part of the state: twenty minutes from Worcester and seventy from Boston, but mostly through pine forest and past ranch houses flying American flags, maybe with a trailered boat or a midsized RV in the front yard. The forest broken up by occasional strip-mall zones with a Target, a Staples, a Panera Bread.

To out-of-staters, Massachusetts is Boston, Cape Cod, and the Berkshires, without much in between. You'd be surprised how many people out my way visit Boston once a year—a family trip to a Red Sox game, maybe, or dinner at a dress-up restaurant—and like it that way.

This was my place. Cities don't suit me.

Harmon was the same way.

He relaxed and talked.

And talked.

Around the time Kenny's TV series hit, Harmon was like a million other guys: watched football all day Sunday, thought he was an expert.

He took to playing an occasional parlay card because Willy, the bartender down at the Golden Dragon, sold them. You paid ten bucks for the card. Picking three games against the point spread won you sixty bucks. Picking five earned two hundred. The big kahuna, the play that most of the jerks at the Dragon went for—because it was only ten bucks, right?—was to pick eleven NFL games on a given weekend, including the Monday Night finale, for a payday of forty-five hundred enchiladas.

Nobody ever won, of course. Picking football games against the spread is like picking stocks: Everybody from the top gurus to a blindfolded chimpanzee hits about 60 percent, and anybody who claims to do consistently better is a liar.

The worst day of Harmon Kollar's life, he now knew, came when he correctly picked eleven games in only his third time trying.

"You thought you were a big man," I said, rolling north and east on Route 70, thinking of a friend named Dixie who lived here in Clinton. "Thought you knew what you were doing."

Harmon nodded. "Guess who hand-delivered my forty-five hundred?"

"Big Joe Redmond."

"Yup."

"You were already a cop, right?"

He had been. One of Bryar's eight uniformed patrolmen. Harmon hadn't appreciated how good he had it as a small-town cop back then: annual cost-of-living raises, fresh cruisers every thirty-nine months, a health-care package that was basically free from his point of view. All the stuff that'd been dribbling away since the bottom fell out in '08.

Although the Golden Dragon parlay cards had always seemed innocent—everybody from the grade-school principal to the deputy chief played one, and bought a round if he won a few hundred bucks—Harmon's meeting with Big Joe had felt wrong enough so that he made sure he was out of uniform and in his own car when it happened.

In fact, Harmon had requested a car-to-car meeting, the type uniformed cops know well, where you put driver's window to driver's window. Back then, Big Joe was driving a crew-cab Silverado, burgundy with chrome rims, a beautiful truck. Since Harmon had been in Tricia's little whatevermobile, Joe—who Harmon then thought of as a contractor, a damn successful one but just a contractor who wore a flannel shirt and a fleece vest like anybody else—sat a full eighteen inches taller than the youngish cop, elbow on his sill, looking down with amusement on his phiz.

"So there he is," Big Joe had said, window to window in a convenience-store lot. "Smartest guy who ever played a card. How'd you do it?"

Harmon had said something about dumb luck.

"Don't sell yourself short," Big Joe said, producing a business-sized envelope. Waggling it, gesturing with it, in what Harmon saw as a deadpan tease, Big Joe wondering if Harmon would lunge at the envelope and its forty-five hundred-dollar bills, one hell of a lot of tax-free dough.

Harmon held his water, didn't grab at the envelope.

"You're bein' modest," Big Joe said. "Nobody hits eleven games through shit luck. I guess you learned the game pretty good out there in Michigan, huh? Guy like you, smart, well liked, guy like you could do all right in this town."

"Guy like me could do even better if you handed over that envelope."

Everything stopped. It was the type of wise-ass comment that Big Joe didn't hear often.

And didn't appreciate when he did.

But Harmon hadn't known that.

Yet.

So everything stopped, and exhaust fumes hung in the nighttime air, and nobody said anything, and the hair on Harmon's arms prickled just a little as he got an inkling of what Big Joe was all about . . .

. . . and then Big Joe cracked up, pounding his steering wheel, whacking the envelope on his sill. "Smart and well liked and a funny fucker to boot! I'm telling you, Kollar, you could do all right around here."

Then he looked at the envelope as if trying to remember what it was.

He waggled it a few final times.

"Fair and square," he finally said, extending it out and down in what Harmon later decided was intentional slow motion. "What's won is done, my old man used to say."

The ever-loving envelope stopped moving. "However," Big Joe said, locking eyes with Harmon, "there's a lot more goes on in the back room of the Dragon than these parlay cards. You know the cards are for shitheads, right?"

Harmon flared red. "I play one most weeks."

"Don't take it personal. I play one, too. For laughs. For something to talk about. What I mean, the cards are for . . . well, shitheads. Nobody ever wins, and when they do they blow it on a round of Scorpion Bowls. A guy like you, Kollar, a Michigan Freaking Wolverine, a guy knows what he's doing . . ."

"Yeah?"

Big Joe looked around and shifted in his seat. "Before I say more, no offense, what am I talking to here? Am I talking to John Law? Or am I talking to Harmon Kollar, a good guy lives over on West Upton Road?"

"You're talking to a guy who plays a card every week and doesn't care who knows it."

It was the right answer. "That's who I thought I was talking to. Had to check, though." Big Joe leaned until his chin nearly touched his door, and he lowered his voice. "Cutting to the chase, if you're ever feeling sporty, you can do a lot better in the Dragon than these cards."

"You're saying I can put down a real bet."

"Hell yes it's what I'm saying. That sound interesting to you?"

"It might."

Big Joe cut loose a big grin. "Knew it!" he said, slapping his truck's door with the envelope. "Don't tell any of the shitheads, okay? We keep it pretty low-profile."

They sure did: At that point, Harmon had been a working cop in town for going on five years, and he'd had no idea. "How do I . . . how does it work?"

"What you do," Big Joe said, "you come in when Willy's behind the bar, and you say, 'It looks a touch inclement outside.'"

Harmon said nothing.

"And make sure you're carrying an umbrella. A red one."

Harmon said nothing.

Big Joe said nothing.

Then he cracked up, that grin again. "I'm fuckin' with ya! Fuckin' with ya! Almost had ya, didn't I? Nah, just grab Willy and tell him what games you're looking at. He'll tell you what line we're using. Be cool about the whole thing, that's all we ask."

Far as Harmon was concerned, that must have been the end of the story. Because he was quiet for a long time as we drove Route 62 east, through a town called Berlin. We passed a farm stand, closed for the winter, where I once bought a slice of pie for a very bad woman.

"I'm going to guess at a few things," I said, swinging onto I-495 south for the run back to Bryar. "You started putting down bets, *real* bets, at the Golden Dragon."

He let out a long sigh and pinched the bridge of his nose. "I did. I did. Money trumped duty. No, that's not it, long as I'm telling you ugly truth I ought to be keeping to myself. It wasn't the money, it was the idea of not being a shithead. You know?"

"You knew Big Joe was a jerk. It's obvious from the way you talk about him. But you wanted in anyway. You wanted to be one of the guys who knew what went on in the back room."

Harmon said nothing.

"You bet," I said. "And you lost."

Harmon said nothing.

"Then you lost some more."

Nothing.

"You wound up in Big Joe's pocket."

"I did."

"And?"

"WBFS was in the shitter by then," Harmon said. "The business hadn't done well right from the get-go, that's no secret. When the gambling debts got ugly I started robbing Peter to pay Paul. Pulling out money that wasn't exactly mine to pull. I sold trucks. I did a stupid refi I'll never get clear of. That kind of thing." He chuffed a half-laugh. "It was around then things with Tricia really went south, too. When it rains it pours."

I found myself sitting very still at the mention of Tricia. Wanting more info, but not wanting to tip my hand that I wanted it.

When Harmon said no more about her, I circled back to something I'd wondered about anyway. "Why a moving company? I mean, of all the things?"

"I've wondered myself. About a thousand times. It seemed like a business a guy like me could do all right in. Buy a fleet, hire a bunch of strong college boys, football players looking for work. How hard could it be?" Again that half-laugh, this time with more bitterness, nearly a sob, folded in. "Pretty damn hard."

"It's always more complex when you're in it," I said, thinking of my own shops. "Fixing cars is the only thing I'm good at. So I opened a garage. Suddenly I was a manager and a shrink and an IT guy and a paper pusher and a toilet scrubber. Doubt I spent four hours a week fixing cars."

If he heard that, he ignored it. "Pretty goddamn hard," he said to himself, staring ahead.

I wondered if Harmon had another reason to open a business: to try for a little success of his own. Back then, Kenny was pulling big money in Hollywood. Harmon's NFL dream had died when his legbone snapped. Being a small-town cop was okay, but it was *only* okay. You could see where he'd dream of a breakout success. If you knew Harmon, you could also see where the dream might not be thought through very well.

Neither of us spoke again until I pulled into the parking lot and idled next to Harmon's truck.

"I don't talk like this, Sax," he said, looking straight ahead. "I don't spill my guts. It's not what I do."

"That makes two of us."

"I did it because you got me, fair and square, the other night at the Dragon. I know you've pulled off some impressive stuff. Dumb, amateur hour, but impressive. You would have learned about my gambling sooner or later. I'm respecting that, and I'm telling you"—Harmon shifted in his seat, and we locked eyes—"this deep shit I'm in had nothing to do with my mother. I worked overtime to shield her from it."

"Since we're talking this way, I've got to say it," I said. "Eudora's property must've looked tasty to these casino operators. The sale could have squared you up and then some."

He went red but held my eyes. "I won't deny it. I wanted her to sell. She said over her dead . . . she said no, and we both know she was stubborn as hell. So I'll say it again: My problems with Big Joe had nothing to do with anything else."

Harmon Kollar climbed out of my truck and into his.

I turned around and left.

CHAPTER TWENTY-FIVE

I used to think I was good at spotting liars.

I used to think I was a tough hombre, too.

When you get lied to enough and get the shit kicked out of you enough, you stop thinking those things.

Harmon Kollar had sought me out and told me a bunch of truths he didn't enjoy admitting. Then he'd looked me in the eye and sworn he wasn't Eudora's murderer.

Maybe he was telling the truth. Maybe he wasn't.

When it came to lying, I'd heard it all, seen it all, from drunks and junkies. One favorite tactic: Tell the embarrassing story, the one that makes you look bad. The idea being this: *See? If I confess to stealing from the collection plate, I'm letting it all hang out. There's no reason for me to lie about the other thing.*

Bullshit.

I admitted it to myself, though: Harmon's from-the-chest tears at the funeral, combined with what he'd just told me about the gambling, rang true. They made me want to look elsewhere for suspects.

In any case, nothing he'd said changed my priorities or my plan. The next item on my agenda was still this Rose Monteiro, widow of Paulo.

Why?

Checklist:

Russ Budde had pointed me at Ruthie Luciani, and Ruthie had pointed me at Rose. So the Bryar old-timers, the ones who knew all the stories and skeletons, were trying to tell me something. I'd be a jackass to ignore them.

Andy Spoon, Eudora's first husband, had strong-armed Paulo Monteiro out of property that was now worth something.

Paulo, and now Rose, apparently ran a gang.

I knew enough about Brazilians in general, and Brazilian crooks specifically, to tell you this: They do not forget *anything*, and they especially do not forget being ripped off. Don't take my word for it. Check the police logs in São Paulo, where intra-favela blood feuds run three generations without letup.

Final item on the checklist:

McCord had confirmed what I suspected—while Los Bajamaros had no official presence in Massachusetts, they had co-op deals with the Brazilians. That was a possible link between Lobo Soto and Rose Monteiro, and *that* was worth digging into.

I'd blown an hour and a half with Harmon, but there might still be time for a visit to Monteiro before the early sunset.

Thinking all this through, I was just pulling my cell to call McCord for research help when it rang. A local number I didn't recognize. I clicked on, said nothing.

"Conway?"

"Tricia? How'd you get this number?"

"I got it from Kenny. Was that wrong?"

"No."

"I felt somewhat girlish after our chat yesterday. It's a feeling that's neither customary nor comfortable for me. If I said more than I should have about my marital situation, let me apologize."

"Don't worry about it. I just saw him."

That got her attention. "Oh? Do tell."

"Not much to tell." I was already regretting mentioning him.

"And yet I'm dying of curiosity. Did my name come up?"

I needed to change the subject. "You near a computer?"

"Sure. I'm at home."

"Google Rose Monteiro. Throw in Paulo, Worcester, Brazilian, maybe gang."

There was a longish pause. Then Tricia said, "Oh my God. What are you getting yourself into?"

"Got an address?"

"It looks like they own a limousine company on Albany Street, is that what you want?"

"Sure."

"Does this make me your sidekick?"

I heard the smile in her voice.

Felt one of my own as I said, "I guess it does."

Worcester's a funny place. It's got everything you'd expect in a decent-sized city, but there's no logic or plan to it. Nothing connects to anything. You'll be walking through a flat-out ghetto, turn around, and realize you could throw a baseball to City Hall, or to a ritzy college.

So I wasn't surprised when Executive Transport, the Monteiro limo outfit on Albany Street, turned out to be three hundred yards from a couple of expensive restaurants Charlene used to like.

Maybe she still liked them. I wouldn't know.

Tricia had stayed on the phone while I drove, scanning newspaper stories from a couple years back and summing them up for me.

Rose Monteiro was a piece of work. When hubby Paulo had turned up missing, she'd gone on trial for Murder One and Conspiracy to Commit. According to the prosecutor, Paulo had made the mistake of playing house with his mistress, a second cousin half his age, then crying poor-mouth when Rose had demanded a divorce.

Rose'd had Paulo strapped to a lift in Executive Transport's maintenance shop one night, the prosecutor said. That's where poor old

Paulo had died. Although not until he'd explained, in exacting detail, where he'd stashed all the money. Account numbers, PINs, everything.

The way the prosecutor told it, Paulo likely *wished* he was dead for those last few hours, before Rose finally nodded and had her man slash hubby's throat.

Trace evidence showed hubby likely bled out into the oil-change pit.

Tricia was smart and quick. She'd skimmed more stories. The prosecution's problem, she told me, was that no body was found, so the case was built around a tiny amount of blood and the claims of thugs, nearly all of them illegals, who'd worked for Paulo, then for Rose, and had finally been turned by the cops when they were picked up for minor crimes.

In other words, the prosecutor wound up asking the jury to believe a half-dozen savage crooks who'd been lying about *everything,* right down to their own names, for twenty years or more.

Rose Monteiro's high-priced defense team blew holes in the allegations and embarrassed the prosecution. The jury came back inside an hour. Rose walked.

Now here I was, in a field of auto-body shops and warehouses and paint-supply operations and other small industrial outfits, all backing up to train tracks.

Executive Transport was a well-run business. I saw that at a glance. You learn to spot the signs.

For starters, even though not one customer in a hundred would visit this place—it would be a Web site-and-telephone business—the two-story brick building was spotless, power-washed within the last few years, the mortar touched up as needed, the parking lot freshly paved and striped.

The joint had a private car wash, the kind you find attached to gas stations, with two shivering bastards—low men on the totem pole—wiping down each Town Car, Suburban, and Escalade that rolled through. Each wiped-down vehicle was driven by a man in a blue blazer, who would park, hop out, and trot into the building with a clipboard in hand.

The drivers mostly looked like retired guys filling up their hours. I wouldn't mind doing that kind of work someday myself, but I'm not sure what my prospects are for retirement.

After looking the place over for five minutes, I swung into the lot and found a parking space with VISITOR stenciled at its head.

I didn't imagine it'd be easy to get to Rose Monteiro, but if I could vamp my way into the building and catch her attention, I had a puncher's chance.

Still.

Why not take a precaution? This lady doesn't screw around. Be smart for once.

I texted Tricia. *Going in Exec Transport, Albany St Worc, right now. If I don't call or txt in 30 mins, call Worc cops. Also call this number:*

The number belonged to McCord. Wasn't much he could do at a distance of three thousand miles. Then again, he'd magically tracked me down in Los Angeles, so you never knew.

Tricia came back right away. *Srsly? Like a Cold War spy thriller.*

I sent back *Srsly.*

I climbed from my truck, pulled open a door, stepped into the main garage area of Executive Transport . . .

. . . and heard her before I saw her.

"Two TCs and a Sub isn't *good* enough, Robert. Client specified three TCs, client *gets* three TCs."

She had a voice like a crow being run across a cheese grater. I swear, it made me clench my jaw.

I walked toward the voice, which was around a corner, while poor Robert mumbled about wheel bearings and tie-rod ends and an alignment. I decoded as I walked. TC would be Town Car, Sub would be Suburban.

As I rounded the corner, the crow on a cheese grater said, "Well, it'll have to be one hell of a quick alignment, then. Sixty State Street, Boston, seven thirty sharp. Make it happen."

She spun to walk away, this woman who ran her shop hands-on and apparently tortured her cheating husband to death.

She walked into me.

Her nose banged square into the zipper of my jacket.

"Ouch," said Rose Monteiro, taking a step back, looking daggers at me as she straightened her huge glasses.

Instinct told me the way to play it. Monteiro wouldn't respect a yes-man, a bower-and-scraper. She would respect power. She was used to having her ass kissed. The way to stand out, to show I wasn't another Robert, was to not pucker up.

So I ignored her at first. I looked over her head at Robert, bald with a halfhearted comb-over, who stood just in front of a black Town Car on a blue lift. He looked like somebody'd let all the air out of him.

"Mark the tie-rod threads real careful with plumber's tape," I said, still looking past Monteiro. "Then tighten the new ends to the marks and skip the alignment for today. It'll be fine long as your driver stays under seventy. Save you forty-five minutes."

We stood still and quiet for maybe ten seconds.

In another corner of the garage, an air wrench whined and a compressor kicked on.

Monteiro whirled again. "See?" she said to Robert, hands on hips. "*See?* More of that, less of this." She made an exaggerated wilt-and-mope.

Then she spun for a third time, to face me again. "You here about a job? Because if you are, you're hired."

That voice. *Yuh HOI-uhd.*

Poor Robert.

I said, "Talk to you in private?"

"Private? I'm a Revere girl with five brothers and I married a Brazilian, I don't know from private. You want private, go to confession." It had the feel of an old joke, Rose looking around for approval as she spoke, getting a weak smile from Robert.

I waited until she was done grandstanding.

Finally she looked at me. Her smile, which never had touched her eyes, was long gone. She was ready to be obeyed now.

"Los Bajamaros," I said. Real quiet. She could barely hear me over the air compressor, I knew.

She could read my lips, though.

Her eyes went hard and sharp. "Upstairs."

In tight black skirt, bare legs, and black high heels, she clack-clack-clacked across the shop floor and up a flight of corrugated iron stairs to a balcony that ringed the place.

It was carpeted up here, and much quieter than the lower level. Rose led the way to an office and waiting area. A gal who looked like a junior version of Rose—the dark hair, dark eyes, thin face, even the big glasses—didn't look up from her PC as we passed.

The big guy who stood outside a closed door did. He looked me over but good. Not trying to hide it or be anything like polite, he pulled his phone and snapped my picture as I waited for Rose to let me into her office.

Which had a pair of arched windows looking over the parking lot, Albany Street, and train tracks.

"Sit," she said and made her way around her desk. "Los Bajama-ros. Mexicans out of the Valley. Boss man's a smart little fucker name of Lobo Soto. What about them?"

So she wasn't going to play dumb. I liked that. Respected it.

Part of me wanted to stall or jump around, do something to take control—but I didn't *have* control. Not much. There was at least one armed man eight feet away, and Rose Monteiro didn't vibe as a patient woman.

What I did have was info.

So deal it out like playing cards. Watch her reaction. See what works and what doesn't.

"Lobo Soto and Los Bajamaros," I said, "kidnapped Kenny Spoon. Not because of a grudge, not for direct ransom. Strictly for a third-party payday. It's what they do."

"Kenny Spoon the TV guy from around here, the has-been. His mommy just got shot. It's all over the news. So I'm figuring out why you're here. But who *are* you?"

I said my name.

She waved a disgusted hand. "Conway Sax, Joey Spumoni, Dick Hertz from Holden. That's not what I meant and you know it. Who *are* you?"

"I'm a mechanic."

Deadpan. "A mechanic. And a good one, I guess, from the way you just wised up Robert."

I shrugged.

Rose shook her head. "You're more than just a damn mechanic."

I said nothing.

"The thing is, I know your name. From somewhere. How would I know it?"

"I'm the guy took Kenny Spoon away from Los Bajamaros."

"I wouldn't know anything about that."

I looked at her until she dropped her eyes.

"Tommy outside is running you right now," she said, nodding at the closed door. "We're tied into some serious databases. Your name's familiar, Sax."

I said nothing.

Rose sighed, put two fingers in her mouth, whistled.

The office door opened. Tommy took one step in and stared at his phone. "Sax, Conway," he said. "Did a bit at Walpole. Manslaughter."

"You don't say," Rose said.

"Self-defense," I said. "I got rung up by a DA who needed to make a splash."

" 'Course you did, dearie. 'Course you did."

Tommy never looked up. When he decided we were finished, he

went on. "Did his parole, made it off paper. Works as a grease mon-key here and there, but never for long. Owned his own shop a couple times, but they didn't last either. He . . . maybe I shouldn't say this next thing, Rose."

"Say it."

Tommy shrugged. "The thing in Springfield a while back? Our col-league, the gentleman who owned a club? And had a son? And unfor-tunate events befell them?"

"Yeah?"

"Sax was in the thick of that mess, but he skated. The staties held him, then released him. The DA charged him, then pulled the charges. The *Herald* named him, then stopped naming him."

Rose thumped her blotter. "*That's* why I knew your name. The Char-lie Pundo thing. Thanks, Tommy."

He stepped backward and closed the door.

"Mechanic my ass," Rose said.

CHAPTER TWENTY-SIX

I am a mechanic," I said. "And yeah, I was in on that Springfield thing. But not the way you think."

"I don't care what happened out there. Or how, or why. *Especially* why. I'm a pragmatic girl, always have been. *Why* is for shrinks and bedwetters. Alls I know is Charlie's out of the game, and so's his weirdo son. Same pie, bigger slice for me. You're starting to look interesting to me, mechanic."

She leaned forward, resting elbows on blotter, and did what she could—not much—to soften her voice. "Man walks in a place like this, looking like half a con and half a cowboy, no wedding band, turns out he can take care of cars and take care of himself. What *else* can you take care of, Sax?"

"Um," I said. I spent half a second wondering how old she was, then another half deciding I didn't care.

Those eyes were pretty once you got past the goofy glasses. I'm a sucker for long lashes.

And the top, or blouse, or whatever women call shirts. What with the leaning forward.

And that pulled my memory to the skirt, and those heels, clack-clacking across the concrete floor.

And if you want the truth, it'd been awhile. For me and Charlene, I mean. Since there *was* no more me and Charlene.

I hadn't thought about that, hadn't felt like I was missing much.

Until now.

I may have gone red.

Rose may have gotten a kick out of that.

I took a breath. "You haven't asked why I'm involved."

Her eyes switched modes just like that. She'd been having some fun with me, but fun was over. "I haven't asked," she said, " 'cause I don't care."

"Los Bajamaros killed Eudora Spoon. That's right. An L.A. gang did a hit not fifteen miles from here as the crow flies. How do you feel about that? That something you're okay with?"

Did her pupils tighten up? Did her jaw shift just a little as she clenched her teeth?

I thought they did, so I pushed harder.

"The triggerman died when I wrecked his car," I said. "But there was another Bajamaro there, and he got away."

Rose sat very, very still.

"Lobo Soto himself," I said.

The office felt warm.

Outside, a freight rolled past at walking speed, groaning and clicking.

"You need to be very careful what you say in here," Rose said. "In this office. In this building."

"So I hear," I said, pulling my phone. I called up my text message to Tricia. I turned the phone so Rose could read it, then pushed it across her blotter. "That careful enough?"

She read it, squinting, checking the time stamp against her wrist-watch—a vintage man's Rolex OysterDate that slopped around like a bracelet on her thin wrist.

I said, "I've got what, six minutes before I need to get in touch with my friend?"

"You shouldn't be saying the things you're saying," she said in a different voice, a formal voice. She was wondering, for the first time, if I was wired.

Or maybe she was realizing she'd have to have me killed.

Or maybe both.

"Here's what I'll say." I rose as I spoke. "Eudora Spoon, Kenny's mother, was a friend of mine. Everybody who killed her is gonna pay. The triggerman paid already. Lobo Soto's gonna pay. Whoever ordered the hit is gonna pay."

Rose stared at me, saying nothing.

"I know you've got a deal going with Los Bajamaros," I said. "They scratch your back out in L.A., you scratch theirs around here. So it's hard to imagine you didn't sign off on the hit."

"And if I did, I'm gonna pay?"

"Bet your sweet ass."

"Why, thank you," Rose said.

I didn't smile. "I've got this pal, a smart bastard, helps me out once in a while. Know what he says all the time?"

"What's that?"

"'The enemy of my enemy is my friend.' I guess it's a famous line. Ever heard it?"

"I think so."

"On the off chance you *didn't* know about this hit," I said, "here's something to think about." I grabbed a pen and wrote my cell number on her blotter. "Who'd make a better enemy right now? Lobo Soto, three thousand miles away? Or me, right here in Worcester County? Who do you want for an enemy? Who do you want for a friend? Pick one."

I stepped toward the door.

"Wait," Rose Monteiro said.

I didn't.

Instead I passed Tommy and walked down the stairs, out the door, to my truck.

Didn't breathe until I was a block away. I truly had believed she would kill me.

I called Tricia with an all clear. She just about fainted—I'd left only a couple of minutes to spare. She demanded I come by to explain what had happened, sweetening the deal with a dinner offer.

It was past five, the sun was down, and I was starving. So I drove back to Bryar while I thought. Rose Monteiro made me paranoid enough to bounce around Worcester side streets for ten minutes looking for a tail that wasn't there.

Funny thing: Until this morning, I'd never heard of Rose Monteiro. Eight hours later, it was hard for me to picture a scenario where she didn't either play an active role in Eudora's murder or, at the very least, sign off on a Bajamaros hit.

I had no evidence that Monteiro and her crew would directly benefit from the death, but everything else pointed that way: the Monteiros' ugly history with Andy Spoon, the Bryar old-timers' tips, Rose's acceptance of my presence. It was as if she'd known *someone, sometime,* was going to brace her on the murder.

But why kill Eudora? What would push Rose in that direction?

I realized there was a giant hole in my knowledge. Eudora had told me of Kenny's kidnapping. As she knew I would, I'd dropped everything and rattled off to Los Angeles in full rescue mode.

Kidnapped *why,* though? What was the ransom demand? I thought through every word we'd exchanged, and I was damned if Eudora had ever said Kenny was being held for X dollars, or until Eudora agreed to Z.

Damn. How had I let that slip?

You let it slip because you couldn't wait to go steaming off to fight somebody else's war.

Hell.

New agenda item: Find out exactly why Kenny was snatched. Best to ask Kenny himself about that.

For now, though, I worked around the hole, focusing on what I did know and seeking spots where Rose Monteiro and her crew fit.

It was easy to picture a scenario where Rose & Company wanted something—Eudora's land being the obvious candidate, land Rose thought had been stolen from her family, land which was now worth a fortune to the casino people—and asked Los Bajamaros to snatch Kenny as some sort of leverage.

That went south when I cut Kenny loose.

Next thing you knew, Lobo Soto himself, plus an ex-marine shooter, were setting up a sniper's nest in Bryar, Massachusetts.

Had a deal between Los Bajamaros and the local Brazilians gone sour?

Had Rose wanted Eudora hit, and called in Los Bajamaros as a make-good after they lost Kenny?

"Holes," I said out loud. "Too many holes." For now, what I needed was answers from Kenny and to keep leaning on Rose Monteiro. Her reaction to our meeting could tell me a lot.

Or get me killed.

The enemy of my enemy is my friend.

She made a hell of an enemy.

I pictured Randall saying it. He loved to whip out quotes like that, spout them like they were no big deal. Maybe they weren't to him, but he knew they were Greek to me, and he liked playing professor. I pictured this tic of his: When he goes into professor mode, he pushes a pair of glasses up the bridge of his nose.

Trouble is, he doesn't wear glasses.

CHAPTER TWENTY-SEVEN

Missing Randall hit me like a punch in the kidney.

He's the son of Luther Swale, my former parole officer. Randall got his right foot blown off when he kicked a trash-can lid in the wrong village in the wrong part of the world. Hadn't been in the army four months when it happened. If he felt sorry for himself, he hid it well. Came back stateside, learned to use his prosthetic well enough to win bar bets because none of the drunks believed one of his ankles was made of titanium and high-tensile-strength plastic.

Randall's the smartest man I've ever met. When he got out of the army, he had an inch-thick stack of letters from colleges, offers of full academic scholarships.

He let the letters sit. He maybe let them sit too long. Instead, he spent time helping me out of jams and getting tangled up with older women who were crazy about him but who he never truly let in.

It'd all boiled over a while back. I'd gotten in over my head, had asked Randall for help. His reward: shotgun pellets that flayed his torso and head.

He'd lived. No thanks to me.

I was dead to him.

I didn't blame him.

But I missed him.

And his help.

Two grown men. Stubborn as can be. Pissing time away because it's easier, in some bizarre way, to clench the teeth and the heart than to say you're sorry.

Before I could outthink myself, I speed-dialed his cell.

Voice mail.

I nearly clicked off. His call log would tell him I'd reached out, right? I would officially be the better man even if I hung up right now.

By the time I thought all this through, Randall's short message had played and his beep had beeped.

Don't outthink yourself. Just this one goddamn time.

"It's a crying shame is what it is," I said, swinging into Tricia's driveway. "Too proud to come in out of the rain, the both of us. Jack-asses." Pause. "I miss hanging around with you."

It may not strike you as much, but it sure was hard for me.

I clicked off, shut down the truck, and went inside.

"I'd ask if you mind," Tricia Kollar said, opening a Corona, "but I don't *give* a rat's fanny if you mind. Today I refused a shipment of pillows, fought with Captain Clueless at Corporate over these awful framed prints he's jamming down our throat, and pressed charges against a shoplifter while her three-year-old cried giant toddler tears. And that was *before* you put me in charge of calling in the cavalry in case this awful Rose Monteiro decided to murder you. It's past five, snow's coming, I'm not driving anywhere, and by God I want a beer."

As she said all this, she strode to a sectional, pivoted, sat down hard, twitched her feet onto a hassock, took a long sip, and sighed.

Man, did I like her, looking at her there in flannel sweatpants and a ratty sweatshirt and fur-lined moccasins. You'd be surprised how many people won't drink in front of a drunk. I prefer folks who handle it the way Tricia was.

"Bottoms up," I said, and sat kitty-corner across from her.

"It's starting," she said, looking west through the window well. She'd dimmed the lights inside and turned on the high-powered floods outside, so we could see the first fat flakes, looking like ticker tape, flutter to the driveway.

We were quiet maybe twenty seconds.

Then we said, at the exact same time, "I love this part."

Then we whiplashed to stare at each other, our eyes big.

Then we laughed.

"Things get so quiet when the snow starts," I said.

"And if there's one thing you appreciate, it's quiet."

I said nothing.

Tricia took another long sip. "I hope chicken Caesar salad's okay."

"It's fine."

"First things first, though. I, your trusty sidekick, demand a full accounting of your recent foray into hostile territory."

I hesitated. I prefer to keep my cards close.

On the other hand, Tricia had helped me out.

And McCord was in California.

And who knew where Randall was.

And Tricia looked relaxed and open and eager.

And freckled.

Something about that spray of freckles across her nose. Even in winter, when most people's freckles disappear.

So I told it.

Every word of it.

There were a lot of words.

I even surprised myself, when I wrapped up, by looking Tricia in the eye and saying, "I thought she was going to have Tommy shoot the back of my head. I really did."

"Dear *God*," Tricia said, eyes wide. She had gone for a second beer at some point. Now she set it on an end table, crossed the room, knelt near me, and put a hand on my forearm. "How do you put yourself in these positions? *Why* do you put yourself in these positions?"

"I did it for Eudora."

She looked in my eyes for what seemed a long time. "Simple as that?"

"Simple as that. Everybody pays."

"No gray areas?" As she spoke, she shifted her hand from my forearm to my head, pushing her fingers through my hair.

Her face was close to mine.

The lights were so low in here.

We looked at one another.

"No gray," I said. "Not this time. Everybody pays."

It came out an odd cross: half croak, half holler. I felt the shake in my voice, saw I was thrumming.

It killed the moment.

As Tricia sprang up, slapping her thighs and saying, "On to dinner!" and quick-stepping across to the kitchen, I wondered why I'd killed it.

I wished I hadn't.

CHAPTER TWENTY-EIGHT

It was one of those prepared supermarket dinners, so Tricia just needed a few minutes to warm the chicken and dress the salad.

I thought about the big hole in what I knew—why had Kenny been snatched in the first place?—and called his cell. He said he was right across the road at Eudora's place. I asked could he come over. He said sure, he could use the excuse to walk the greys, he'd be by after he ate.

I relayed all this to Tricia as she set the table.

We were uncomfortable after the moment I'd botched. Or scotched. I still wasn't sure which. I wanted to say something about how married means married, no gray area, but I couldn't put the words together.

Tricia had cranked up every light in the joint. All we could see in the window wall now was our own reflection: a pair of stiff-legged people trying to pretend what had happened hadn't happened.

A few minutes later, we were finally crunching away. "Good," I said. "Thank you."

"Oh, I knocked myself out. Slaved over a hot stove all day."

"I did about a week's worth of talking over there," I said, nodding at the living room. "Now you."

"Me what?"

"You talk."

"About?"

"You and Harmon. From there to here. You were a cheerleader, he was a jock. Answer me this for starters: You always say you were an *ironic* cheerleader. What's that mean?"

"A fair question. I never *embraced* cheerleading, do you know what I mean? I grew up in Ann Arbor, and I'm not kidding when I say half the little girls there can picture no greater glory than cheering for the Wolverines on Saturday. Me, I went through all the programs, the comps, the traveling teams, the summer cheer camps . . . but I never connected with that group. I always felt like I was observing the scene from above, mocking it even as I engaged in it. My friends were goths and skatepunks, and I liked nothing more than expounding to them about the phoniness of it all. Does that answer the question?"

"I guess. It's sad."

Tricia laughed. Her eyes did not. "Sad how?"

"Sad to do something but not let yourself really get into it. To not let yourself enjoy it all the way."

Tricia ate a bite of chicken very slowly, pausing to pair it with a crouton, looking at me all the while. "A girl could be forgiven for seeing you as a simple man," she finally said. "And there's nothing wrong with being a simple man. But you're not one."

"So now I know what an ironic cheerleader is," I said. "Another question. You dropped out after a couple of years to marry Harmon and come back here. That doesn't fit. It's not you."

"It's not?"

"You know it's not. You're smart as hell. Got college degree written all over you. So why?"

"I stand by my declaration that in the case of Conway Sax, still waters run deep. You have a way with the deceptively probing questions, sir."

I said nothing.

Tricia set down her fork, put her elbows on the table, and rested her head in her hands. "So there I was, living the dream of so many vapid Michigan girls, flouncing it up in my pleated skirt for the maize and blue. Even better, I'd snared a cute football player as my very own boyfriend. Life was good."

I put down my own fork.

"I was also having an affair with my art history professor," Tricia said, not looking me in the eye. "TA, actually. He was twenty-four and tall and Austrian, with this accent—"

"TA?"

"Teaching assistant. College professors don't teach anymore, did you know that? They publish unreadable books and snipe at one another in meetings. Graduate students do the teaching. As you might imagine, I tried very hard to be sophisticated for my Austrian TA. That meant accelerating my ironic-cheerleader act. I spent hours, entire *weekends,* smoking Gitanes in the awful little room he rented and saying the meanest things about cheerleading and cheerleaders. About Michigan football and college football in general. About . . ."

Her voice had gone tighter and tighter.

"About Harmon," I said.

"About Harmon." She rasped it.

I waited.

She began to speak, then stopped.

Then again.

Finally, with effort I could see, she said, "Harmon didn't know any of this. He suspected nothing. He was a sophomore football player at the University of By God Michigan, and he was getting laid, and that was all he needed to know. The Wisconsin game was a very big deal, his first start. I skipped that game. I went to a panel discussion in Toronto instead. The topic, if memory serves, was Martin Luther's contribution to the spread of Mannerism."

"You went with your TA boyfriend."

"It was the first weekend of football I'd skipped since I was eight."

"And Harmon busted his leg."

"And Harmon busted his leg. And I've been making up for that weekend in Toronto ever since. And I thank you so very damn much for bringing it up. Are you finished?"

Without waiting for an answer, she snapped to her feet, zipped away both plates, and made for the kitchen.

Hell.

I sat, wondering how I'd turned everything so rotten with two questions.

A knock at the front door saved me, giving me something to do.

"Kenny," I said over my shoulder.

"If he's got those damn dogs," Tricia said over the water she was using to rinse dishes, "tell him they stay outside."

That slowed me up for a second. Had she forgotten it was snowing? The dogs would be cold.

"Thank you," Kenny said when I opened the door. "I know I took a while. I underestimated the difficulty of navigating the drive."

I knew what he meant. Harmon's house, yard, and business make for a cockeyed layout. Blasting through granite to create roadway isn't cheap. When he built the compound, Harmon economized by doubling up: The access road for the storage operation was also his driveway.

It was a terrible decision, as a bunch of people tried to warn him. Storage customers had their own padlocks and twenty-four-hour access to their units, so vehicles could conceivably roll past the master bedroom at three in the morning. As it turned out, they almost never did, because Wolverine Bros. Freight & Storage tanked right from the start. But Harmon didn't know that when he was planning.

Even worse, the twisty, hilly driveway was hell on the moving trucks, a fleet of twenty-six-foot Fords and Volvos. It took some fancy driving to get one up or down without scraping rock. He learned pretty quickly that not all his drivers were up to it.

Anyway, trudging up that drive couldn't be easy when snow was actually falling. A pair of skittish greyhounds couldn't help, either.

Before I could mention what Tricia had said about the dogs, the pair of them bolted into the entry. Once I closed the door, they just stood there, nervous. I didn't see where they were doing any harm, so I grabbed an old sweatshirt from a hook, used it to rub melted snow from their backs—Dandy gave me a big old lick on the cheek—and left them there while Kenny and I went to the living room.

Where Tricia had recovered. She hugged Kenny, leaned back, and asked how he was doing.

"As well as can be expected," he said. "Better, actually. I'm occupying myself with the surprisingly complex details of a family death, and it passes the time, though it does occasionally make one feel ghoulish. Today I contacted a tech support specialist and enlisted his help cracking Mother's many computer and online passwords."

"You staying sober?" I asked.

Kenny looked at Tricia, half-smiling. "He minces few words. Had we noticed this?"

"We had."

"You want to go to a meeting," I said, "or you just want to talk? Call me. Doesn't matter when."

"Thank you. I truly am doing well. Nobody's more surprised than I by this development, but there it is."

I waved an arm and we sat on the sectional.

"Why'd Los Bajamaros kidnap you?"

Instead of answering, he raised an actor's eyebrow at Tricia.

"No words minced," she said.

I ignored that, keeping my focus on Kenny. "What was it all about?"

"Mother didn't say?"

"I didn't ask."

"That was foolish."

"Yup. Quit screwing around. Why?"

He folded his arms across his chest. He wore a sand-colored sweater, one he'd left behind when he headed west or one of his father's. Either way, there were moth holes in the elbows.

"And if I say it's none of your damn business?" he asked.

"None of my business? None of my *business*?" I ticked off items on my fingers as I spoke. "I hauled you out of that miserable joint, two on twelve. I did a *Smokey and the Bandit* bit that totaled my rental and damn near got me shot. I introduced you to Shaky Pete, who sobered you up. And Erin, who looks to be the best thing in your life, is being watched over by McCord. You owe me an awful lot. You're lucky I'll settle for an explanation."

CHAPTER TWENTY-NINE

Color drained from Kenny's face as I spoke. "Okay," he said. "Okay."

He licked his lips.

I waited.

"What gets my Irish up," he finally said, "is the widespread assumption that the fiasco was all about me. Kenny the has-been. Kenny the pill-head. Kenny Spoon from the where-are-they-now shows on E!"

"Tell me more."

"Once Los Bajamaros had me imprisoned," he said, "nobody ever spoke to me. But on the ride over—Erin and I were out for frozen yogurt when two of them simply touched a pistol to my ribs and invited me to climb in their ridiculous lowrider, there must have been two dozen people around, can you believe it?—one asked the other in Spanish why they'd snatched me. I have enough Spanish to get by, who doesn't in L.A.? The second one said my brother had something or had to *do* something, that was all Lobo had told him and that was all he needed to know."

"I'll be damned."

"Join the club."

I spent the next ten minutes asking questions from different angles, trying to get Kenny to remember more.

Or maybe I was playing the cop's trick of trying to catch him in a lie.

His story about the kidnapping never changed. He was minding his own business with Erin, getting frozen yogurt, when they snatched him up. Other than the burst of Spanish in the car, nobody ever told him jack shit about why he was where he was.

After three or four rounds of questions, Kenny grew annoyed. He announced we were through talking, rose, put on his coat, leashed the dogs, and left.

"Huh," I said.

I was so lost in thought I was surprised when Tricia said, "Huh what? Share your observations."

"How'd that story vibe to you?"

She selected her words carefully. "It had the ring of truth, but . . ."

"But he's a pro actor," I said.

"Precisely. If he's telling the truth, Kenny's kidnapping may have been a—call it a lever. Intended to move Harmon in some direction."

"But Kenny would know we'd think that way," I said, "and the whole story may be bullshit."

We were quiet a while.

Tricia was easy to be quiet around.

I liked that.

"What's our next move?" she finally said.

"Take a hard look at Rose," I said, rising. "See if today's meeting makes her jump in any particular direction. And by the way, it's *my* move, not *ours*."

She made an exaggerated pout, kind of kidding but kind of not. "I'm being demoted already from my sidekick position?"

"You want to be a sidekick," I said, "do some more googling. Find me a home address for Rose Monteiro. She'll be in Worcester or a suburb of."

She brightened some. "When do you need the info, chief?"

"She strikes me as a workhorse," I said. "I'll want to be on her by breakfast time. Thank you for dinner."

I bent over and kissed the top of her head before leaving.

Just the top of her head.

My phone buzzed as I headed for Framingham.

McCord.

I clicked on.

"How's Erin?" I asked. "And what's that noise?"

He ignored the second question. "Her boss told her to take a few days off. I guess her shiner made 'em uncomfortable at work."

"What's that noise?"

"They came back."

I straightened up. "What?"

"Erin said it was the same pair from before. They must've cloned her garage door opener the first time, 'cause that's how they got in. At two this morning."

"You were there this time."

McCord said nothing.

"Poor bastards," I said.

"Far as I know," he said, "they'll live. But they did tell me what I asked them to tell me."

I imagined how that interrogation had gone and said again, "Poor bastards."

"First thing you need to know," he said, "they got no idea where Soto is. They convinced me he's not in L.A. Took 'em a while, but they convinced me. At first the Bajamaros assumed he'd split for Mexico, but I guess there's no sign of him there."

"The gang's worried about the boss man, so somebody made those poor saps go back to Erin's? See if they could pick up his trail?"

"Yup."

"What were the odds Erin would know anything? Bajamaros must be pretty desperate for info."

"Yup."

Huh. "He's most likely taking a low-profile cross-country drive," I said. "He's a smart guy. He's no *pistolero* gangbanger. He could pull it off."

"Or maybe he went to ground in your neck of the woods," McCord said. "That'd be safest."

"If he had a safe place."

"So does he?"

"I'll look at that."

That damn noise. Almost like a waterfall, but not quite.

"Another thing they told me," McCord said. "Last few years, Soto's been on a big push to go legit."

"You told me that already."

"Know what his new specialty is?"

"Tell me."

"Casinos. Slots. Legalized gaming."

"That's a big deal right here. Right now."

"I know, I googled. That's why I thought you should know. Los Bajamaros don't do as much chop-shop bullshit or street-dealing bullshit as they used to. Some, but not as much. Instead, they look for places where gambling's on the ballot. They go in and make it happen. They take home an upfront payday plus a tiny slice of the action. A consultant's slice. A *legal* slice. It worked in Idaho, then it worked in South Dakota."

"Now Soto's been making it happen right here in Bryar," I said.

"Like you said, he's smart."

I thought and drove.

"What the *hell* is that noise?" I finally said.

"Well," McCord said.

"Sounds like a waterfall."

"It's a bathtub. Filling."

"A bathtub," I said.

McCord said nothing.

Then it came to me.

"You and Erin," I said.

"Proximity," he said.

I sighed. "You sure everything's okay, lover boy? What if Los Baja-maros take another run at you?"

"That would be dumb."

I thought it through. Decided I agreed.

"Hard to picture you fitting in a bathtub alone," I said. "Let alone with somebody else."

"It's a big bathtub," McCord said. And clicked off.

It'd been one hell of a day, and it had one surprise left.

When I tried to pull into Floriano's driveway, Randall Swale's silver Hyundai blocked my way.

I backed into the street and parked there. I may have smiled.

He was in the dining room. They all were. Randall, Floriano, Maria, and Dozen talked and laughed around tiny coffee cups and tiny plates full of tiny jelly cakes. Warm light, crumbs and elbows, good times. People who liked each other and had missed each other.

"Look at what dragged in *el gato*!" Maria said to me, pointing at Randall. She'd been working on her English and had been getting brave.

"Mom!" Dozen said, stretching the word.

Randall laughed, rose, looked at me.

In Portuguese, Floriano told Dozen to help his mother clear the table.

Randall stepped around the table, stepped to me, shook my hand. "I'm sorry as hell I missed the funeral," he said. "I was in the air."

I said, "From?"

"San Francisco."

"Stanford?"

"Among others. Long story." As he spoke, he steered me into the parlor, which Floriano and Maria had set up with a mish-mosh of

hand-me-downs and castoffs that worked fine. Brazilians shake their
heads at the stuff we throw away. They all drive pickup trucks, they
all have a strong brother or cousin, and they all furnish their homes
free of charge.

Speaking of Floriano—he'd vanished. Smart man, can read a vibe.
Other than dish clinks and radiator hisses, the first floor was quiet.

So were Randall and I.

Sitting in a wing chair, he crossed his legs, giving me a look at his
ankle. It was quite a machine.

Dale hopped on the arm of Randall's chair. Randall scratched Dale's
ears. Dale didn't mind.

"You got my voice mail," I finally said.

"And one hell of a voice mail it was."

I looked at my friend. He's a dead ringer for one of the guys on that
old TV show *The Wire*. A bad guy who's really bad, but somehow you
like him anyway. Women come up to Randall on the street, make big
eyes at him, and tell him how much he looks like the dude.

The tiny shotgun-pellet scars near the hairline at his left temple
didn't hurt his looks much. If you didn't know what to look for, you
could miss them.

Sitting here now in a warm parlor, watching him scratch my cat's
ears, I tried to tell him how sorry I was about those scars. I tried to tell
him I missed him. I tried to tell him that when I felt like talking to
anybody—it doesn't happen often, but it happens—he and Sophie
were the first ones I thought of. The *only* ones I thought of.

I said nothing.

The words would come halfway up my chest, then get lost in a tight
throat and tight shoulders and a tight jaw and a feeling that if I said
anything more, one damn word, I'd bawl like a baby.

So I said nothing.

That was okay.

Randall knew.

"Your voice mail," he finally said, "made reference to jackasses. To overproud men who'd rather get soaked to the skin than admit it's raining."

"Something like that."

"Point taken."

Then Randall Swale let me off the hook simply and completely, just by slapping both his thighs.

The double slap was sharp enough to send Dale running.

The double slap said *That's enough of that.*

The double slap said *Time to move on.*

The double slap said everything.

Randall's like that.

I said, "I wouldn't mind telling you what's going on around here. Regarding Eudora and such. If you've got time."

"Nothing but, compadre."

"You remember McCord?"

"State trooper, New Hampshire. Retired because his boss was a dipshit."

"He's in on this."

"Lucky McCord."

I told it. I told it all.

Except about Tricia. Her I kept to myself.

CHAPTER THIRTY

"Mother of mercy," Randall said quite a while later. It was going on eleven, and I'd been up since before five, and man was I tired.

"Your take?" I said.

"My take, first of all, is I'm so sorry about Eudora. I only met her once or twice, but I know she meant a lot to you."

I nodded.

"She was the grande dame of the Barnburners," he said. "She died in your arms. She bled to death pressed against you. Are you okay?"

I nodded.

"Are you *okay*, Conway?"

I said nothing.

I licked my lips.

I wished for a glass of water.

"No," I finally said.

"Good," Randall said.

I popped eyebrows.

"Only a liar or a psychopath could answer yes."

"I'm no liar."

He let the comment hang, then made a slow smile. "I'd forgotten you can be funny in your own way. Want to talk about it? About her?"

"No."

"Of course you don't. In that case, what's the plan?"

"I'm going to keep an eye on Rose Monteiro. See how she reacts to our meeting."

"Want help?"

"I can handle it."

"You sure?"

"I can handle it."

He frowned in concentration, leaned forward, and rubbed his hands while he thought things through.

I watched closely.

Finally he pushed those imaginary glasses up his nose, and I knew I had him hooked. Partners again.

Good old Randall.

"Who's investigating the murder?" he asked. "I assume Harmon's not in charge."

"You're right. State cops took over. Lead investigator's a gal named Venezia. Smart. Kind of cool. Funny thing, though. She's a trooper, not a detective. Wears the uniform and everything. Never seen that before."

"Did you have a full and frank discussion with this Venezia? Did you tell her everything there was to tell?"

"Of course not."

"Of course not," Randall said. "Reason, please?"

"I tried to tell her about Soto and she didn't buy it. After that, why should I bang my head against a wall helping the cops?"

"Fair point." Randall sighed. "What *do* the staties know about Soto?"

"They must know his rep, because they ID'd his partner, the shooter. Ex-army, current Bajamaro. And when you look at Los Bajamaros, you're looking at Soto. And like I said, his gang is doing strong-arm work to get casinos built. No way will the cops miss all that."

"Wow."

"And we know Los Bajamaros work for Monteiro and vice versa. So we've really got something worth teasing out there."

"Another angle: Who's in charge of Eudora's estate?"

"For now, it seems Kenny's running the show. That's what he implied tonight, anyway."

He frowned. "As executor? From what you've told me about him, I find that hard to believe."

I shook my head. "No way he's the executor. But he's keeping the household going. Paying this month's bills, watching her dogs. Like that. Seems to have grown up some."

"Thus emerges a plan, or a reasonable facsimile thereof. Learning more about Eudora's estate, specifically Harmon's standing regarding same, is priority one."

"Don't overlook Kenny. He sure has made himself at home."

"Kenny the whining, naked kidnap victim? Don't tell me you see him as a player."

"This whole mess started when I headed west to fetch him."

"Until thirty seconds ago, you made it sound as if he has trouble tying his shoes. Can you picture him arranging an elaborate double-cross scam?"

I shrugged, knowing how sketchy it sounded. "You'll drop everything and help me out? Just like that?"

"There's not a lot to drop. My, ah, college career has been settled, but it doesn't begin until September."

"Hot damn." I shook his hand. "Stanford?"

Randall looked away. "No."

"Brown? Duke?"

"No and no."

"Don't tell me you went for Purdue."

"Try Framingham State."

I laughed.

Then took a good look at my friend's face.

I stopped laughing.

"It's a long story," he said. "I'll explain sometime."

The room went quiet but for a steam radiator.

"Conway," Randall said.

"Yeah."

"Should we be doing this? Should *you* be doing this?"

I said nothing.

"Or should you call Venezia, make a clean breast of everything, and return to your life?"

Ain't much to return to.

I didn't say it out loud.

Said nothing instead.

"These are old patterns," Randall said, "and unhealthy ones. Galloping off to fight somebody else's battle. On a swaybacked steed, as the man wrote, with a rusty lance."

"What man?"

"Never mind. I say again: Should we be doing this?"

"She bled out against my chest," I said. "She was there. Then she wasn't."

Randall looked at me and nodded.

There was sadness in the nod.

Then he left me sitting there while he found Floriano and Maria to say good night.

There's nothing wrong with Framingham State.

Nothing at all.

Hell, I'd been thrilled when my son, Roy, was accepted there, though he lasted only a semester and a half.

So I couldn't tell you why it was that twenty minutes later, when I hit my knees and leaned on my cot in the hard basement dark, Randall Swale was right at the top of my prayers.

CHAPTER THIRTY-ONE

It was the next morning.

Rose Monteiro lived in a Worcester neighborhood five minutes from Holy Cross, the Catholic college. Nice area: up on a hill, east-facing view of woods and athletic fields and, right now, sunrise.

Most of the homes, including Monteiro's, were three-story Victorians painted in period-correct funky colors. Hers was the queen bee of the street. Broad wraparound porch, huge windows, handsome roof with an arch that must be a bear to reshingle.

The only wrong note, the sole concession to working as a gang-ster in a neighborhood of college administrators: Where the other houses made do with white picket fences or hedges, Rose's property was wrapped by a six-foot wrought-iron fence, gated at the drive-way.

A rap on my truck's passenger window just about made me spill coffee.

Tricia Kollar. Her face half sheepish, half defiant, fully made up.

Fully pretty.

I sighed, set my coffee in the cup holder, leaned across, and opened the door. Didn't have much choice unless I wanted to draw attention to myself in an upscale neighborhood.

"Sidekick's privilege," she said. "I found you the address as requested, so I get to ride along. What do you say?"

"I say I'll drive you back to your car."

"Nonsense. Family is family. As a Kollar-slash-Spoon, I hereby vote myself in."

I turned my head to look up the hill at Rose's gate. It'd be a hell of a thing if she up and drove away while I palavered with Tricia. "You know what she did to her husband," I said. "This ain't no Afterschool Special."

"Noted. And I'd like to present a thought."

"What?"

"Her security types seem competent. Won't they have identified your truck yesterday?"

She was right about that, and I'd considered it, but I hadn't had time this morning to swap cars with anybody.

"*My* car," Tricia said, "is parked three behind yours. Neither Rose Monteiro nor her security detail have ever heard of it or of me."

Wasn't much I could say to that. When you're right you're right.

So at quarter of seven, when the black wrought-iron gate rolled noiselessly away and a pair of licorice black Cadillac CTSs trundled onto the street, I was behind the wheel of Tricia's Infiniti.

The first ten minutes of the drive were the toughest. Lots of stop-lights meant lots of opportunities to lose the Caddies. Worcester's the Wild West where driving is concerned—you never know who's going to do what.

So I stuck to the rearmost Cadillac's bumper, ran reds where necessary, and hoped Rose's driver would write me off as just another nut-job commuter.

"Oh my," Tricia said once, jamming down an imaginary brake pedal.

"Worcester," I said.

Soon we hit Route 146. My tail job grew a lot easier. Tricia stopped working her imaginary brakes.

This road defined the Blackstone Valley, running south by southeast all the way to Providence. Two lanes in either direction, it was an easy seventy-five-mile-an-hour run. I gave the Cadillacs a quarter-mile leash. I changed lanes, ducked behind other cars.

When we passed the exit for Purgatory Chasm, a state park, Tricia said, "There's a place Harmon and I used to go down here. Back when we used to go places."

"Slatersville Diner?"

She whirled in her seat. "How did you know?"

"He dragged me there once. Wouldn't stop talking about the place. Let's wait and see, though. They could be headed anywhere."

But as exits clicked by and we passed the WELCOME TO RHODE IS-LAND sign and the Caddies slowed, it became pretty clear we were headed for the Slatersville Diner.

It's of those old-school jobs, a converted aluminum trailer up on blocks. Just outside Woonsocket, it's plunked down in an elbow of a tiny river—a stream most of the year, truth be told—that feeds into the Blackstone.

A few years back, somebody wrote a long article for *New York Magazine* about the joint. The article was titled "The Last Real Place," and it was nothing but a love letter to grease and home fries and waitresses who call you hon.

Ever since the article hit, the hillbillies who've run the joint since 1953 can't cook up enough eggs and burgers and fried chicken for all the Brooklyn hipsters who make the pilgrimage north with the price tags still on their Woolrich jackets. They come in trying to look rugged and authentic, like they just cleared a stand of trees, but some of 'em give away the game by asking what's gluten free.

The Slatersville Diner had been Harmon's favorite. I'd come with him just that once, when we were making a half-assed effort to like one another. It'd been clear he was a regular, joshing with the waitress and the cook, nodding hellos to the locals.

Me, I wasn't sure the place was worth the drive from Bryar, let alone Brooklyn. In the spring, maybe, when the river was pretty to look at—

but I'd bet a hundred dollars that if I blindfolded you, you couldn't tell Slatersville Diner scrambled eggs from anybody else's scrambled eggs.

Sure enough, the Cadillacs crunched into the diner's gravel lot. I drove past without looking at them. Tricia took my cue and did the same.

This was hilly country. I took a hard right when I could and climbed a road that paralleled the one we'd just left. A quarter mile or so brought us to a perfect vantage point. Plow jockeys had created a twelve-foot mountain of crusted snow in a wide spot in the road. I hid the car behind the mountain and left it running so we could move fast if we had to.

Tricia and I climbed out and stood near a wooden guardrail. From here we could look down through leafless trees at the diner, and the altitude difference was enough so that nobody inside would spot us.

Other vehicles in the diner lot: a Volvo wagon, a nothingburger Taurus, a couple of contractors' trucks with graphics on their doors.

I pulled my phone, opened a notes app, and began typing.

Tricia said, "What are you doing?"

"Getting the info on those pickup trucks."

"Why?"

I shrugged. "Better to have it than to not have it. Besides, see the white one?"

It was a GMC longbed with graphics that read, under a phone number:

O&S Landscaping

Mulch - Mow - Yard Cleanups

Stonework - Plowing

"I see it."

"That's a 508 number. And the prefix makes it from our neck of the woods. Marlborough, I think."

"So?"

"There are plenty of places that serve scrambled eggs in Marlborough."

"But contractors go all over, don't they? Wherever there's work?"

I shrugged. "Like I said, better to have it than not."

Then we watched.

"Your stomach is growling," Tricia said after a while.

I said nothing.

Five minutes later she said, "Do you often leave cars running the way mine is?"

"When there's a reason," I said, not peeling my eyes from the diner.

"It gives me an odd feeling. Like leaving for a trip and wondering if you left the iron on."

"In the Arctic Circle," I said, "the truckers start their rigs in October and don't shut 'em off until May. If they turn off the engine, they won't be able to fire it up again."

"I would not enjoy the Arctic Circle."

That hit me a certain way. I guess I laughed some. With eyes still on the diner, I reached an arm across Tricia's shoulders, pulled her to me, and kissed the side of her head, laughing the whole time.

She stayed where I'd pulled her.

It was a nice fit. Warm. Natural.

I felt Tricia's stare.

I moved my arm real quick.

We both cleared our throats.

"Let's focus," I said.

"Yes," Tricia said. "Let's focus."

Twenty minutes later, the diner's spring-loaded screen door opened.

I ducked behind the wooden guardrail, pulling Tricia down with me.

Tommy stepped out first. He was pretty good: He glanced at every vehicle in the parking lot, making sure they were all familiar.

He wasn't *that* good, though. A little comfortable, a little sloppy. His gaze never rose our way. We were just eyeballs and foreheads behind a guardrail, and I doubt he could've made us out at that distance. Still, he should have looked, should have quartered the area.

Like I said: sloppy, comfortable, going through the motions.

That was good to know. I filed it away.

Rose Monteiro stepped from the diner in black high heels that she placed very carefully on each step while Tommy followed, his hands at the ready in case she slipped.

Rose: black stockings on those nice legs, the stockings running up to a black fur coat whose colors and textures and depth shifted like something out of Harry Potter. I don't know diddly about fur, but I know what money looks like.

Giant sunglasses hid her eyes.

Bringing up the rear was a man who could have been Tommy's brother.

The three of them did not speak as they walked across the lot. As I'd expected, Tommy helped Rose into the backseat of one car, then climbed in ahead of her as the other man hopped in the other car.

Then the diner's door opened again.

"Holy shit," I said.

"Who is that?" Tricia said.

Out of the Slatersville Diner, wearing black pants and a canvas car coat two sizes too big, stepped Lobo Soto.

CHAPTER THIRTY-TWO

Without acknowledging the Cadillacs, which were pulling out, Soto took a key from his pocket and strode to the white pickup that I'd pointed out to Tricia.

"Come on," I said, trotting to her Infiniti.

"What for?" Tricia said. "What's next?"

It's Soto's time to pay.

I didn't say it out loud. Instead I popped the car in reverse and began a three-point turn that'd take us down the hill.

I was moving fast now.

"Conway, you're scaring me."

"Everybody pays." This time I did say it out loud.

"Conway, stop. Think."

"Nothing *to* think. Yesterday's meet with Rose was to flush her, see which way she jumped. It worked. Straight to Soto she jumped."

"That's not exactly iron-clad, is it?"

"Well, I'm not exactly the DA," I said, cutting hard left, onto the diner road. "It's enough for me."

We picked up speed. It was a winding road, with a high crown and blind corners and lots of salt.

I'm not big on race-driver sayings, but here's one that plays out every time: Amateur drivers take the slow turns too fast and the fast turns too slow.

These were fast turns.

I was absolutely flying, going seventy-five in places you would've gone thirty.

"You're scaring me," Tricia said.

"You signed on for this. This is what you wanted."

"It's not, Conway. It's not! I want you to slow down and *think*, for the love of God!"

I wasn't in the mood to think, but it must have been Tricia's lucky day. Because just as I barrel-assed around a blind off-camber right-hander, catching a glimpse of Soto's truck, feeling the Infiniti's front end get light, I spotted a young mother at the foot of a driveway.

She had two little kids. Girls.

They wore matching purple coats.

She was clutching them, an arm around each, animal terror on her face as I scrabbled past, looking for traction at eighty miles an hour.

Shame swamped my red-mist anger.

I looked to my right at Tricia, and the look on her face sealed the deal.

She had resigned herself. She thought she was going to die in the passenger seat of her own car.

"Hell," I said.

I lifted.

"I'm sorry," I said.

I found a place to turn around.

"What are you doing?" Tricia said in a very small voice. "Where are we going?"

"Breakfast," I said.

She wasn't hungry.

She nursed coffee and watched me eat while we talked.

Tricia said, "What were you planning to do?"

"Everybody pays."

"So you've said. Specifically, though. What were you going to do?"

"Soto first," I said. "He's a threat, plus he was closest. I would have rammed him. Spun him out, maybe flipped him. Then . . ." I shrugged, sipped.

"You would have . . ." She glanced around the diner, leaned in, hunched her shoulders. "Killed him."

I said nothing.

"And then it would have been Rose's turn."

I said nothing.

For a while.

Thinking about Tricia Kollar. About trust. About how nice it'd felt when my arm was around her. She'd just tucked right in there.

"How much," I finally said, "do you know about what I do? The Barnburners stuff? Between Harmon and Eudora, you must have heard something."

She took her time, thinking, maybe editing before she spoke. "I know you help Barnburners out of jams. Eudora said you were a fanatic about it. And Harmon may have said once or twice that but for Charlene's high-priced lawyers, you'd still be in state prison." She blew on her coffee, sipped, met my gaze. "He may have said that was a good place for you."

"So you know plenty."

"Theoretical knowing is not at all the same as what I just experienced. Not in the slightest."

I ate.

"Let me put some pieces together," Tricia said. "You believe your conversation with Rose yesterday alarmed her."

I nodded. "Enough for her to call a risky meeting with Soto, who'd gone to ground."

"What about, though? What is the nature of their partnership?"

"Picture this," I said. "Say Rose Monteiro wanted Eudora's land.

Partly for business reasons—casino developers are drooling over it. And partly to settle a thirty-year blood feud that began when Andy Spoon swindled Rose's husband."

"But you said Rose had her husband . . . you know. So why does she care if he got swindled?"

"Blood is blood," I said, shrugging. "It's okay for me to kick the snot out of my little brother, but if *you* kick the snot out of my little brother, I'm coming after you. Get it?"

"Fair enough."

"To get this land, Rose needs some kind of lever over Eudora. Kenny somehow becomes the lever. Rose has no pull in L.A., but she does have a co-op deal with Los Bajamaros."

"So Lobo Soto and company kidnap Kenny. Why, though? What exactly is the nature of the lever?"

"I'm still shaky on that," I said. "At first, I thought it was just that Eudora wanted to connect with her kid before she died. Rose and Los Bajamaros were going to hold that over her. Sign over the land or you'll never see Kenny again."

"But Kenny cast doubt on that with his story last night. He says he was kidnapped because Harmon was supposed to do something, or maybe sign something."

"And you and I agreed his story sounded solid."

"But we also agreed that as an actor, he was perfectly capable of fooling us."

I sighed. "I wish you'd let me stay after Soto. He'll be even harder to find now."

"Well," Tricia said, "you've got the information from his truck."

"And I'll check it out. But I don't expect much to come of it."

"What else do we do now?"

"Don't pull that again," I said, and may have smiled. "Me, not us. And what I do is go after Rose Monteiro."

"Bodyguards and all?"

"Everybody pays."

"I don't know how much I know about you," Tricia said. "And the funny thing is, I don't know how much I *want* to know about you."

I paid. We left.

"Diet Coke," Tricia said. "Right?"

I said sure and leaned on the kitchen counter.

I'd driven her home. Had climbed from her car, stretched. I'd gotten the feeling we were in something that neither of us wanted to end. Had accepted her invitation inside.

"This morning feels long and short both," I said. "You know?"

"I do."

Two words.

Two words only.

But.

It's hard to explain, but the way she said it.

The things we'd done that morning. The things we'd shared.

The way she looked at me from beneath her eyelashes.

The way we talked about Charlene and Harmon. Like they were exes from a hundred years ago.

All this told me, as Tricia handed me a soda, what was going to happen.

My stomach rolled like a high-school boy's.

I didn't want my soda anymore.

I set it on the counter and leaned.

Tricia leaned next to me.

We looked through the window wall at the Blackstone Valley.

Maybe her hip was touching mine.

Or maybe I imagined that.

Tricia stepped from the counter. She faced me. She looked up from beneath her lashes again and put a little palm on my heart. "There's one thing I need to know," she said. "And I don't think you'll lie, because I don't think you could. Not about this."

"What?"

"You and Charlene. Is anything there? Is anything left?"

"No," I said.

"Yes," I said.

"No," I said.

In slow motion, or it seemed that way, Tricia set her water glass on the counter to my left.

"No wins," she said. "Two to one."

And she stood on tiptoe to be kissed.

And I kissed her.

CHAPTER THIRTY-THREE

Well," I said.

"Well," Tricia said.

"I should go," I said.

"You should go," she said.

"Time is it?"

She rolled away, squinted, rolled back. "Nearly seven."

"Jesus."

"We fell asleep."

"We earned it."

She laughed some, finger-combing my chest hair with one hand.

I climbed from the guest-room bed—hours before, Tricia had begun steering us, half undressed, toward the master bedroom, but she'd changed course, and that was for the best—and began to dress. The only light came from an oversized alarm clock on the nightstand, but I still found myself hunching, my back turned to the window wall. I wondered if you ever got used to living in a glass house.

Something swept over me. In pants but no shirt, I half sat on, half fell to the bed. Elbows on knees, face in hands. I must have mumbled.

She said, "What?"

"I never wanted to do this again."

"You were going to become a monk?"

"That's not what I meant."

Tricia knee-walked across the bed. She leaned on my back and wrapped her arms around me. "What *did* you mean?"

I felt her breath on my ear.

I put a hand on her forearm and pulled her even closer.

Against my back like that, she felt so good. So warm.

"I never wanted to dress in the dark again," I said, "and tiptoe out carrying my shoes. Thought I was done with all that."

"So don't tiptoe out. Stay here where you belong."

"Can't."

"You're going to visit Rose Monteiro, aren't you?"

I said nothing.

"In your world," she said, "everybody pays. With Lobo Soto in the wind, it's Rose's turn."

"Something like that."

"Bodyguards and all."

"Yes."

"Do you have a gun?"

"No."

"And yet away you go."

"Yes."

"And there's not a damn thing I can say to stop you."

I rose, dressed, left.

Forty minutes later, I parked a few houses up from Rose Monteiro's place, glad I'd seen her home in daylight. I had what felt like a good plan for getting inside.

Job one: Move, and soon. While plenty of cars were street-parked here—Priuses and little Honda SUVs and a few unkillable Volvo 240s—this was the type of neighborhood where a man sitting in a pickup truck would light off a call to the cops.

I reached under the dashboard, near the pull for the headlights, and found my Gerber lock-blade knife where I'd rigged it the day I bought the truck. It's a nice piece: light, barely three inches long when it's closed, wicked two-inch blade.

Just west of Victory Lane, Indiana, a man on a train had once told me if you needed more than two inches of blade, you didn't know how to handle yourself. I believed him, because he seemed to handle *him*self okay. He'd just used his short knife to take away my liquor and my last six dollars, and he was forcing me to exit the boxcar because he didn't like the looks of me.

The train was doing about thirty-five at the time, headed northeast for Fort Wayne.

But that's another story.

From beneath my bench seat I pulled mechanic's gloves. Put them on, killed the truck's dome light, climbed out.

I heard a sound from my left. Turned away from Rose's place without looking at it, walked uphill. A man with a gray beard was walking a tiny white yapper of a dog. The man was talking on a cell. We nodded to each other. The dog yapped at my foot.

I walked another fifty feet, stopped, and looked over my shoulder. The man and his yapper disappeared around a corner.

I turned and walked back the way I'd come. Passed my truck. Scoped my planned approach, making final adjustments as I neared Rose's yard.

Her next-door neighbor's picket fence ended just a foot from her own wrought-iron job. Looking around, seeing nobody, pausing not at all, I stepped onto the picket fence's horizontal support rail. Wrapped my work-gloved hands around a pair of wrought-iron uprights—they were spiked, but only for show—got the sole of my right boot against an upright, pushed and hoisted.

Lifted my left boot over the spikes, got it on the square one-inch tube that served as the top horizontal support.

This was the tricky part. My left boot wanted to slip from the support, and once I swung my right boot, I would be committed to the move. I'd either drop over neatly or have a serious crotch problem.

I dropped over neatly and backed away from the fence, as sure as I could be that nobody'd spotted me.

I learned in my B&E days that once you're in, the first chore is to set up your way out. Looked around the yard, found a stout cast-concrete birdbath. It was in two parts. I lifted the top, the bath itself. It didn't interest me—I set it down.

The lower piece was about as tall as the picket fence. It'd do. I carried it to the corner I'd used to get in, set it down, practiced stepping on it, felt satisfied.

I turned and approached the building, staying low. It was hard to see much of anything inside the house: The hill I was climbing made for a lousy angle. As I worked my way closer, I realized the yard had been sprinkled with evergreen trees and shrubs to obscure the view from the street year-round. Lousy landscaping, smart security.

Cleared a final trio of low pines, got my first good look.

Two-car garage, detached, with old-fashioned barn-style doors that were closed.

In the driveway, next to a low flight of porch steps: a Cadillac CTS in black. It would have Executive Transport livery plates, and it would belong to one of the guys I'd seen at the Slatersville Diner, probably Tommy.

The home's first floor was dark, at least in front. On the second floor, a pair of shades on my side were drawn, with lamp-glow behind them.

The rest of the second-floor shades were open.

Security tip: Close all the shades when you close any of them. The drawn shades told me Rose Monteiro's whereabouts as clearly as a neon sign would've.

A picture formed in my head. Tommy would be Rose's number one bodyguard: half security, half butler. She'd be up in that shades-drawn room for the night, reading or watching TV. He'd be somewhere in the back of the first floor—the kitchen table, something like that. I wondered if he slept here. Probably not: If so, he would have snugged the Cadillac close to the garage instead of leaving it by the porch stairs.

I approached the house. Had to step slow slow slow: despite the whipsaw-winter thaw, a half inch of snow remained in shaded areas. It had crusted at nightfall, so each time I planted a boot, I needed to press down gently or risk making noise.

I crossed the driveway, stood where a decorative tree shielded me from what I could now see was the kitchen. Checked out the setup. Rose's bedroom windows were at this corner of the house. The porch railing and the rain gutter above it were old-school sturdy, and the roof above the porch featured a gentle pitch. If I had to, I could climb up there.

Good to know.

Continued the prowl around the house's backside. Duckwalked beneath kitchen windows, then saw exactly what I'd pictured: a window near the kitchen, facing the wooded back yard, with a bluish TV glow.

Duckwalked to the glowing window, raised my head slow slow slow.

I smelled Tommy before I saw him.

Smelled his cigar, anyway.

It's funny how things change. In Massachusetts, where I've lived for a long time, the smell of cigarettes just about knocks you over. It's that rare. And indoors? Forget it. Even in AA, where everybody used to smoke like a cold diesel engine, you have to step outside to catch a whiff of cigarette smoke.

Cigars are even harder to come by. Especially indoors.

So the smell caught my attention.

No wonder I smelled it: Tommy's head was no more than two feet from my nose. He lay in a recliner with his back to me, looking at a college basketball game on a giant flat-screen TV across the room. All I saw of him was a bald spot and his slippered feet.

I heard nothing. Squinted at the TV. An icon in its lower left corner showed it was set on mute.

Huh.

Took a chance, stood a little taller, and saw Tommy's cigar.

It made me smile.

Because it was burning away in an amber-colored ashtray on a side table.

Its ash was a full three inches long.

Tommy, top bodyguard to Rose Monteiro, had dozed off. Had left a cigar burning in a hundred-and-thirty-year-old wooden house.

Tough to find good help.

CHAPTER THIRTY-FOUR

Time to visit Rose.

I retraced my steps, walking in my own tracks to minimize noise.

The porch steps creaked, but only a little.

The porch railing was rock solid, as expected.

I stood on the railing near a support column, knowing I'd need it for traction. I'm not weak, but I'm also not light.

Or young.

I reached for the gutter above with both hands, took two deep breaths, and did a pull-up. Got my chin level with the gutter. Searched for that column with my left boot, found it, used it to scrabble. Threw my right boot up and over.

In a relatively comfortable position now, I stopped moving and reminded myself to breathe. Couldn't be sure how much noise I'd made, though it didn't strike me as much. Needed to listen for movement in Rose's bedroom.

Ten seconds. Nothing.

Another ten. Nothing.

My comfortable position wasn't comfortable anymore, and as far as I could tell, Tommy was still snoozing.

So I torqued with shoulder and knee and ankle until I was spread out on the roof. Then I belly-crawled, both to stay low and to spread my weight for minimal creaking.

I was crawling toward the front of the house, away from Rose's room. Why?

Because her bedroom windows were sure to be locked.

The picture coming into focus showed an underused house. It was likely just Rose rattling around the place, with Tommy doing body-guard/companion work each day and going home each night—after waking up in his recliner and switching off ESPN. The pair of them would spend most of their time in a few rooms at the back of the house, away from street traffic. Almost like an old married couple who ought to move to a smaller place but couldn't pull the trigger.

Point being, if I was going to find an easy way in, I was going to find it at the front. In a guest room, maybe, or a no-longer-used kid's room. A neglected area where, if I was lucky, a window might be unlocked or open a few inches.

Sure enough.

I scored with the second window I tried on the front side. Up here, you had a nice view of Holy Cross and a chunk of the city. Felt like you were on top of the world. When I was a kid, I would've found my way out here to goof off or smoke cigarettes.

Rose had to have grandkids.

I bet they'd wormed out here more than once. Just for kid kicks.

I wasn't surprised to see a corner of a screen sticking out. Which meant I wouldn't have to do any slicing with my knife.

I bent the screen's aluminum frame one-handed, got my other hand against the window casing, and pushed up.

The window rose three inches.

Which was good.

Groaning like a drunk frat boy while it moved.

Which was bad.

I went still and silent again. Listened for twenty seconds.

Heard nothing. Pushed.

The window went up, shuddering the whole way.

Or maybe I imagined that.

I slipped in feet first, let go of the screen, closed the window.

It was darker in here than it'd been outside, so I blinked and breathed and listened for maybe thirty seconds.

Good thing, too: When my vision adjusted, I saw that the middle of the big room was dominated by a kid's train and tracks on a four-by-eight-foot table. The table, set up for little kids to enjoy, was only two feet off the floor. It was easy to picture myself tripping over it.

I sidestepped it on my way to the door.

Then felt naked.

Touched the folded knife in my pocket.

Still felt naked.

I know what you're thinking: When you've got revenge on your mind, how the hell do you go after a Rose Monteiro without a gun?

Here's the best I can do for an answer: I've always had something against them. Guns are for dopes. What's the song say? A pistol can get you into trouble, but it can't get you out. I've seen too many drunken assholes empty revolvers at each other at a range of two feet—without hitting anything but the poor bartender.

I will admit, though, that maybe twice a year I wish I had a gun in my hand.

I wished for one now.

And the year was young.

I looked around for something, *any*thing. Spotted a capsized toy train, a single car that had been separated from the bulk of the set. Hefted it.

The train was heavier than you'd think, an old toy made of honest metal. It was about the size of a cop's flashlight, with the same heft.

So I gripped it in my right hand as I sidestepped from the playroom and down a long hall, toward Rose Monteiro's room on my left.

I took long steps and transferred my weight slowly. The narrow-pine floor, runner-covered, wanted to squeak. My light steps didn't let it.

After ten seconds that felt a lot longer, I had an ear to her door. Blue light at my feet said the TV was on. Reality-show voices confirmed it.

Took two deep breaths. Grasped the cut-glass knob with my left hand. The knob was on the right side of the door, so it was an awkward move, but it let me keep my weapon—okay, my toy train—in my right hand.

I turned the knob and pushed the door and stepped into a suite of rooms in one fluid move, raised my train like a club, moved around a corner to a queen-sized four-poster bed . . .

. . . which was empty. Tousled sheets and blankets, dented pillows against a headboard. But empty.

Behind me, in the blind spot created when I opened the door—my most vulnerable spot, the one Randall's taught me to check first—came the *schick* sound of a semiautomatic's slide being pulled.

The door was kicked shut.

"Is that a vintage Lionel 2023 Union Pacific Diesel in your hand?" Rose Monteiro said. "Or are you just happy to see me?"

CHAPTER THIRTY-FIVE

H ell," I said.

"Turn around and sit and put down the train," Rose said. "Not on the bed, for Chrissake, Tommy just greased the undercarriage last week. Set it on the table there."

I did, next to a book that taught you to eat what cavemen ate.

She was sitting in a chair that looked old and French and expensive.

Her satin slippers and satin robe and long satin nightgown were pink.

Her gun was black.

"Looks like Tommy fell asleep again," she said. "The lummox."

"What gave me away? Squeaks?"

"Not squeaks, exactly . . . shifts. Live in an old house long enough, it talks to you."

Without asking permission, I plucked a clicker from the tangle of sheets and killed the TV. Now the only light came from a bedside forty-watt bulb shielded by a pink lampshade.

We sat and looked at each other.

"What now?" I asked after a while.

"We took a harder look at you," she said. "That situation from a while back, the colleague of mine who retired, your part in his send-off—they interested me. Fascinated me, if you want the truth. So we reached out. We made calls. Turns out you're an ex-NASCAR stud, huh? My husband loved that stuff. Me, I get a headache. Fifty jellybeans driving in circles."

"Forty-three."

"Never correct a woman holding a Springfield Armory .45," she said. "We also learned you're some sort of superdrunk. Batman for alkies is what we heard. What the hell is that about?"

"Long story."

"I bet." She looked at the gun in her hand, hesitated, set it on her thigh. She did leave her finger on the trigger guard.

Her robe shifted a bit as she did all this.

She did have some legs.

"It wasn't smart," she said. "Coming here. I would've thought you knew better."

"Rose Monteiro," I said. "The pretty-legs gangster lady who bled out hubby in an oil-change pit."

"So you did know better," she said, maybe smiling half a smile at the pretty-legs crack. "But here you are. Why, Sax? This have something to do with your Batman-for-drunks shtick?"

"Call it shtick if you want," I said, "but my friend Eudora is dead. And everybody who needs to pay is going to."

"And I'm on the list?"

"At the top."

"So you broke into my house to beat me to death with a model train?"

"Any tool at hand."

I guess the look in my eyes slowed her some. "Most men threatening to beat someone to death," she said, "they come off weak and silly. Not you. You're a serious man, I'll give you that. But fill me in. How'd I make this list?"

"Andy Spoon flimflammed your husband out of the property on 142. It was the last time, maybe the *only* time, Paulo Monteiro got the short end of a deal. He didn't like it. He didn't forget it. Neither have you. You wanted the land back for business—to sell to a casino developer. But you also wanted it for pleasure—to hose Andy Spoon's widow. Trouble was, Eudora didn't want any part of a casino in Bryar. She wouldn't go along."

Rose stared at me a full thirty seconds.

"You know what?" she finally said. "You're half smart and you're half right. That's a dangerous combination. I give you credit for the legwork, but guess what?"

I said nothing.

"Eudora Spoon was hot to trot," Rose said, a mean smile curling up one cheek. "By the time we approached her, she'd already done a plot survey and environmental-impact study on her own nickel. She was prepping the property for sale to the highest bidder."

"Bullshit," I said.

"No bullshit," Rose said, holding my gaze, full of confidence. "Drop by the shop sometime, I'll show you the plot survey. Hell, I'll show you the preliminary P&S we were working on. We had a ways to go. These things take time once the lawyers start chipping away at each other. But we were on our way."

It seemed impossible, but Rose Monteiro's eyes and posture and manner—her pleasure at letting me know how goddamn wrong I'd been—convinced me.

"Wait, though," I said. "You met Lobo Soto this morning. Breakfast, Slatersville Diner."

Her eyes clouded. I'd finally surprised her. "You tailed me? Not bad. Damn that Tommy. Getting soft in his old age."

"You must've called the meeting," I said, " 'cause Soto's gone to ground. Nobody in L.A. knows where he is."

"So you figured you spooked me yesterday," Rose said. "Then I reached for the smelling salts and called a big meet with Soto, my murder partner."

"Something like that."

"This is where you're half smart and half right, and this is why it's a problem. Yes, Soto was interested in Bryar. He was greasing the skids. For me, but especially for one casino outfit, the one with the inside track. And yes, Los Bajamaros and me have an arrangement of professional courtesy."

"But?"

"But that's all we had," Rose said. "I didn't call that meeting, Soto did."

"Why?"

"He had run afoul of my good graces."

"How?"

"None of your fucking business how," she said. "Now before you leave, Sax, I'm gonna tell you one last thing out of the goodness of my heart. Maybe it helps you, maybe it doesn't, and I don't much care which."

I waited.

"Blood is blood," Rose said.

"I've heard that more than once lately."

"Blood is blood, family is family. When it's good, there's nothing like it. But when it's bad"—she shrugged—"nothing's uglier. You'll be leaving now."

I stood. "Pretty cryptic."

"Blood is blood," Rose said. "Family is family. And liars are liars, especially when they're pros."

"It feels weird to say this," I said, "but thanks."

"Don't thank me. And don't pick up that train."

"I can put it back."

Rose Monteiro shook her head. "You'll just drop it on my carpet," she said, "when Tommy knocks you out."

Then he did.

*　*　*

I woke up to cold and pain and heat and light.

Cold: It was February and it was nighttime and I was lying on a thin layer of salted ice in a parking lot.

Pain from my head. I touched the back of it and felt a sticky lump the size of half a Superball.

I sat up.

Then threw up. Just like that.

With that out of the way, I turned around in slow motion—my joints felt like someone had poured sand in them—and squinted and shielded my eyes.

My truck was on fire.

Nothing fancy. I had to guess, I'd say Tommy had found a plastic gas can in Rose's garage, driven me here, dragged me to the pavement, splashed gas in the F-250's interior, lit a match, and walked away.

I stood.

And threw up again.

But stayed on my feet, patting my pockets.

They'd left me my phone. For that matter, they'd left me my knife.

Professional courtesy.

I walked away from the fire, half surprised the cops weren't here yet.

My timing was good. It turned out the parking lot serviced a baseball field. As I took a left and walked west, still with that sand-in-the-joints feeling, deep blat-blat sirens told me the fire department was almost here.

I found a street sign, read it. Found a basement business, ducked down its stairs. Pulled my cell.

My thumb hovered.

Randall was the one to dial, of course.

I dialed Tricia instead.

CHAPTER THIRTY-SIX

Calling Tricia was a mistake, it turned out.

She made me talk all the way back to her place.

Randall would've known better.

Especially after I rolled down the window and puked a final time.

After telling Tricia all about the meet with Rose, and speculating as to how Tommy had creamed me—my guess was that he'd woken in his chair, heard us, and crept up a back staircase to another door to the master suite—I got to the hint Rose had dropped about family.

"Blood is blood," Tricia said. "There's that damn phrase again. A family favorite."

"I'm more focused on the other thing she said. About liars being liars, especially when they're pros."

"Meaning?"

"An actor's a paid liar."

"*What?* Kenny?" It surprised her enough so she swiveled her head and swerved, which didn't help my stomach any. "But Kenny's incompetent! Kenny's . . . well, you're the one who found him in Booth Two, drunk as a skunk with a comic book on his lap."

"Rose vibed like a woman speaking truth," I said.

"Vibed? Pardon me, but that's weak. She's lied to you before, if memory serves."

I shook my head and shifted, impatient. "Sure she has. But last night she had nothing to fear and an ace up her sleeve. Could've had me killed and dumped in a pond just like that."

Tricia nodded slowly, thinking it through. "With that ace up her sleeve, there was no reason for Rose to lie to you."

"Exactly," I said. "So picture it: What if Kenny had Los Bajamaros kidnap him? They're West Coast. He's West Coast. So there's your access. And it might explain why Erin didn't exactly beat the bushes searching for him. When I asked about it, I thought she was ashamed she'd let him go off on a bender. Maybe that wasn't it. Maybe she was in on the scam."

"Why would Kenny pull something like that, though? That's the real question, isn't it?"

"It is. And I don't know the answer. Here's what I do know: Money changes people. Makes 'em think new ways, do new things."

"Meaning what?"

"I told you Eudora was dead set against casinos in general, and one on her property in particular. Turns out she was doing everything but pouring the foundation to get one started."

"If Rose Monteiro is to be believed."

"I was there, and I believe her. My point is, don't put anything past Kenny if the payout's big enough. Hell, don't put anything past anybody."

"Even you?"

"I'm different."

"I'll say."

"Maybe that's why I live in my buddy's basement and the Worcester FD is spraying down my truck right this minute."

We were quiet the last half mile.

Finally, cutting left into her driveway, Tricia said, "The elephant in the room. I'll raise it if you won't."

"What elephant?"

"Harmon."

"Oh."

"Yes, oh. It's hard to imagine Eudora making all these grand plans without his knowledge, isn't it?"

"You didn't see it happening. Neither did I."

"Still."

"I know," I said. "You've got a point."

"Harmon as suspect," Tricia said in a very small voice, "complicates matters."

"Yes."

"For us."

"Yes."

Tricia shut off her Infiniti. We sat in silence.

I rubbed my eyes. "I need to call the cops and report my truck stolen."

"Will anybody buy that?"

"Not really. But it's what you do."

She leaned and kissed my cheek. "I'm here," she said. "Hell or high water, I'm here. Make it a quick call and we'll get some ice on your head."

"Um. Harmon?"

"Night shift. Four to four. Ain't that a shame?"

She climbed from the car and went inside.

Something nagged at me.

Where *was* Harmon? For a cop whose mother'd been murdered, he sure was keeping his head down. I hadn't seen him since the day after the funeral.

Maybe he was working the case on his own, on the side, the same way I was.

Or maybe he knows about you and Tricia.

My face went red.

I shook my head, not wanting to think along those lines, and pulled my cell.

I called to report the stolen truck, then stood in Tricia's driveway and breathed.

Jeez, but it was warm for February. I took a bunch of deep breaths to clear my head, and I couldn't even see my breath-vapor.

Here's what I did see, though, when I pocketed my phone and looked across 142:

Eudora's house.

Being run by Kenny.

It had worried me. It had worried everybody who knew him. He could barely scramble an egg, barely latch a window. Nobody really trusted him to run Eudora's house, especially with those dogs. At the funeral, a few of us had hinted he should either stay with Harmon a while or let somebody move in to keep him company.

He'd waved off the help with increasing stubbornness, finally coming right out and telling us to leave him the hell alone.

Standing where I stood, hands in pants pockets, I stared at the house.

Maybe it was because I was thinking about Kenny Spoon in a whole new way, but I'll be damned if things didn't look serene down there.

Not that I could be sure, of course, not at a hundred and fifty yards. Still . . .

A steady plume of smoke rose from the aluminum chimney, which meant Kenny had figured out the wood stove. The Mercedes was neatly angle-parked at the foot of the porch steps, the way Eudora used to have me park it to unload groceries.

Warm light came from the living-room picture window that faced me. A person who had to be Kenny, though it didn't quite look like him, sat at a round wooden table. Doing paperwork, maybe. There'd be plenty of that.

Kenny rose and crossed from my right to my left, headed for the kitchen.

One of the greyhounds—Cha Cha, I was pretty sure—hopped up

and followed. Alert, ears pricked, like there was the possibility of a treat.

Now *that* was impressive. If Kenny Spoon had earned the trust of a greyhound whose longtime owner was suddenly gone, he was doing something right.

People surprise you if you let them.

I looked at my watch. Ten past midnight.

Much earlier that day—well, it was now the previous day—I'd meant to drop in. Check up, look Kenny in the eye, shake him down for pills and booze if need be.

But the day had gone in a different direction.

That's one way to put it.

I'm an early riser. It turned out Tricia was not.

The next morning, I used that to my advantage. Texted Floriano at quarter of five. At five thirty, with no questions asked, he pulled into Tricia's driveway in his own truck. Behind him was a white F-150, one of Floriano's landscaping trucks, idle for the winter.

The cousin driving the pickup shut it down, handed me the keys, and climbed in beside Floriano. Floriano got himself turned around and drove down the way he'd come.

He'd removed the magnetic signs from the truck's doors. It even looked like he'd run it through a gas-station car wash on the way here.

Good old Floriano.

My first move with the new wheels was to hit an eye-opener meeting at a senior center over in Northbridge. Me, three junkies, and a fat businessman who stank of gin and spent the hour weeping silently.

Then I drove back to Bryar to see Kenny Spoon.

It was sunless and windy but warm when I knocked on Eudora's front door.

No answer.

Knocked again.

Nothing.

Huh.

I was about to twist the knob, just to check, when I heard a commotion around the front side of the house, the Route 142 side. I walked toward the noise, and there they were: Dandy and Cha Cha on their matching leashes, Kenny in his moth-eaten sweater.

It's hard to explain how I felt as the three of them cleared the final hump. I was upwind, so the greys didn't sense me, but Kenny paused atop the hump, smiled big, and waved before closing the final twenty yards to the house.

That hump, that little rise. Eudora'd been at its crest when Lobo Soto and his pal blew a hole in her.

The rise had likely saved my life, cutting the shooter's line of sight as I slid backward with Eudora pressed to me.

When they kicked me from the Grafton jail, the cop at the front desk had held up my bloody jacket with two fingers, had made a question with his eyebrows.

"Burn it," I'd said.

Now here I was, wondering if Kenny'd been behind the whole operation.

If he was, he would pay.

But I had to be damn sure.

All this passed through my head as Kenny neared me.

Something was different, off, unexpected.

It hit me: There was no moping here. Dogs reflect the mood of their master. Dandy and Cha Cha were having a fine old time, taking their usual morning hike, snuffling around in what little snow remained, rushing me with wagging tails when they finally saw me.

As for Kenny . . . he looked *great*. Clear eyes, a little new weight and a little windburn in his cheeks, a sturdy chopping stride.

How many days ago had I found him in a Van Nuys jackoff parlor, bare-ass naked, reading comic books and clutching a Scotch bottle?

Wait.

The image had jogged something. A memory? A mismatch? *Think. It's important.*

But it got away from me, the way things do, dammit.

Anyway, it hadn't been many days. This was a major-league shift, especially for a man who'd lost his mother.

Unless the loss of the mother wasn't bad news—was in fact very good news.

When Kenny clapped to get my attention, I realized I'd zoned out.

He was smiling. "I *said,* hot chocolate for us and kibble for the hounds?"

I said sure and followed him inside. Looked around while he fed the dogs.

The place was cozy. Neat as a pin. Glasses and dishes in the dish drainer. I've been around drunks long enough to look for wine and highball glasses, and there were none in view. Atop the round table: Eudora's laptop, plugged in and charging, and three manila folders thick with papers. Those would be utility bills, bank statements, all the things that need sorting after a death.

"How are you doing?" I asked, turning to face Kenny.

Wait.

Something else was different.

I watched him make a cup of cocoa from one of those single-serve coffeemakers everybody has now. He looked at me and held up a cup, silently asking did I want one. I shook my head but kept looking at him.

He made a twisted little smile and scratched the back of his head, and only then did it hit me.

Kenny Spoon had cut his hair.

It's a little thing.

Unless it's not.

CHAPTER THIRTY-SEVEN

The bowl cut had been Kenny's trademark for what, fifteen years? He'd made a mint with it. The blond bowl had been part of the is-he-gay-or-isn't-he routine that somehow made him even dreamier to fourteen-year-old girls.

Naturally, he'd hung on to the hair way too long. First it made him an easy mark for *Saturday Night Live*. Then for those Hollywood-scoop TV shows and magazines.

Then nobody bothered making fun of him anymore.

I had a feeling that was the part Hollywood types truly feared.

Here he stood with something just this side of a buzz cut, self-conscious, knowing I was staring.

What do you say?

"Looks good," I said.

"It feels funny."

"I cut mine the same way."

"I noticed."

"What you do," I said, "first time you feel like you want a comb or a brush, you get it cut again."

"That," Kenny said, "is the perfect Conway Sax approach to hair care. I would expect nothing else."

I didn't know if that was a compliment or not.

"You seem," I said, sweeping an arm that took in the neat table and paperwork and laptop, "you seem . . . in *charge*."

"My blushes, Watson."

"Who's Watson?"

"Never mind."

"I gotta say it, you seem *different*. You seem *sober*."

"And you seem surprised. Which is surprising, given that it's you who frog-marched me into AA."

"You complaining?"

"Not a bit. On the contrary. You saved my life. Truly. I've . . . I've been to a couple of meetings on my own."

"I guess I had . . ."

"Low expectations?"

"Yeah," I said. "Yeah, I guess so."

"Even now, I detect skepticism."

"I've been around a long time, Kenny. Seen a lot of good starts. You're sober today. Good for you. Keep comin'."

"Fair enough," he said. "Today I'm sober."

We stood.

In the wood stove, logs shifted.

Kenny said, "Was there anything else?"

"How are things going?" I asked, edging around the table, hoping for a look at the laptop. "Paperwork and bills and closing accounts and all that? Slip up on that stuff, it can cost you down the road. I've seen it before."

"It's a chore, but I've found nothing surprising or onerous. At this point, I'm just tidying things up so I can hand it all off to the executor. Let it become her headache."

He tried for casual, but as I shuffled, trying to get a peek at the computer, he shuffled, too, trying to beat me there.

Kenny won our little race.

When he did, he slapped a few keys. "The curse of the senior citizen," he said. "I doubt she's updated a program or applied a security patch since she brought this damn thing home. I keep power-cycling, updating this and that."

The laptop's screen went from Windows Blue to black just as I stepped next to him. He folded his arms and met my gaze.

We both knew he was hiding something, lying about something.

Kenny had the advantage: He knew what it was.

I ran options in my head. There wasn't much I could do right here, right now—I didn't have enough information to start throwing curveballs at him.

No, best to play it cool. Let Kenny Spoon win a round.

I would come back for another round when I was better armed.

I made two minutes' worth of small talk about the dogs and left.

When I cleared the final curve at the top of Tricia's driveway, she was walking toward her car. Dressed for work: gray slacks under a black blouse, name board affixed. She held in one hand a funky bag. It was half the size of a paper grocery-store sack and cut the same way, but it was blue and thick-looking. It looked silly to me. Then again, purses, like ladies' shoes, are a universe I don't need or want to know about.

She dropped the bag when she saw me, looking flustered. "I thought you'd gone!"

"I dropped in on Kenny. Truck's still here." I nodded at it. "Thought that'd clue you in."

"Still," she said, trying to smile, "a girl would appreciate a note." She looked down at her shoes and sidestepped a puddle that was more like a stream. "According to the radio, whipsaw winter's going even crazier. They say we're in for a three-day run of sixty-five-degree days, maybe even seventy."

"Shame to spend a day like that working."

"Indeed," she said, smiling again, the smile getting sly now. "I've got a much better idea. Something I've been meaning to show you."

"I was kidding," I said. Actually, as I'd crossed 142, I'd been hoping she'd be gone. I'd been planning my next move on Kenny. I really wanted a look at that laptop, and I wondered how much time I had before he wiped its hard drive or turned it over to the executor. "Got a few things to—"

I didn't get to finish, because she planted a big old kiss on me, pulled away, tapped an index finger on my lips, and darted into the house, hollering over her shoulder not to move a muscle.

I didn't move a muscle.

In a few minutes she was back, lugging a canvas bag stuffed full of something or other. "I called in well," she said. "And you know what? It felt great. Want to see my tree fort?"

What the hell?

Curious, I followed her up the driveway toward the storage units. Truth be told, I would've followed her to Timbuktu.

Tricia angled left, toward the sign that hung above the road, then stepped off the paving onto dirt and granite. We were near the first E in WOLVERINE.

I got nervous—the angle was steep, and she wasn't more than a dozen feet from the drop to Route 142.

"Scared?" she said. "Don't be. Come on!"

Then she surprised the hell out of me by climbing the E.

"Well, I'll be damned," I said. Whoever'd made the sign had built in a ladder made of inch-thick pipe. It made sense from a maintenance point of view. I started to look around at the other letters for similar ladders, but Tricia was ordering me to haul my ass up.

I hauled.

To the top of the E, which was a platform no bigger than six feet by six. Dead flat, no railings.

A man could get vertigo up here.

"Well, I'll be damned," I said again. "*That's* a view."

I was looking southwest over the Blackstone Valley, and even in winter the rolling hills were something. On a clear day like this, I knew I could see all the way to Rhode Island.

Noise startled me enough so that I did a little dance. Which wasn't comfortable, not one bit, three stories above the road.

The noise came from a battery-powered air pump. Tricia had un-rolled an air mattress—it, the pump, and a ratty blanket had been in the canvas bag—and was inflating it.

The racket was over in a minute.

I said, "What gives?"

"This was Harmon's favorite spot," she said. "It was *our* spot."

"Well . . . what am I doing here, then?"

She ignored that. "Look around. Tell me what you notice."

I didn't do a lot of looking around.

Because Tricia stepped out of her shoes and began to undress.

"Um," I said. "What am I supposed to notice? Besides the obvious."

She giggled, stepping out of her slacks, folding herself onto the air mattress, and pulling the beefy blanket over her. "Casa Eudora is in-visible from here."

It was true. A bend in 142 and a pair of granite outcroppings made Eudora's place disappear from this vantage point, though it wasn't more than a couple hundred yards away.

"Harmon's favorite spot and mine," Tricia said when I looked at her again. "Our only secret. The one ever-loving place we could run to and pretend Eudora and her money and golden-boy Kenny and *his* money didn't exist."

I wasn't sure why she was telling me all this. Maybe she was trying to show that where Harmon had *been* her man, I was her man *now*.

If that was her play, the words weren't making me feel the way they were supposed to.

If you want the truth, words weren't very important just then.

Tricia Kollar was important.

CHAPTER THIRTY-EIGHT

Her hands were folded behind her head.

And she was smiling, which somehow made her freckles look both innocent and wicked.

And beneath that blanket, she was naked.

She extended her arms. "Come to me."

I began to.

"Nuh-uh-uh," she said, waggling a finger. "No clothes allowed under here."

What was I supposed to do?

What would *you* do?

That smile. That spray of freckles.

All my urgency, all the puzzles melted away.

And I stripped, with my back to Route 142 and the Blackstone Valley and all of Rhode Island.

And I joined her under the covers.

A funny thing happened sometime during the next half hour.

The air mattress popped.

When it did, we laughed and kept right on doing what we'd been doing.

Now, with the both of us spent and resting—or trying to on a plywood platform that wasn't very comfortable anymore—I reached awkwardly, peeling up a corner of the deflated mattress, and took a look.

"Aha," I said.

"Aha what, exactly?"

"Whoever made the sign cheaped out on materials. This isn't marine-grade plywood, see?"

"Can't see, don't care," she said with a smile in her voice.

I ignored her. "What with the weather and the sun, the plywood's buckling. It's forcing the screws to back out. And a screw popped the mattress."

"Fascinating."

I dropped the mattress corner and rolled onto my belly. Tricia, on her back, had thrown a forearm across her eyes to block the sun. I scrunched over to put her in shade.

"Thank you, kind sir."

"Something you said before," I said.

"Oh God, I'm blushing. If I hollered the wrong name, I'm going to throw myself off."

"No no no. *Before* before. About Kenny's ridiculous money."

"Yes?"

"Why did Kenny bankroll all this? He and Harmon weren't close. They were half brothers with that age difference, and you've told me they envied the hell out of each other in a weird way."

"I'm not sure it was envy. It was more that each resented the other's gifts."

"Still. Between the house and the business and this idiotic sign, Kenny must've shelled out a million anyway."

She barked a laugh. "Try two point one."

"Proves my point. Why?"

She curled a finger through my chest hair, not knowing she was doing it, and thought awhile.

"Why do twenty-one-year-old football players buy a house for their mama and Range Rovers for all their cousins the day of the NFL Draft?" Tricia finally asked. "Because they can. Because everybody wants to be a hero."

"There's something to that," I said, "but it's not enough. It doesn't fit Kenny. Now that he's cleaned up his act, I see how smart he is. Smart and shrewd."

"It was very difficult for Harmon to ask Kenny for anything. He never had before. Kenny's success really stuck in his craw." Tricia laughed a little. "Speaking of craw-sticking, do you know the story behind the company name and the sign?"

"Tell me."

"Kenny had only one condition when he loaned Harmon the two-million-plus."

I waited.

"Harmon had always dreamed of the company name: Wolverine Freight & Storage. Bizarrely, he believed his fifteen minutes of football-factory fame might drive some business his way."

"That's kind of sad. The punch line, I'm guessing, is that Kenny made him add 'Brothers' to the name."

She nodded. "Oh, how it pissed Harmon off. To share the limelight with Kenny, who'd spent a year prancing through Michigan's theater program. Even at his most beneficent, Kenny had to slip little brother the needle."

"Huh."

Tricia shifted uncomfortably on the deflated mattress. "I'd ask why the sudden interest in Kenny, but I do believe I can guess. You've zeroed in on him as a suspect, haven't you?"

I said I guessed so. Told her about the silent, unacknowledged race Kenny and I had just held to see if I could glance at Eudora's laptop before he shut it down.

"Thin gruel," she said when I finished.

"I've seen thinner pay off. I'm going back. Gonna have my look at that computer."

"Seriously? What's going on *now,* this moment, that you need to look at it?"

"I think she's got records, e-mails, letters on there that point to Kenny. I think he's wiping out anything he thinks he can and generally using his access to clean up after himself. I need to have a look. That means getting him out of there, and I know how."

"It's all so . . . so damn Gothic, so damn *Dateline NBC.* Half brothers and family secrets and matricide."

"And a secret fort hidden fifty feet above Route 142."

There was a long pause. A couple of cars zipped by below, underlining my point.

"Where the lonely lady entertains gentleman callers," Tricia finally said, some spirit creeping back into her voice. "But only big, raw detective types."

She snuggled closer in a way that made me forget all about busting into Eudora's place.

"I'm not a detective," I said. "I'm a mechanic."

"Even better," Tricia said.

"I'm going inside," she said a while later. "I'm going to call my assistant manager and tell her I've made a miraculous recovery. Then a shower, and then it's off to work. You do whatever you must, detective who's not a detective."

She hurried her clothes on beneath the blanket. Then she kissed my forehead and climbed down the ladder.

Me: dazed. Wondering what the hell was going on. Wondering could I really be falling for somebody? Now? In the middle of something like this?

Why not?

I rolled onto my belly and watched Tricia make her way toward the house. I smiled when she walked past the big bag she'd dropped in the drive. She wasn't a hundred yards away, but I didn't want to holler from the secret fort. I grabbed my pants, found my phone, speed-dialed.

She picked up, turned, waved. "You rang?"

"You forgot your purse."

"Pardon?" Then she saw what I was pointing at, took a few steps, and swiped up the bag. "*Purse?* Try insulated lunch bag." She half-snorted, half-laughed. "*Purse*. Men."

She clicked off and stepped into the house.

Half an hour later, after stowing the air mattress and showering and dressing, I picked up Tricia's landline.

My cell rang. It was Sophie. I set down the landline and clicked on my cell.

"I bear news," Sophie said first thing. "Harmon Kollar news."

"*What?* None of this is your business, kid."

"I began to wonder," she said, ignoring me, "why he hasn't been confirmed as police chief."

"Budget."

"Maybe. Maybe not. Did you know the Bryar Police Department has been sued twice in cases involving one Harmon Kollar?"

I said nothing, but hell no, I hadn't known that. There couldn't be many who did know, either, or the small-town rumors would have spread.

"Did you know," Sophie said, "both cases involved allegations of brutality by Brazilians?"

"Where the hell'd you get this?"

"PACER and ChoicePoint."

"What are those?"

"Databases. Good ones, the type for which businesses gladly pay."

It clicked. "Charlene has 'em. Uses 'em for background checks on employees."

"*Prospective* employees."

"You must have sneaked a peek at her laptop. Dumb move, kid. She'd kill you."

"If she found out. Which she won't." Sophie sighed. "Eye on the ball, Conway. Did you hear me? Harmon Kollar, Mister Boring but Clean, has a history of beating up Brazilian guys who happen to get caught speeding in Bryar. Or had."

"Had?"

"Both cases are old," she said. "It's as if young Patrolman Kollar was a hothead, a prejudiced jerk, but saw the light."

"Maybe he got something out of his system," I said.

"The Come-to-Jesus speech," Sophie said. "And it worked."

"But now that he's up for chief, history's biting him in the ass."

"I thought you should know."

"Kid," I said, "if your mother ever hears about this—"

"When," Sophie said, "is the last time a parent outsmarted her child regarding a technology issue?"

She clicked off.

I may have smiled.

But not for long.

Because it was a lot to think about.

Eudora Spoon's first husband had cheated a Brazilian out of his land.

Eudora Spoon's cop son had, for a while anyway, gotten his kicks beating up Brazilian dudes.

What had Tricia said the night before? *Harmon as suspect complicates matters.*

He sure as hell did.

Wouldn't it be something if Harmon was involved in his mother's death.

And I made him pay for it.

And the world learned I was messing around with his wife.

Wouldn't that be something.

I took two deep breaths, squared my shoulders, made up my mind.

I would look at Harmon. Would look at him in a whole new way. Would follow this mess wherever the facts took me.

For now, though, nothing was different. My reasons for suspecting Kenny Spoon hadn't gone away.

So pick up the landline and hit *69 to block caller ID.

I dialed Eudora's number from memory. While the phone rang, I made my lips the shape of an Edsel's grille and held them there.

Kenny picked up. Which was lucky. Not everyone does when they can't see who's calling.

"Mr. Kenneth Spoon?" I said.

The Edsel grille routine completely changes your voice. It just *does*. Try it sometime. "This is," Kenny said.

"I'm calling for Trooper Venezia. She would like you to come to the Millbury barracks for an interview. Do you know how to get to the Millbury barracks, sir?"

"Wait. *What?* When?"

"Immediately, sir."

"What the hell for? Do I *have* to? Is this . . . I mean, do I need a lawyer? What does she want?"

"Did Trooper Venezia recently interview you, sir?"

"I spoke with her a few days ago, sure."

"This would be a follow-up interview. That is all the information I have, sir. Do you know how to get here?"

"I'll GPS it. *Jes*us."

"Thank you, sir."

CHAPTER THIRTY-NINE

I was hoping Eudora wouldn't password-protect her laptop.
She did.

That was the bad news.

The good news: She hadn't gotten the memo on what makes a good password.

Pet names make lousy ones.

The worst, in fact, other than *password* or *1234*.

So fifteen minutes after my bogus call, sitting in her dining room with her screen glowing sky blue at me—having watched from Tricia's kitchen as Kenny drove off in the Mercedes—I looked at the dogs on the rug and keyed *dandychacha* into the password box.

No dice.

chachadandy

No dice.

ChaChaDandy

Bingo.

I felt pretty smug as Windows welcomed me and the computer's desktop filled in.

I popped a memory stick in a USB port and checked my watch. The run to Millbury and back would take Kenny at least an hour—

probably much more as various baffled cops tried to track down Venezia.

Eudora made it easy. Kenny had lied when he said her computer was a mess. She'd run a tight ship, with lots of subfolders inside her Documents folder, the titles dated and self-explanatory.

I began to open and read the docs that looked promising.

"Holy shit," I said out loud.

My voice attracted Cha Cha. She stood with her head near my left hand. Without looking away from the laptop I said, "How about that, hound? How about you?"

I scratched Cha Cha's head.

She didn't mind.

She whurffled and flopped on her side, maybe eighteen inches from my chair. Dandy tiptoed in, looked at the both of us, and did the same.

Fifteen minutes later, I had everything I could possibly need on the memory stick.

I also had a whole new outlook.

On Kenny.

And Harmon.

I checked my watch again. Time to get out, think it all through, and then decide what-all to do with what I had.

Cop work is easy.

Justice is hard.

I clicked to shut down the laptop.

Dandy raised his head, jangling his collar some.

Cha Cha did the same.

I heard tires on the driveway and looked out the window.

At Kenny.

Who was rolling past in the Mercedes, staring at me.

Busted is busted.

So I sat at the table while Kenny entered the house and fended off the greys, eventually settling them with a treat apiece.

"Nice try," he finally said, plopping onto the sofa. "It should have worked, but Venezia herself called as I wended my way toward Millbury. Bit of damn inconvenient luck for you, really."

The laptop had powered off. I tapped its lid. "I know everything, Kenny."

Give him credit for a good deadpan. "What's to know?"

"You don't want to spill because I may be bluffing," I said. "But if you set your palm on the laptop, you'll feel it's warm."

He said nothing.

"Her password was ChaChaDandy. Two capital Cs and a capital D."

"You sly fucker," Kenny said.

"Eudora had a lot of people fooled," I said. "Even Rose Monteiro, who thinks she knows everything, believed your mother was prepping the property to sell to a casino."

He said nothing.

"Turns out," I said, shifting in my chair—enjoying this, truth be told—"she was going to make damn sure no casino ever came near the place."

He said nothing.

"By turning the site into a greyhound rescue operation."

Kenny couldn't hold it in anymore. "Can you *believe* it? It's worth five million if it's worth a nickel. And there's already a dog place not fifteen minutes away."

I nodded. "Greyhound Friends over in Hopkinton. Eudora hauled me there more than once. Said they're doing God's work."

"Fine." He folded his arms and puffed his lower lip, the pouting Hollywood baby back now in a big way. "Let them do God's work. Let me put a few shekels in my pocket for once in my life."

"Once? Seems to me you had more than your share before you pissed it away." I sighed and tapped the laptop. "Remember, I read up. Your mother *trusted* you, Kenny. For all your bowl-cut Peter Pan bullshit, you were the one she believed in. Not Harmon. She never liked the way he put the arm on you to fund his house and business, even if the rest of the world saw him as the steady one. That's why she wanted you back here. That's why she was setting you up to usher the deal through."

We were quiet awhile.

Dandy tiptoed over, sniffed Kenny's rear end, and tiptoed away.

"What's your next move?" Kenny asked.

"Talk to the executor of the estate," I said. "Maybe talk to a reporter. Get this story about the greyhound rescue operation out there. I've got all the important docs on a memory stick, in case you were wondering."

"If this were one of those silly late-Victorian plays, or perhaps a postwar film noir, I would produce a tidy little pistol and demand said memory stick."

"I don't know much about Victorian plays," I said. "But if you pull a gun, I'll take it away and bust out your teeth with it."

"That you could, sir. You'll find no argument here. The gun is entirely hypothetical."

"If it makes you feel any better," I said, "I was half convinced you worked with Soto to have yourself kidnapped. That you set the whole thing up."

"You thought *I* had Mother killed?"

"Pretty much."

"Fuck you, Conway Sax."

"Now I see you wouldn't have worked it that way. Once she died, her estate plan kicked in. Legal beagles started running everything. Your best bet was to change her mind while she was alive."

"The thought had occurred. What's your point?"

"Somebody else might've had a different viewpoint."

He raised his eyebrows to ask the question.

I said, "Seen Harmon lately?"

CHAPTER FORTY

"Harmon?" Kenny said. "We've never been close, but it's hard to imagine Harmon doing something so ugly. That's not . . . *him*."

"I would've thought so, too. But now I wonder." I gave Kenny a thirty-second rundown on Harmon's history of thumping Brazilians, then another thirty on his gambling debts. Made sure to let him know most of those debts came about *after* Kenny's big loan.

"You don't say," he said, his eyes narrowing. "That was a lot of money to me. Even then, even when I was rolling, that was a chunk."

"Piss you off?"

"Of course. No. I don't know. Yes, but . . ." Kenny's face went soft-focus, and he made a what-can-you-do shrug. "The weakness of the flesh and all that. I don't imagine I'm in much of a position to condemn."

It was a good answer.

I could almost like Kenny.

I said, "What if the debt got unbearable? What if Harmon got desperate for a way out and teamed up with Soto? What if they were using you as a lever to force Eudora to change her will?"

He thought that through. "That might explain why Harmon's name came up when Los Bajamaros kidnapped me."

I nodded.

"But how would Harmon have come across a Valley thug in the first place?"

I shrugged. It was a good question.

Kenny shook his head hard. "If that was the pairing, call me a naïf, but I think it more likely that Soto was running the show, using Harmon's gambling debt to control him. Now that their plan appears to have gone tits-up, I'm worried about what Soto may have done to my brother."

"Half brother," I said.

"Brother," Kenny Spoon said. "Blood is blood."

I decided I *did* like him some. In spite of everything.

People change if you let them.

I rose. "I need to go after him."

Kenny stood. "Then what?"

Everybody pays.

I didn't say it out loud.

Instead I shook Kenny Spooner's hand.

The gesture came across as formal somehow.

I felt it.

I could tell he did, too.

Where was Harmon?

For an acting chief of police whose mom had been a high-profile murder vic, he was keeping a hell of a low profile.

"Huh," I said out loud, sitting alone in the truck. "Guess we know why."

First move: Text Tricia. *Looking for harmon, what's cheaterbeater say?*

While I waited for her reply, I thought it through.

Once you added it up, it made too much sense to ignore. Harmon's life wasn't working out so hot. His business had tanked. His marriage was tanking. There was a hold up on his big promotion due to some ugly history, and even if he got the promotion, his department was a joke. He was deep in debt to a creep who could lower the boom anytime.

Now that I knew a little more about him, patterns emerged. Harmon liked to come across as the noble son, the one who stuck around to take care of Mom after she lost her husband.

But.

He was always looking for somebody else to do his heavy lifting.

First, he'd talked Kenny out of a couple million for a business and a dream house. The house was a white elephant, and Harmon had quickly proved he couldn't run the business to save his life. To boot, he'd funneled some of the loan straight to Big Joe Redmond the bookie.

It was easy to picture a scenario where Harmon had bided his time, waiting for Eudora to die. When the casinos called and Eudora came down with cancer, he must have thought he'd hit the lottery.

So imagine what went through his head when Eudora, mostly to be contrary, decided to turn her land into an animal shelter.

It'd been too much.

It'd pushed dull old Harmon Kollar into a bad place.

As usual, it turned out he'd bitten off more than he could chew. Kenny had been right to suspect Lobo Soto was running the show. Hell, he'd been right to wonder if Harmon was okay. The minute Soto viewed Harmon as a liability, the lawman was in deep trouble.

Tough. If he set up Eudora, he's got to pay one way or the other. Maybe he'll pay courtesy of Lobo Soto. Maybe he already did. So be it.

But I had to know.

My phone binged.

Text from Tricia. *He's right in Bryar, 186 mendon rd. Why do u care?*

I texted thanks, ignoring her question, and googled the address.

It was the Golden Dragon.

So there you had it. Full circle.

Harmon was with Big Joe Redmond.

There were two vehicles in the Dragon's parking lot. One was an old Buick that I knew Willy, the manager and barkeep, had inherited from his mom.

The other was a Ram 2500 in burgundy. Crew cab. Chrome twenty-two-inch rims that had to cost six grand the set.

Big Joe Redmond's truck. I'd watched Harmon toss an envelope full of vigorish into the cab of that truck. It felt like four years ago, but it was only four nights.

Harmon's truck wasn't here, but that didn't mean anything.

I parked and headed for the back door, trying to build the head of red-mist anger I would need to pull this off. Strode past a Dumpster, into a kitchen that smelled exactly like the Dumpster, past a vending machine that sold lottery tickets, into the office that doubled as storage space for kegs and hard liquor.

Willy sat behind a desk angled kitty-corner to face the door. He saw me first. I hadn't been inside the Dragon more than three or four times, and not for a year, but he nodded and called me by name. His hair had gone nearly all gray, but he still wore it in the same flyaway semi-Afro. Like Don King, the regulars always teased him.

The one who had to be Big Joe sat in a scrounged ladder-back chair. The way he turned his entire torso to look at me hinted at neck trouble, maybe back trouble.

I smiled at him. Not to be nice, but because of the way he looked as he rose and extended his hand.

I'd heard his name around town, but I'd never seen him.

When a guy's called Big Joe, you figure the nickname could go a couple ways. First, he could be a shrimp. The old opposite nickname, like a man-mountain called Tiny.

What you really expect—what *I'd* expected, anyway—is a former football type, an offensive lineman whose shoulders have long since turned to belly. The kind of guy who built a rep as a bar fighter mostly by mauling and bear-hugging.

Big Joe Redmond was not that.

Big Joe Redmond was a beanpole. Six foot six, thin as a stiff rope, overdeveloped forehead that hinted at a childhood gland problem. There was really only one good nickname for him, and since nobody called him by it, it had to piss him off.

"Lurch," I said. Big smile. I extended my own right hand.

He dropped his. "Willy," he said, "what happened to the last guy called me that?"

"That'd be before my time, Big Joe," Willy said. Expecting trouble, he was closing apps on his laptop, trying to shut it down.

"Nah," Big Joe said, "it was only last spring. Loudmouth softball player from Whitinsville, remember? Called me that once, then again after I asked him to stop, all polite and shit?"

"I disremember," Willy said, slapping shut the computer, rising, and tucking it under an arm.

"Like hell you disremember. Fat fuck left his front teeth sticking out of your bar, how you gonna disremember that?"

"Willy needs to get out front and start the lunchtime setup," I said, leaving my eyes on Big Joe. "Don't you, Willy?"

"Damn right I do," he said and crossed the room, keeping me between him and Big Joe.

I asked him to close the door on his way out.

He did.

"Nobody needs to see what goes on in here," I said, scouting the office as I spoke.

"Consider yourself lucky. What do you want? Tell me quick, before I run you out of here."

I ignored him. The office was decent sized, twelve feet square, but between the desk and the ladder-back chair and the liquor cases, floor space was tight.

That worked in my favor.

My plan to throw Big Joe off by treating him like a mutt was working. He didn't know who I was or what I wanted. He set hands on hips—I swear his elbows stuck out three feet apiece—and said, "Look, ace, what the *hell*—"

Before he could finish, I stepped in and hit him with two short rights. The first one, to the belly button, doubled him over. The second one, a few inches higher, took his wind. Made him helpless as a baby.

CHAPTER FORTY-ONE

Big Joe Redmond clutched at his stomach. Clawed at it, pulling at his skin like a twelve-year-old on a playground.

Instinct is funny that way.

He staggered as much as he could in the tight space. I made a couple of quick moves to get the chair behind him, then let him fall into it.

Now I had some altitude on him.

While he gasped and pulled and made fishmouth expressions, I stood over him.

"Where is he?"

Big Joe stared, gasped.

"Look," I said. "What's happening here doesn't have a whole lot to do with you. I take no pleasure in it."

He finally caught his wind, taking that beyond-deep breath that told him he was going to live after all, and made eye contact.

"But what I need," I said, while he breathed so hard he just about sucked in my jacket, "is information. Need it fast, need it right. Okay?"

"I don't even know who you are," Big Joe said, "but you're dead. You are a dead man. I'm looking at a corpse."

I sighed. Decided Big Joe wasn't going anywhere in spite of his tough talk, made a very fast search of the joint: kitchen, restrooms, bar-and-eating area.

No Harmon.

I stepped back into the office and stood before Big Joe. Something I'd said a few seconds before came back at me. *I take no pleasure.*

The hell of it was, it was true.

It wasn't always.

I used to get kicks this way. When I was younger. When the transfer of power from the other guy to me felt like a big deal.

It didn't anymore.

This was strictly business. Here in this dumpy Chinese joint, Joe Redmond was king. He called his customers shitheads, and they took it because they had to. Here in this shitty little keno joint, with watery ginger ale and carp in brown tanks gasping for oxygen and Saginaw Fence jerks stopping by Thursday night to drink half their paychecks, Joe Redmond was one hell of a swinging dick.

The fastest way to break him down was to treat him like half that.

I'd done that.

Right here in this office with its yard-sale chair, its yard-sale desk, its gimme calendar from Miller Lite.

With its cases of booze.

Cases.

I could smell the liquor. Beneath the cardboard, beneath the sealed necks, I could smell it, I swear to God.

I didn't want to be here. Let Big Joe Redmond be big. Let him be tough, too tough to call Lurch even though that was the first thing you thought when you looked at him. Let him beat up plumbers from the local thirty-five-and-older softball league.

Let me be somewhere else.

Let me be *anywhere* else.

Let me be with Tricia.

Big Joe was moving his mouth.

". . . got your tongue there, hombre? Picturing your coffin? A cheapie, a pinewood special? Because that's what *I'm* picturing, once I get done with—"

I slapped him with my left hand.

I'm a big fan of the open-handed slap. Hurts the slappee like hell, doesn't bust up your knuckles.

More important, it unmans a guy.

See, when you punch a man, all he does is lose a fight. Big deal.

Slap a man, though, and you've humiliated him. You might as well flip and spank him.

The slap shut Big Joe's mouth.

I slapped him again, with my right this time. *Hard.*

Ever whapped a soaking-wet T-shirt on a flat rock? That was the sound, right there.

Spittle flew from his mouth onto Willy's desk.

I slapped him with the left.

The right.

A couple more. Quick ones now, some rhythm behind them.

I slapped until I saw what I needed to see: Big Joe Redmond crying.

Sometimes I hate what I do.

I snagged a bar rag from a corner, passed it to him, gave him thirty seconds.

"I'm sorry," I said. "If I knew any other way."

"What do you *want*?" No eye contact. Big Joe was all done with bluster for the day.

I leaned a hip on Willy's desk and folded my arms. "Harmon Kollar owes you," I said. "He started with parlay cards. You got him betting NFL games against the spread. He lost, like they all do. Then he started chasing to get whole, like they all do. Now he's in deep."

"So?"

"How deep?"

"A hundred and twenty this week. Next week? Depends if he scrapes together the vig to keep it from snowballing. Sometimes he makes the vig, sometimes he don't."

"Tell you the truth, I would've thought it was more. One-twenty doesn't seem . . . crippling."

"This ain't Vegas, case you hadn't noticed. One-twenty's about ten times what anybody else has ever owed me."

"So where is he?"

"The fuck should I know?"

Something about Big Joe's eyes. Baffled, scared, humiliated. For the first time since Tricia's text message, I felt doubt. What if . . .

"His phone, then," I said. "When's the last time he was here? He must've lost his phone."

"He ain't stepped in the door for . . . hell, not for a long time. He pays me off in the parking lot."

"So he dropped his phone in the parking lot."

I knew how weak that sounded even as I said it. A phone dropped in the Dragon's lot would get run over by a pickup truck or snagged by a drunk.

Something was wrong.

Either Harmon had figured out how to end-run the Cheater Beater, or the app itself had screwed the pooch.

And here I was, wasting time and feeling like a jerk.

There wasn't much I could say to Big Joe. So I said nothing. Just whirled to leave.

A flyer, masking-taped to the wall, caught my eye. It was the same hot pink as the yard signs you used to see all over Bryar. It featured an old-fashioned drawing of a woman, someone from an old magazine ad or *Father Knows Best,* wagging her finger. The caption beneath the woman read:

Casinos in Bryar? Not in my town, not on my watch!

Below that, in block letters:

NO ON 2.

Somebody had used pencil to draw a giant cock and balls on the woman. Of course. What else would you expect in the back room of the Golden Dragon?

As I made my way toward the parking lot, Willy was lighting Sterno candles that would heat trays during the lunch buffet. Without looking up, he said, "You asking the wrong one about Harmon Kollar's debt."

I stopped. "Good ears."

He may have smiled some. "Good ears, tight lips. Why I'm still around."

"Are you the one I should be talking to? You sly devil?"

He snorted. "Naw. I'm just what you think I am. Big Joe, though. He ain't what everybody think *he* is."

"Everybody thinks he's a bookie."

"He a *errand* boy is all. Do what he told, then come back here and play the tough man."

"He's sure got everybody fooled," I said, "because it's a small town, and I never heard that before."

"He work hard at it. His dignity all tied up in it. His what they call sense of self."

I smiled at that, in spite of everything. "Who's he work for?"

"I don't like sayin'."

"Come on, you took it this far."

"Used to be for Paulo Monteiro."

I stood there. Stunned. "Rose," I finally said.

"I didn't say that," Willy said. "Now did I?"

"Hell no you didn't," I said, clapping him on the shoulder as I left.

CHAPTER FORTY-TWO

In my truck, I started a text to Tricia. My best guess: The Cheater Beater had some sort of History feature, and she'd pulled that up when she meant to pull Harmon's current location.

Before I could hit SEND, though, Randall called. I had a hell of a lot to fill him in on.

Because I now had a firm link from Harmon to Los Bajamaros.

And it ran straight through Rose Monteiro.

I was babbling this to Randall as I beelined for Framingham.

"Slow down, kemo sabe," he was saying. "A little less foaming at the mouth and a little more connecting of the dots, if you please."

I took a deep breath and dropped the F-150's speed a few miles per hour. As usual, Randall was right. It wouldn't do me any good to get bagged speeding just now.

"When Eudora got killed," I said, "Harmon's reaction, his grief, struck me as . . . appropriate. Not too much, not too little. So right off the bat, I wasn't looking at him. I was looking at Lobo Soto, of course, but mainly I wanted to know who he was working for."

"Or with," Randall said.

"Sure. Ruthie at Town Hall pointed me toward Rose Monteiro, and for a while that looked like my best bet. But it turns out Eudora was playing Rose like a fiddle."

"How's that?"

I realized Randall didn't know about Eudora's plot surveys and environmental-impact studies and all that. I explained as fast as I could.

"Okay," he said. "Where does this take us?"

"Rose thought Eudora was prepping the land for sale to the highest bidder. And from the docs I found on Eudora's computer, I can see Eudora *wanted* Rose thinking that way. Eudora was showing some leg to ease the pressure."

"Rose knew she had the biggest checkbook," Randall said, "likely working with one of the casinos. She assumed she was in line for the big score. From her point of view, whether it happened before Eudora died or after didn't make much difference."

"Right. She could afford to let the cancer do its thing. She thought she was locked in to avenge the time Andy Spoon ripped off her husband *and* make a tasty profit."

"Where Eudora actually planned a greyhound shelter, bless her soul. And you say she set up Rose to think this way?"

"It's pretty clear when you look at her laptop."

"Smart broad."

"Yup. Anyway, I chased Rose down pretty good, and she convinced me she didn't work with Soto to kill Eudora. Not directly, anyway."

"Then you posited that Kenny was the one. That he'd orchestrated some sort of James Bond–style double-cross with a twist, kidnapping himself. That struck me as a reach."

"It was. The estate-planning docs show his best bet was to talk his mother into changing her will. Eudora had a weird soft spot for him. He knew it, and used it. Maybe he could have persuaded her, we'll never know. Too late now. The will drives everything from here on out."

"Barring the inevitable lawsuits."

He was right about that. "Could be," I said. "And I'm no lawyer. But it all looks rock solid. Anyway, then I thought of Big Joe."

"Why him?"

"I figured maybe he'd set up the Kenny kidnap plan because Harmon was missing payments."

"I would've thought he'd be an early suspect."

"Maybe he should have been," I said. "But remember, I was pretty much ignoring Harmon at that point. I guess I was ignoring his problems, too."

"What changed your mind?"

I hesitated.

A text from Harmon's wife. Who I'm sleeping with.

"The important thing," I said, knowing Randall had picked up on my hesitation, rushing past it, "is that I learned Big Joe, the toughest hombre in Bryar, is just an errand boy. A collector for Rose Monteiro."

"So what you were babbling about before," he said, taking his time, thinking as he spoke, "is a chain running from Bryar's acting chief of police through Big Joe, who's connected to Rose Monteiro."

"Who's connected to Los Bajamaros. It was the middle link that was missing before. The question was always who from around here had access to Lobo Soto's boys."

"Now that you know Harmon enjoyed said access, you're convinced he killed his mother. Riddle me this, though. What did Harmon gain? Wouldn't he have been in the same boat as Kenny? Trying to talk sense, as he saw it, into his mother?"

"Fair point. Maybe he went off his rocker just a little bit when he learned about the greyhound plan. Maybe we'll get to ask him about his reasons."

"Or maybe we won't," Randall said. "Maybe asking Harmon anything at all is pretty low on your priority sheet."

"Maybe." I was on Route 9 east now, well into Framingham. I stopped at a traffic light.

"What next?" Randall asked.

"We talk to Rose Monteiro."

"Talk?"

"For now," I said, "We just talk. She's got to know where Harmon and Soto are."

"Why?"

"One of the things these gangs do with their co-op agreements is set up safe houses for each other. Only the locals know the terrain well enough."

"And you saw Soto in Woonsocket yesterday, so he's still in the area."

"And I'll be damned if anybody's seen Harmon the last few days. I think the pair of them are holed up together."

"Huh." There was a long pause. "So now we're off to visit the husband-killing gangster lady?"

He put an extra hair of emphasis on "we," and I appreciated that.

"Could be rough," I said. "After I climbed up on her roof, I'm guessing she read her guys the riot act."

"So be it."

"Twice a year," I said, "I wish I had a gun."

"Say no more."

"You? Seriously? Where . . . ?"

"Don't ask," Randall said, "don't tell."

He clicked off.

That goddamn kid is something.

I spent the final few minutes of the drive to Randall's place thinking about this buddy of mine, a former Barnburner who's crazy for surfing. When his wife left him, he quit his marketing job and moved to Narragansett, Rhode Island, which is a big east coast surf spot. This buddy is pushing fifty, but he now works selling skateboards to teenagers, surfs most mornings in a wetsuit, and considers himself a success. And he's sober, so who's to argue?

There was a time this buddy and I took a lot of drives to AA commitments, just the two of us, and he used to talk surfing until I wanted to stick gum in my ears.

His favorite topic was the feeling of catching a wave at the perfect moment. Not too soon, not too late. Pushing over the ledge, he called it. Describing this moment, he used all sorts of Mother Earth mumbo-jumbo and sexual terms. I'll spare you the terms, but the gist was that if you nailed the wave just right, it felt like being in bed with someone when you know something great is going to happen but it hasn't happened yet.

The first time I heard the spiel, I said something about the wave cresting. Just trying to sound interested.

"Cresting?" My buddy looked at me like I'd just spit on his dashboard. "*Cresting?* Have you been listening *at all,* compadre? If you wait for the crest, you have missed it, you have blown it, you have well and truly pooped the bed. You might as well be skim-boarding on the beach like a German tourist."

I said I was sorry, but he ignored the apology. "No, the crest is too late, far, far too late. What you want . . . it's the time between the swell and the crest. Call it a . . . a *pre*crest." He played a little drum solo on his steering wheel, smiling big. "Yes! The precrest."

Well.

Right now, in my truck, I felt this whole mess precresting. Everything about Eudora's murder—the hush-hush casino push, Harmon's disappearing act, the Bajamaros tie-in—was building, getting set to tip.

If I waited for the crest, I'd be too late.

CHAPTER FORTY-THREE

Randall rents an upstairs apartment from a sweet old couple in Framingham's Saxonville neighborhood.

I watched him rattle down the outdoor black-iron staircase with a laptop bag in one hand. "And away we go," he said, tossing the bag on the seat between us.

"Not yet," I said, and pulled away.

"Pardon?"

I touched the laptop bag. "Makes me nervous. Hang on."

A few hundred yards down the road was a tired strip mall with a Walgreens, a dry-cleaner, a florist. I pulled into its side parking lot, where a green Dumpster was shielded from neighbors by a six-foot wooden fence. The fence shielded us, too.

I touched the laptop bag again. "Are they wrapped in rags?"

"No, but—"

"They should be." I reached beneath the bench on his side and rummaged for a T-shirt.

"For crying out loud," Randall said. "We're not crossing the border, we're driving to Worcester. Can you relax?"

"Right now," I said, "you're not an army officer on the rise. And you're not a smart kid with scholarship offers. You're a black guy cruising around in a pickup truck. Nothing lights up a bored cop like a cruising black guy." As I spoke, I took an old gray T-shirt that said FLATOUT, with a big red 05 below, and ripped it into two pieces.

Randall folded his arms and said nothing.

He's smart, but he's young. Thinks he can make the world a certain way by wanting it to be that way. Thinks he can live in a world where cops—white ones and black ones—don't pull over black guys just for riding around in landscaper trucks.

I unzipped the bag, looked around to make sure nobody was watching, and wrapped each Beretta 92FS in half a T-shirt.

"Sidearms," I said, hefting the second 92, "for officers in the United States Army."

"You are correct, sir."

One of the guns fit beneath the dashboard on the passenger side. I tucked it there. The other would have to go beneath the seat on my side. I cursed, wishing for my own truck—I'd rigged a sheet-aluminum hidey-hole that bolted to the frame.

For now, this would have to do.

I tossed the laptop bag in the Dumpster and returned to the truck.

We said nothing as we drove west.

I finally cleared my throat. "Framingham State," I said. "Good school. I was happy when my kid got in, and kind of pissed when he dropped out."

"But," Randall said, half-smiling.

"But it's not good enough for you. You know it. What happened?"

"Early in my grand college tour," he said, "I fancied I detected something in the eyes of the Admissions Office types. A certain disappointment."

"Why's that?"

"I have no limp, as you know."

"So?"

"I came to believe they were disappointed," he said, "that my missing parts weren't a bit more . . . public. A bit easier to show off."

I didn't get it. Maybe my face told Randall that.

"I'd been advertised as a twofer, you see," he said. "No, even better, a *triple* threat. An African American male with excellent high-school grades and a disability."

"Aha."

"Yes. In these interviews, my disability wasn't pulling its weight. Eyes darted toward my pant legs. More than once, the line of questioning betrayed a certain skepticism on the interviewer's part. I believe they would have been happier had I hopped into the office on my good foot and slammed the other on their fucking desk, Conway."

That caught my attention. Randall doesn't curse much.

"Late in the tour," he said, "I tried a cynical experiment at two colleges. Damn good ones, I might add, an Ivy and a near-Ivy. Upon sitting, I immediately crossed my legs to put this"—he slapped his prosthesis—"unmistakably on display. Fits of Admissions Office euphoria ensued. Red carpets were unfurled. They damn near offered to carry me about those campuses in a sedan chair."

"I know what you're getting at," I said. "But so what? They wanted you to front their catalog. Big deal. Say cheese and use them for a freebie college degree. Isn't that how it works?"

"Unquestionably. The cynicism, though. It doesn't feel right. It doesn't feel good. It doesn't feel like *me*."

We'd reached Executive Transport in Worcester. I parked at the curb forty yards away. We idled.

Randall sighed. "So it's Framingham State on my own merits. Not to mention my own nickel. Student loans until I'm forty. Oh joy."

"To prove a dumb-ass point that you'll never talk about again," I said.

"Touché," he said.

"Rusty lance. Swaybacked steed."

"*Double* touché. A point well scored by the man who wants everybody to think he's a dimwit."

"Hush up and grab your piece."

I may have smiled as I said that.

CHAPTER FORTY-FOUR

W ho the hell is this?" Rose looked from me to Tommy, curling her lip. "And how the hell'd he get up here? How the hell'd *they* get up here?"

I almost felt bad for Tommy.

"He's Randall," I said, "and he's with me, and he's nonnegotiable."

"And he dislikes being referred to in the third person nearly as much as he dislikes novels written in the second," Randall said. "And he adds parenthetically that for a criminal who's suffered several breaches recently, your perimeter security is pitiful."

Rose and Tommy stared at him.

"True," I said. With my left hand, I showed Rose the gun we'd taken away from Tommy without any fight at all.

She curled her lip at him some more.

"If I thought you had any idea Soto and Harmon were going to kill Eudora," I said, "you would be dead right now. Do you understand this, Rose?"

She held my eyes and tapped long, intricately painted fingernails on her desk. "Yes," she said after a while.

"I think you've got an agreement with Los Bajamaros. I think Soto asked you to line up a safe house for him. You thought his crew was in town just to do some muscle stuff around casino deals. And that was okay by you, because you thought you had an inside track on Eudora's land."

"I didn't *think* I had an edge," she said. "I *did* have an edge."

This wasn't the time to tell her about the greyhound shelter. "Maybe you did," I said. "Point is, you set up the safe house. You lived up to your agreement. That was important to you."

"And you want an address."

"I do."

She tapped those fingernails. "How far would you go to get it?"

"We can find out."

"How about him?" Shifting her eyes to Randall for a moment.

She was smart. She'd read Randall as the weak link.

"You lived up to your agreement, Rose." I tried to soften my voice some, and maybe I did. "It was important to you. You thought Soto was here to bribe a selectman, or to make a lowball offer on some poor sucker's home. You didn't know he had a sniper setting up to shoot an old woman in the spine."

Rose said nothing, but her fingernails hovered.

"I knew her ten years plus," I said. "She talked to me while she bled to death."

In slow motion, Rose uncapped a pen and pulled toward her a notepad with her initials and a big pink rose. Wrote on the top sheet, ripped it off, slid it my way.

I picked it up. "Marlborough. *Muitos brasileiros lá.*"

She nodded. "Hope you got a good memory, Sax. Because that paper stays here."

I memorized the address, held the paper for Randall to do the same, passed it back to her. "You don't want Bajamaros blowback."

"Bet your ass I don't. Last thing I need." She handed the sheet to Tommy, who ran it through a small shredder.

"Thank you," I said. "One more thing."

"Fuck you one more thing!" She leapt from her chair, and I may have started some at the from-out-of-nowhere fury.

"Sax," Rose said, leaning on her desk, her little forearms shaking, "do you have any goddamn idea how lucky you are? Do you have any goddamn idea who I *am*? What I *do*?"

"I know plenty," I said.

"People who walk in here . . . hell, who climb in the window of my fucking house, where my grandbabies play when they visit? Those people don't walk out, Sax. They don't boss me around, telling me they need this and they need that and I gotta do this if we wanna stay friends. They just . . . *don't*."

I said nothing.

"So what makes you different?"

I said nothing.

"I blame myself," Rose said. "I'm a big girl, or supposed to be. I'm too big, no, lay it on the line, I'm too *old* to go all gushy when some half-a-cowboy walks in and starts bossing me. The way I fell for it this time around? That's fool-me-once."

She sat. Locked eyes, made sure she had my full attention. "There won't be a fool-me-twice. Understand?"

I said nothing.

"I ever see you again," she said, "I wanna see you the way I see everybody else in this office. Hat in hand, feeling lucky to get an appointment, scared shitless you won't get out."

"You'll never see me again," I said. "Period."

Rose was quiet as Randall and I stepped from her office.

Tommy tried to look tough as we passed. But it was too late for that. Too late for him.

"Wow," Randall said when we were clear of the building. "I thought for a moment we were going to be executed by reinforcements."

"Me, too."

"And you pushed your luck anyway."

I shrugged. Unlocked the truck. Climbed in.

* * *

"Staples?" he said ten minutes later. "Mind if I ask what we're doing here?"

"Be right back."

In five minutes I was.

As he had after the scolding about the guns, Randall sat stone-faced, arms folded.

The pouting, the minor whining. This wasn't Randall. He'd been in hairy situations, overseas and with me. He'd saved my ass twice, and dodged gunfire to do it.

This was different.

We weren't driving to Marlborough to do a little recon, or a stakeout.

We were driving there to kill two men.

In cold blood, or something like it.

Randall knew that. And at a subsurface level he didn't recognize, he knew it was wrong for him.

Yet he wanted to be there for me.

The tension between the two things was making him weird.

Which reinforced a decision I'd already made.

We drove east on Route 20.

I was pretty sure Randall didn't know Marlborough well. Decided to test him to make sure.

"From what I remember of Marlborough," I said, "the safe house isn't really a house. It's some small-potatoes garage around the corner from the airport."

"Marlborough has an airport?"

That was the answer I'd wanted to hear. It proved he didn't know this town.

"Rinky-dink," I said. "One runway, puddle jumpers only. Point being, the safe house is right there. Gonna drop you around the backside. I'll take the front."

"Fair enough."

Then we were quiet again.

Soon I peeled off Route 20 and passed the airport.

"Rinky-dink indeed," Randall said.

I took a left, drove a few hundred yards, U-turned, pointed. "Second from the right."

He looked things over. "The pines will make a nice screen."

"And there're no windows on this side," I said. "Piece of cake. Let's get going. Got your piece?"

"Of course."

He swallowed. Nervous as hell, and couldn't admit it to me or to himself.

He wouldn't be nervous for long.

"Work your way close but not too close," I said. "Wait behind that dump truck for my text. Should take me about ten minutes to set up."

"Okay," Randall said.

He climbed from my truck.

He seemed to want to say something, standing there, working his Adam's apple.

I took off. Drove a hundred yards, pulled over. Dialed Randall's number while watching him in my rearview mirror.

"New plan," I said when he clicked on.

"What?"

"You'll want to clear that gun and dump it. Down a sewer or something, where no kid can find it."

"What the hell?"

Then he got it. "Conway, you mother—"

I clicked off.

Ten seconds later, as I hit Route 20 again and turned left toward the real safe house, my cell rang again.

I didn't answer.

CHAPTER FORTY-FIVE

Ten minutes later, I half-regretted ditching Randall.

Turned out the safe house was in a tough spot. It was buried in a hilly, maze-style neighborhood of roads that curved and angled so that nothing led where it ought to.

More bad news: By reading mailbox numbers, I figured out the place was an outbuilding tucked up a surprisingly long driveway. On my way in, I'd have to thread between a pair of ranch houses. On my way out, I'd run the same gauntlet.

I didn't have much choice, though. One more slow-roll through the neighborhood would be one too many, the one that would prompt a suspicious mom to call the cops.

Besides, I've found you can get away with a lot in a plain white pickup truck. Without exactly lying about it, you can make people think you're a home inspector, an insurance adjuster, a guy selling seamless gutters . . . just about anything.

Especially if you juice up the act with an aluminum clipboard.

Which I just happened to have. With a pad of generic inventory forms and a gel-tip pen. From Staples.

The clipboard was the type whose cover hinges to expose a shallow box.

Randall's Beretta fit in the box. Barely, but barely was enough.

I straightened in my seat, put a lemon-puss expression on my face, and drove right between those ranch houses, not looking left or right. I rolled up the long drive, crossing three or four little snowmelt rivers on the way.

Parked trucks and machinery told me right away this oversized lot was used as a storage and staging area for a landscaping outfit. Which made sense when you considered the Bajamaros-Brazil tie-in: there may be a Brazilian in Marlborough who doesn't work landscaping in the summer, but I've never met him.

At the top of the drive, I made a one-eighty that did two jobs: it gave me a good look at the safe house, and it got my truck pointed the way I'd come.

The building itself: a crummy cinder-block deal, thrown together on the cheap. Its roof tried to look like a barn's but didn't have much luck. The only decent part of the setup was a pair of roll-up garage doors, oversized in height, which meant somebody worked on big trucks inside. Or used to.

In front of those doors sat a white longbed GMC pickup with graphics that read, over a 508 phone number, O&S LANDSCAPING.

Bingo. The truck Soto had driven to and from the Slatersville Diner meet. Call it confirmation.

Next to the truck: a slammed Honda Civic hatchback, primer gray, with a big dumb exhaust pipe and bigger, dumber wheels.

No sign of Harmon Kollar's F-250, but there could be a dozen explanations for that.

I scanned the building, looking for my opening.

I spotted it near a second-floor window. May have smiled while I slipped a blank form into the clipboard's teeth.

I made no attempt to hide. The opposite, really. I slammed the truck door and stood by the building's corner, looking up, frowning. Slipped the pen from my shirt pocket, began checking random boxes on the form. Sensed movement in a second-floor window that wasn't quite in my line of sight. Ignored the movement.

Two minutes later, a man-door between the two rollup doors opened. A young guy stood there, a little guy, maybe five-three, wiry the way those Brazilians are—they never impress you with a Mr. Olympia look, but they'll do any labor you can name all day long.

He wore sneakers that nearly looked like football cleats but not quite, beat-up jeans, and a T-shirt that said HONDA PERFORMANCE DEVELOPMENT. Had a scraggly half-beard, stoned eyeballs.

No, not stoned. Something else. Something uglier. They were eyes that'd gone too hard too fast.

I wondered what had done that to the kid's eyes.

He scratched the beard. "You look for something, man?"

"I'm not," I said, smiling. "Well, I am. On behalf of National Grid, that is. And I found it, friend. And believe me when I say I don't give a hoot one way or the other, but what I found ain't good news for whoever owns this joint. Would that be you? I'm guessing no, but I've been wrong before."

As I spoke, I used my pen to point upward.

The kid looked annoyed, but he stepped away from the building, letting the door shut behind him. That was good. It told me the door was unlocked. Since the kid was obviously unarmed—no room to hide anything in the T-shirt and tight jeans—it told me they were getting lazy here. Lazy and bored. Standing watch over Soto and Harmon was a shit job, and this was a shit place, and this kid, sent out to get rid of the stranger, was low man on the totem pole.

I said again, "Would that be you, friend? The owner?"

"Uh? No. No. What is it?" His gaze was following my pen.

"What do you do, then, work here? Who *is* the owner?"

He was getting annoyed. "Uh? *Nao sei*. Don't know. What *is* it, man?"

I laughed, obviously faking it, transitioning into prick mode, hoping the kid had enough English to pick up on it. "Sorry, amigo. I don't talk to laymen often as I should. You're stealing your electricity back here. Or *someone* is. See how it's jerry-rigged from the house out front?"

He saw it because it was true. Once you were looking for it, you didn't have to be an expert to spot the home-brewed rat's nest of wires I'd been indicating, or to follow it to the house that shared the lot.

"I tell my boss," the kid said. "I just work here, you know?"

"That your boss right there?" I asked, using the pen to point at the GMC pickup. "I make you for the owner of this little rice-rod. So I'm guessing your boss is inside, staying warm. But I've been wrong before."

The "rice-rod" crack pissed him off, as I'd hoped it would. Behind the beard, his face went red. He took two steps in my direction. Again I sensed movement from the window above.

"Ain't none of us here own this place," he said. "You know what I think? I think it be best you leave. Amigo."

"Well, now," I said, "just hang on there. What I'm supposed to do, a case like this, I'm supposed to call Dispatch, then sit and wait, not let the violation out of my sight. Dispatch sends a supervisor, and most supervisors bring a cop, account of they've had some rough go-rounds. See, they like to correct the violation same day it's uncovered. Policy, you know?"

"Fock your policy." Another step toward me. "I think it be real good you leave *right focking now,* amigo." He stretched the last word this time, *ameeeeego.*

"Hey, it's not me getting all hot and bothered over a little bootleg electricity. It's National Goddamn Grid, friend, and I was a master electrician, union, for eleven years until Vegas went to shit, and now I'm living with Dad and making eleven bones an hour doing National Goddamn Grid's dirty work. And I'm lucky to have the gig and I earn my eleven an hour, but I do not, repeat *not,* want to cause any more misery than I need to."

The kid stared. I wondered how much of my made-up rant he'd understood.

It didn't matter. Because now the upstairs-window vibe was powerful. I was looking at the kid with the scraggly beard, but I was play-acting for the window.

"You know," I said, tapping my clipboard, "these reports, they get lost sometimes. They get caught in the wind, or I spill coffee on 'em. National Goddamn Grid doesn't like it, but there ain't much they can do about it."

Then I did something that translates real easy: I rubbed the thumb of my free hand across the fingers of the same hand.

We stood there maybe ten seconds.

A puff of wind tried to blow the form off the clipboard. Perfect. I smiled. "See? Out here in the field, just about anything can happen to these forms."

We locked eyes. I wondered again what had turned this kid so dark, so heavy. He didn't look like he could decide which shoe went on which foot, let alone whether to bribe the electrical inspector and how much. Something had screwed him up.

I caught myself holding my breath, wondering which way this was going to go.

From the upstairs window we heard, *"Trazer ele para cima."*

Phew. I recognized *Bring him up.* I've learned some Portuguese because I had to.

Beckoning me to follow, not putting much on it, the kid stepped through the man-door.

I stepped after him.

The garage was cold, and it stank. The main area, to our right, was filled with junk. An engine hoist. The giant rear axle and wheels, no tires, from a semi. Moldering cardboard cartons. Crates and crates, stacks and stacks, of unidentifiable crap. A canary yellow Camaro, second generation, up on jackstands—somebody's dream once, a project car that would never run again.

The cold was the type that starts in the soles of your boots and works its way up and doesn't let go.

The moldering cardboard cartons explained most of the smell.

But not all of it.

The kid led me up a rough set of stairs, then through a door into a slightly—but only slightly—less miserable place. It was a half-assed apartment, drywalled but unpainted. There were yard-sale sofas and chairs, a dorm-sized fridge, a microwave, a sixty-inch flat-screen. To my left were two doors. One would lead to a bathroom, the other to a bedroom.

Harmon and Soto would be in the bedroom.

I had to act fast, before they heard my voice. It was dumb luck that the bedroom had no window, or they would have spotted me outside and I'd be dead.

Trying to think all this through in maybe a second and a half, I missed something until it was too late:

Where was the guy from the window?

CHAPTER FORTY-SIX

Cold pressure on the back left side of my skull answered that one. He'd been hidden by the opening door. My danger area. Randall had told me so a dozen times.

Then I was in a jam.

Because the right move, the natural move, was to keep rolling with the National Goddamn Grid routine, but I couldn't afford to speak. Not with Harmon and Soto six feet away, separated from me only by a thin wall.

So I raised my hands like a bank teller in a heist movie, keeping the box-clipboard in my left.

"*Busca!*" the gun holder's voice said. "*Rapidamente!*"

The scruffy-beard kid searched me, quick and rough and thorough. Then he shook his head.

With his gun barrel still touching me, the man kicked my ankle while bumping my hip. The move dumped me on the plank floor hard enough so I slammed an elbow and dropped the clipboard.

Cupping the elbow as cover, I looked at the clipboard.

Its box hadn't sprung open. Thank God.

It wasn't far from my right hand. Thank God.

"What you come for? Who sent you?" He took a step toward me, holding a semiauto that was big and black and steady.

The man was a lefty.

I had a hard time peeling my eyes from that gun, but not for the reason you'd think. There was something off, something wrong. Something that ought to be clicking in my head but wasn't, not quite.

"What you come for, bitch?"

"National Goddamn Grid." I croaked it, partly to disguise my voice and partly because it just came out that way.

Harmon and Soto. Where are they?

It would've been natural for them to hide in the bedroom at first, when they weren't sure what was going on.

By now, one of them should have stuck his head out the door.

So why not?

Was this more a jail than a safe house? It sure felt like it.

For the first time, I met the gaze of the man with the gun.

Instantly I understood what was wrong with his scruffy-beard partner, the kid.

The man with the gun was very, very bad.

He was evil.

He was rotten and twisted and hateful all the way through.

He was insane, and pleased to be that way.

It's a lot to pick up from a glance, I know.

But I'd seen those eyes before.

Wish I hadn't, but I had.

I'd seen those eyes in a man at a camp full of bums like me in Lowell, back in my bad days. That man lured cats to his refrigerator-box home and tortured them to death. He always did it at three in the morning, when the rest of the camp had no choice but to listen.

That was his favorite part, see. The part that got him off. Making us listen.

We were too scared of him to do anything.

For a while, that is. Eventually we did something about it.

I did something about it.

But that's another story.

This man before me had that man's eyes.

I wondered if Soto and Harmon truly were in the next room.

I wondered if they were alive.

I wondered if I would be in two minutes.

"In five seconds," the evil man said, "I roll you over and shoot you here." He patted the back of his knee. "Blow your kneecap into the floor, uh? Ask him, he seen me do it." Nodding at the kid as he spoke.

I didn't bother asking.

Was working things through in my head.

I had new priorities.

The two men I'd come here for might be in that bedroom. Or they might not. Every second that passed made me doubt it more.

So worrying about my voice sank low on my list of priorities.

At the top of that list was an evil crazy man with a handgun.

What I needed:

First, don't get shot.

Second, get into a standing position, a position where I could do something.

Third, get hold of my clipboard.

Fourth, get out of this building alive.

I had to do all that before I could regroup and nail Eudora's killers.

Did I wish I hadn't ditched Randall?

Bet your ass I did.

"Friend," I said, trying to look like a boy caught with a cheat sheet in his shirt pocket, "you got me. You well and truly got me. Seen right through me, I guess. Can't shit a shitter and all that."

As I spoke, I clambered to my feet—clumsy, sore, embarrassed.

The man with the gun took a shuffle-step backward, which was smart.

But he let me rise, which was dumb.

I hitched up my jeans, picked up the clipboard, smiled, shrugged.

"It's a scam, but I guess you figured that out. What we do, when my brother got canned by National Grid he took a shitload of these forms with him, pads and pads. So what we do, we drive around, 'war-driving' my brother calls it, and we look for who's pirating their electrical. It's easy once you know what to look for. And what we do, we run a little shakedown like the one I tried on you guys, and I got to tell you it works ninety percent of the time. And even when it don't work, when some big dude tells us to pound sand, we don't get busted, 'cause the big dude *is* pirating his electrical, so he's not gonna call the cops, right?"

The gun barrel moved not at all.

"*Coincidência,* uh?" the bad man said, looking at me but speaking to his partner. "You like *coincidência?*"

"I hate *coincidência,*" the kid behind me said.

"Look like we gonna put you on the floor and shoot the back of your knee," the bad man said.

I licked my lips and held my hands up, the clipboard in my right. Tried to look like a con man who was in over his head. "Fellas, jeez. It's a *scam.* He's got . . . he's just got pads and pads of these forms, see, and it's easy money, but I know when I'm licked, whatever you guys got going up here is none of my business, right?"

As I spoke with rising panic, I unclipped the bogus sheet from the clipboard, turned to the kid, thrust it at him.

He ignored it.

I turned to the bad man and took a couple of steps, holding up the form the way you'd hold a cross to a vampire. I was a punk, panicking, babbling, in way too deep . . .

. . . the bad man's alarm bells rang when I was about a yard away, with the yellow sheet blocking my view of his face and his of mine.

His alarm bells were too late.

These movie heroes, it always seems they learned to fight in the navy SEALs, doesn't it?

I laugh at that. I believe there are more SEALs in the movies than there are in the navy.

Then there's guys say they learned to fight in bars, meaning they're drunks who can sucker-punch other drunks.

Big deal.

Me, I learned to fight in hobo jungles. Under city overpasses. On a prison brush-clearing crew working State Route 362 south of Cottonport, Louisiana. I kid you not, just before that state outlawed chain gangs.

Where I learned my chops, there are only three moves.

You pick up a man and squeeze him until he faints.

Or you stick a busted bottle in his eye.

Or you kick him in the balls.

I didn't have a bottle, and I wasn't going to bear-hug a crazy man with a gun.

So I kicked him.

Hard as I could. I kicked with my right leg like an old-school straight-on football kicker, maybe Fred Cox from the Vikings. Fell backward as I kicked, getting every last bit of power into it.

I got him with my bootlaces. I hooked him good. I believe I lifted him into the air an inch, though I may just picture it that way in my mind.

Whether I raised the evil man from the floor or not, one thing's for sure: I blew him up. Probably shouldn't say much more about it. Leave it this way: I kicked him right where I wanted to, as hard as I wanted to, and he went down just the way I wanted him to.

He even dropped the semiauto. Just like I wanted him to.

All this happening so fast, but feeling slow in my head.

A tenth of a second after I hit the deck, I popped back up and jumped on the guy, who'd dropped to his knees. He was just kneeling there, making a noise like a teapot, waiting to topple.

I helped him topple.

Pinned him, got my left forearm across his throat. Wanted to put him all the way out, and quick—I was already thinking about the kid behind me.

Now the evil man was on his back on the plank floor, his legs folded at the knees. I lay on him, driving all my weight onto his neck.

I could bust his throat the way I'd busted his balls.

Or maybe he'd get lucky and pass out first.

Either way was fine by me, but it had to happen soon.

He stared at me, eyes bugging.

Even though I was on top, choking him out, I can admit those eyes scared the snot out of me.

With the last fumes in his tank, the evil man reached with his left hand—I had a knee on his right arm, but the left was relatively free—and made a slow-motion try at thumbing my eyeball.

I saw it coming. He didn't have any real strength left, and my senses were set at max intake, so the clawing hand never had a chance. With most of my body occupied, I stopped the hand the first way that came to mind:

I bit it.

In the webbing between thumb and forefinger.

I bit hard.

And held the bite.

The man made a thin scream.

Each pulse of his black heart grew weaker.

As he finally got lucky and fainted, from lack of air or blood or both, I saw the thing that had tried to work its way into my brain when he held the gun on me.

It was on his wrist.

A watch.

A good old indestructible Seiko 6309, just like mine.

Like the man had said, *Coincidência*?

Like the kid had said in response, I hate *coincidência*.

It had to be Harmon Kollar's watch.

That's when a bunch of things became clear.

"No," I said. "Hell no."

CHAPTER FORTY-SEVEN

With the evil man out, I crouched and spun and reached for my clipboard all at once.

The scruffy-beard kid was no threat. He sat on the couch, pressed against its back cushion, digging with his heels, shaking hard, hands in full *I surrender* pose. If he could've used those heels to push himself through the cinder-block wall, he would have.

That didn't keep me from pointing the 92 at him once I pulled it from the clipboard box. Crouching beside the evil man, I grasped his flopping arm near the wrist, shook it. "This," I said to the kid. "*This!*"

Confusion in his eyes.

I worked free the Seiko's rubber strap. "*This*, for Chrissake. Where'd it come from? *Onde?*"

The kid chinned at the man beside me. "He bring it. Brang it."

"Where from, though?"

He shrugged. "*Nao sei.* Don't know, man."

Something about the shrug lit me off, and in two seconds, maybe less, I was across the room with my gun against his upper lip. "Bullshit. Where from?"

"Okay okay okay!" He closed his eyes and squeaked the words like a girl. "He goes away for a day and does something. When he comes back, he wearing that."

As he spoke, I took care of something I should've done already. Took a quick look in the bedroom and the filthy bathroom. They were empty. Soto was long gone, and I was now pretty damn sure Harmon was dead.

"When did that man get the watch?" I said.

"Two-three days?"

"Which?"

The kid thought, nodded. "Not day of snow. Two days after."

That worked. It was then that Harmon had gone missing.

I stepped to the evil man's semiauto, pulled its clip, cleared its chamber. Pocketed the clip and the bullet. Made sure the bad man was still out—he was, and it was ugly, and I didn't like looking at him—then turned to the kid again. "Way I heard it, this is a safe house. For Lobo Soto. Little guy? Ponytail? Mexican?"

"*Sim*. Mexicano. *Was* a safe house. But the Mexicano and him"—nodding at the bad man—"talk talk talk, all the time. I think they like each other, I think they were like . . . *irmãos*?"

Brothers. I got it. Nodded. "The Mexican was staying here. But he left the day of the snow."

"*Sim!*"

"Two days later, this man gets a call. He takes off. He comes back with a new watch."

"*Sim!*"

A picture was forming. Harmon and Soto had partnered up. After Eudora's death, for whatever reason, Soto pulled a double-cross and sicced the evil man on Harmon.

Next question. Where the hell was Lobo Soto?

"You got anything you want here," I said, "grab it. Time to go. Forever."

"I got nothing."

I made him walk in front of me. When we neared the downed evil man, the kid shook like a hardware-store paint vibrator.

"Don't look," I said. "Step past. Don't look."

He followed the advice.

Not me.

I couldn't.

Because when you do what I do, you need to *know* what you've done. You need to square up and face it, look at it hard.

Even if the looking makes you retch. Makes you hate yourself and everything you've done to get where you are at this moment.

At this moment, you're using your boot to toe aside the limp body of a man you just beat half to death because it's partially blocking the door.

You're standing awkwardly on the toe of your other boot, because blood creeps outward from the man's crotch, and you don't want to step in it.

You don't need to think it all through right now. Now is for doing, not thinking.

But you do need to look at it.

Because the time for thinking will come later.

And there's no sense pretending you didn't do what you did.

Because it all comes back at you one way or another.

It weighs.

A sob snapped me out of it.

When I looked up, the kid was disintegrating.

He cried and shook and muttered in Portuguese.

Maybe a week ago, the kid had been plowing driveways and waiting for the spring landscaping rush. Somebody'd told him about an easy babysitting job: make a couple hundred bucks watching TV in a dump in Marlborough, keeping half an eye on some dipshit holed up there.

He'd shown up.

Then his nightmare had begun.

I guided him toward the garage's man door. Before we stepped out, I turned him to face me.

"Later you get to cry," I said. "But not now. Get it? *Entender?*"

He nodded.

I said, "Where are you from?"

"São Paulo."

"Got a passport?"

He nodded.

"Money?"

"Uh . . ."

I took all I had from my wallet and pressed it into his hands.

"I want you to sleep in São Paulo tonight," I said. "Sell your car. Sell it for cash only. Get to Logan or Providence. Get a plane ticket. Sleep at home tonight. Never talk about this. About any of this. Ever. Okay?"

"*Sim.*"

We stepped through the door. I made for my truck. The kid made for his Civic.

There were no cop cars, no neighbors peeking through curtains. I'd been in the cinder-block building maybe six minutes.

It felt longer.

Did it ever.

The kid fired up his Honda and drove off, his beer-can exhaust making that obnoxious noise they make.

I never saw him again.

CHAPTER FORTY-EIGHT

Soto long gone, holed up elsewhere since the day of Eudora's murder.

Rose didn't know that. She thought he was in the Marlborough safe house—there was no doubt in my mind she truly believed it.

Harmon dead, killed by the evil man I'd stepped over. Killed, most likely, two days after his mother was shot. The day after I spoke with him. The day after he admitted how badly he'd screwed up.

It pointed in a direction I couldn't ignore.

Though I wanted to.

Once I cleared the neighborhood without seeing any cops, I bumped up the volume on my phone. Got a series of bings: text messages from Tricia.

Where are u?

U ok?

Worried!!

The messages made me sad. They more or less confirmed it all.

But I had to be sure.

You don't see many pay phones anymore, and sometimes you need one. So I make a point of noticing them. I'd spotted one at a Shell station on my way into the neighborhood.

I pulled in and shot Tricia a text message: *H wasn't at that address, must've just missed him, where is he now?*

I climbed out, dropped quarters in the pay phone, and dialed the number from Venezia's business card. Was set to hang up if she answered.

She didn't. Good.

After the beep, I used a ridiculous old-lady voice to say "Harmon Kollar" and the safe house address. Three times in a row, real slow, in that voice that made me feel like an idiot—but which nobody, Venezia included, would recognize as mine.

I learned that trick in Walpole.

As I started to climb into the truck, something caught my eye.

The gas pumps, not fifteen feet away. Pump 2 and Pump 3.

Something nagging. Something off.

I stared at the pumps. Had that feeling you get when you know you forgot something but you're damned if you can figure out what.

When I got back to the truck, I had my return text from Tricia.

She'd tried to send me to the Marlborough address. The safe house. The place I'd just been.

She'd sent me there to be killed by the evil insane man.

Right up to that moment, I'd been halfway in love with her.

She must have seen me pull up, because there was no flicker of surprise, no hesitation as she pulled open the front door.

She launched into me. I had to hug her or get knocked over.

I hugged her.

"What happened?" Tricia asked, leading me to the living room. "Did you find him at the second place? Are you all right? You look all right. What's wrong?"

"You sent me two places hoping somebody'd do you a favor and kill me."

"What?"

"Knock it off, Tricia. I took care of them both, Big Joe and the crazy little guy who killed Harmon."

"Harmon's dead?"

"Nice try."

And it was. She ran through a half-dozen facial expressions in the space of a few seconds, and they were all pretty convincing.

Why not? She was a liar, and a damn good one.

"I can't . . . Tell me everything, I insist!" she said. "And what in the world is this about wanting you killed? But tell me about Harmon first. Have you called the police?"

I extended a hand. "Let's have a look at your phone."

Tricia's eyes went cloudy, but not for long. "What *is* all this, Conway? As it happens, I was so nervous I dropped it."

"In the last half hour."

"Right after I texted you. Jesus, what's with the tone? Turn around if you don't believe me!"

Sure enough, her smashed phone sat in pieces on the kitchen island.

"Pretty good," I said. "Of course, a phone doesn't disintegrate that way from being dropped. You whipped it down as hard as you could. But who's going to prove that, right?"

Tricia rushed me again, coming in for a hug. "First things first," she said. "What happened to Harmon?"

I caught her forearms, held her at arm's length. "Booth Two," I said.

Puzzled eyes, the first genuine expression she'd showed me. "Pardon?"

"Yesterday, talking about Kenny. When Los Bajamaros had him in Van Nuys. You said they held him in Booth Two."

"So?"

"That was the *first* booth they held him in. I fetched him out of Booth Three. The only way to know about Booth Two was to be in on it from the start."

"*Spare* me, Miss Marple! Booth Three, Booth Two, John Wilkes Booth! None of it means anything." She folded her arms and turned away, not willing to look me in the eye now.

I gave it a long pause and softened my voice. "The dog thing was the last straw," I said. "Wasn't it?"

Her eyebrows made a question.

"You put up with a lot. For a long time. Dropped out of school when you were twenty, came east to Bryar—Nowheresville—with a husband who turned out to be a dud."

"Conway, what are you *talking* about?"

"You're a smart one. Smart as a whip. Art history. I bet you saw yourself in Paris and Rome. You ended up in Bryar, a thousand miles from family, with a husband who bored you to death and couldn't get past his fifteen minutes of big-time football fame. Nearest you come to using your artsy education is picking prints for Bed Bath & Beyond."

Tricia's eyes went flat. "Get out. I don't know why you're being so awful, and I apologize for whatever I've done to offend you, but get out."

I stood my ground, my back to the window wall. "Kids would have gone a long way toward fixing things, or at least patching them for a while. But that didn't work either. I'm guessing it was Harmon who had the problem there. That made you feel piled on, like you couldn't get a break."

She said nothing. Her jaw took a new set.

"Kenny's money helped some," I said. "Gave you an outlet. This house was your hobby for a while, wasn't it? Harmon was along for the ride. *He* got his little dream business, but he found a way to screw that up, too. All while digging himself a deep hole with damn-fool football bets."

"You can say that again," Tricia said.

I was getting to her.

"When the house was done and the business tanked, you had two choices. Leave him or play the long game, the Eudora lottery. Why didn't you leave him? You had no kids to anchor you."

That did it.

It broke her.

"The . . . lottery, as you put it, was becoming an attractive option." She said it so quietly I strained to hear. She licked her lips and stared at nothing. "There were simultaneous rumblings of cancer and casinos. It looked like . . . it looked like . . ."

"It looked like you were finally catching a break."

She nodded.

"Eudora wanted everyone to think she was prepping the property for a casino sale," I said. "How'd you learn about the greyhound-shelter plan?"

"She *told* me, can you believe that? It was Harmon she was worried about. The silly old biddy took me into her confidence. She thought I was the reasonable one. She enlisted me early on to retrieve Kenny from the West Coast. She trusted him and she trusted me."

"She was half right."

Tricia snorted.

"How'd the Kenny kidnapping come about?" I asked. "Near as I could figure, Harmon linked up with Los Bajamaros through Big Joe Redmond and Rose Monteiro."

She shook her head impatiently. "You overthought it. Six months ago, Lobo came to the Blackstone Valley to discuss civic investments with any town that would listen."

Lobo. First names.

"Civic investments," I said, rubbing finger and thumb together.

She nodded. "Of course. He was gauging which towns, which selectmen and zoning boards, and yes, which police chiefs were corruptible."

"How'd Harmon stack up?"

"Pure as the driven snow, the jackass. But he made the mistake of telling Eudora about his meeting with Lobo."

"And she told you. Because she trusted you."

Tricia said nothing.

"You went to Soto and explained where things stood."

Nothing.

"Soto convinced you Eudora had to die. He thought Harmon would take the fall, especially once the law learned about his heavy debt. A fleet of lawyers would shred the will, and if the greyhound people were a problem, Los Bajamaros would pay them off or scare them off."

"And you screwed up the plan two ways. First by pulling Kenny back here at the worst possible time."

I nodded. "Soto wanted Kenny far, far away to lock in Harmon as the only suspect."

"And then you made Lobo crash, and so everybody learned about his sniper."

"You and Soto have been pedaling like crazy ever since. Cover-ups and Plan Bs and half-assed water-treading."

She folded her arms and said nothing.

"Things got twisted up so bad Soto ended up killing Harmon, too," I said. "And since then, you've been feeding me bullshit Cheater Beater info. Hoping *I'd* get killed."

Nothing.

"Funny how plans turn to shit," I said, "when you kill your mother-in-law and set up your husband as the patsy."

CHAPTER FORTY-NINE

She said nothing.

I made my voice soft. "Everybody pays, Tricia."

Nothing.

"No freebies. I'm going to call the cops now. Just be glad you're not Soto. Where is he?"

"Maybe Mexico by now. En route, anyway."

"Bullshit. He's no more Mexican than I am. He's a California boy. Where is he?"

"He *is*!" her face turned ugly. "And the bastard wouldn't take me along! Los Bajamaros have caches and safe places all over the country, he said. He can cool out in style as long as necessary."

"And here you are."

"And here I am."

"Everybody pays."

As I stepped to the phone, I remembered something. Reached in my right pocket, pulled out Harmon's Seiko—I'd removed it from the evil man's wrist—and tossed it to her. "Memento," I said.

She knew right away what it was.

And she wept.

And for the thousandth time, I realized I won't figure out what makes human beings run if I live to be a hundred.

Which I won't.

She flopped onto the sofa with her back to the window wall.

And she wept.

I sat next to her. Hesitated, then put an arm around her.

She didn't lean into me. Leaned forward some instead. Held a fist-ful of tissues in one hand and Harmon's Seiko in the other. She shook the watch. "You had to show me *this* damn thing. Oh, how he went on about it."

"You're telling me."

She sobbed.

She half-laughed.

She turned to face me.

"What am I crying for? What am I mourning? Riddle me this."

I said nothing.

She wiped her eyes, her face a mess. That half-laugh again. "How do things get where they get? How is it that you visit a little Mexican man, hoping he'll try harder to bribe your husband, and you wind up . . . *here?*"

"I'm calling the cops now."

"Don't you want to see where he is?"

"You said Mexico."

She shook her head. *"Harmon."*

"Jesus, he's *here?*"

"Lobo sent that . . . unbalanced little man here. The little man asked about a storage unit. He persuaded Harmon to show him one, and he . . ."

"He killed him in it. And left him there."

Tricia wept. "Tell me why I'm crying. *Tell me!*"

I couldn't tell her.

But I could take and hold her.

So I did.

I didn't know why then.

I still don't.

I let her cry.

I let her pant.

I let her go calm.

Finally she did.

"Show me," I said.

I followed her into the front hall, where she grabbed a key ring from a hook and swapped her nice shoes for a pair of black rubber muck-boots.

Out the front door, hard right onto the foolish driveway shared by the house and business, up the rise toward the storage units. Tricia's muck-boots were a good idea: It was warm and sunny enough so I didn't miss the jacket I'd left inside, and snowmelt rippled down the tarmac in streams that were an inch deep in places.

Tricia paced along just ahead of me, a woman on a mission. She wore a light sweater over gray slacks, the slacks looking kind of silly with the muck-boots.

But also kind of cool.

She slowed for a cinder-block unit with a maroon roll-up door, A-2 painted on the door in two-foot characters. It was padlocked. She needed almost no time to select a key from the big ring.

The lock swung open. Tricia pulled it free.

I stepped past, bent, tugged the corrugated door.

It rolled up easily enough to surprise me. The effect was like lifting a suitcase you think is full but turns out to be empty: I found myself chucking the door upward too quickly. So I hung on to the handle, trying to put on the brakes.

That's the position I found myself in—tiptoes, one arm stretched upward, my flank exposed—when I saw Lobo Soto.

He wasn't in any Mexico.

Hell, he wasn't two feet away.

That quiet, confident smile on his face.

If it'd been a bullshit cop show or a Bruce Willis movie, he would have made some clever crack. He sure had time to.

It wasn't either of those things.

So he just hit me with a long hunk of hardwood, maybe an ax handle.

Twice.

First, he creamed the right side of my rib cage.

All the pain there is, blue-white pain, cold and hot both, blew up in there.

Then he took his time hitting me in the head.

I turned to Tricia as I fell.

"Hey," I said.

CHAPTER FIFTY

You think you're out for a long time, but you never really are.

I screamed as I came to. Didn't have any choice: It was an involuntary reaction courtesy of my ribs. Ice white pain, like biting down on a gum wrapper times a thousand.

Soto was intensifying the pain by hoisting my arms over my head. My wrists were ziptied together. *Tight,* circulation in my hands already going.

He must have ziptied me soon as I went down, then gotten a shoulder into my belly and lifted me. A corner of my brain realized it was exactly the way I'd lifted Kenny Spoon at Bajamaros headquarters.

Which seemed like a dozen years ago.

So Soto had lots of physical strength for a little guy.

He also had a plan.

While I tried to pull myself together enough to make a move—and failed, the pain and shock winning out—he took another ziptie from between his teeth and attached my wrists to the cold wall behind me. I couldn't see it, but there had to be an iron ring in the cinder block.

Lobo Soto stepped back and looked me over. Made a *not bad* nod, like a man checking out a room he just painted.

Behind him, Tricia used a fingernail to tap her teeth. Started to speak, but stopped.

Then again.

"Harmon was a pansy," she finally said. "You saw what that awful Eudora heaped on him. On *us*. With her holier-than-thou AA routine, and her religion, and her Queen Serene pose. She heaped and she heaped and she *heaped*. And despite it all, when presented with his last best hope, the big dumb doormat refused to stand on his hind legs and *do* something, *take* something."

"Rowr," Soto said.

"Shush," she said, staying focused on me. "I want him to understand. I want him to get it. It shouldn't matter to me. But it does."

While Tricia spoke, I scoped. Lobo Soto had been living in this unit, that was obvious. Space heater, leftover twin-sized bed from some kid's room, a lamp, a table, a chair, an iPad . . . and a bag, insulated. The bag I'd seen Tricia carrying yesterday. I'd thought it was her purse. It was for bringing him hot food.

On the wall opposite, I saw a ring in the wall that had to be just like the one I was strapped to.

The ring gave me hope.

I looked away, not wanting them to read my face.

Soto had caught me looking around the unit. He smiled. "Not a bad setup, eh? We used Rose to spread the word about that bullshit safe house. She fell for it. She's not as smart as she thinks she is. Except for some bonding with that batshit-crazy butcher in Marlborough, I spent most of my time right here. I waited for the first batch of cops to leave this place, then doubled back and kept that damn door shut for two days."

I said, "Where's Harmon?"

"Unit D-8," he said, then chuffed a little laugh. "It's downwind."

"Cops are coming," I said. "Venezia. I called before I went in the house."

"Do tell," Tricia said—and slipped my phone from the back pocket of Soto's chinos. She held it up and wiggled it. "Why, then, is she not on your call log?"

Hell.

"Time to go down the hill," Soto said to Tricia.

"And then Mexico!" She said it like a kid eager for school vacation. Then she thrust her chin my way. "What about him?"

"See how he's on his tiptoes? He can't hold that forever. His arms will stretch, tear at the armpits. Fluid will run into his lungs. He's going to drown in his own blood, baby."

"Oh," Tricia said. I saw a flash of something. Of a human being.

Only a flash.

Maybe I imagined it.

Maybe not.

"You don't really think he'll take you along," I said, "do you?"

"Shut it," he said and took Tricia's wrist.

As he guided her from the unit, she glanced over her shoulder at me a couple of times. I swear she did.

Soto talked gently to her the whole time, reaching up, grasping the door's handle, giving a light tug.

When the door hit tarmac, the unit went black.

CHAPTER FIFTY-ONE

Time to go down the hill, he'd said.

That had to mean Kenny's place.

Because Kenny was a loose end.

Like me.

Jesus.

No time for regret. No time for feeling stupid.

I'm not sure what I would've done without the horizontal beam of light at the bottom of the door, where old weather sealing didn't quite seal. That light gave me a target, a goal.

First job: Get higher. Soto'd been right: I was beginning to shake on my tiptoes. My arches were cramping.

When I gave out and flattened my feet, I was done.

What I'd noticed: Before Soto and Tricia had turned the unit into a hideout, it had been a storage shed for a long time. There was lots of junk stashed around, shoved against all three walls.

Maybe I could use some of that junk to stay alive.

I stood on the toes of my left foot and tapped along the wall with my right, probing for something to stand on.

It wasn't easy. My strength was dropping. My left foot trembled as it supported my weight. The pain in my right flank had dulled and spread.

I ignored all that. Moved my right foot as far along the wall as I could, feeling blindly for something.

For anything.

There.

With my leg extended as far as it would go, my boot touched something. I probed. I toed.

The thing, whatever it was, moved an inch. I couldn't tell what my boot was touching, but it seemed flexible. Movable.

I hooked with a toe, pulled the thing toward me. Slow slow slow, not wanting to lose it.

Then the thing was centered beneath my feet. I probed again. Springy, mushy . . . a picture formed. It was a garden hose. It was coiled, but the coil had loosened while I dragged.

It wasn't much, but if I stood on the coil, it had to raise me an inch or two. Didn't it?

I shifted weight. Sure enough, the coil beneath my right foot jacked me up, taking pressure from my ziptied wrists. Now to move the left foot, the one on which I stood tiptoed . . .

The left foot blew it. It trembled, then spasmed, knocking all the coil out of the hose.

I staggered, twisted, torqued my body . . .

Which left all my weight hanging from a single ziptie, ballooning pain through my hands and wrists.

Don't faint don't faint don't faint.

I stayed alert, stayed alive. But not by much.

Gathered myself, got back to tiptoes. That eased the strain on my wrists. I was no worse off than before.

Except that a couple of minutes had passed. Both feet were cramping like crazy, and my toes were shaking in a rhythmic way. What the gym rats call total muscle failure was coming hard and fast.

And you know what? The worst of it was the goddamn frustration.

I *knew* there were tools at hand. I *had* a sliver of light, from the door, and a sliver of hope, from my glance at the iron ring in the wall opposite.

Would I get into position to test that ray of hope? Or would my toes give out first?

Frustration.

I may have sobbed.

But only once.

I focused. I breathed myself calm, breathed oxygen into my feet, breathed them still.

Then, in a move that seemed to take a hundred years, I transferred weight onto my right foot. It was time to go fishing with my left.

I slid my boot four inches.

Nothing.

Another four.

Nothing.

The farther I slid my left foot, the harder it became to balance on my right. Each shift added pressure to the ziptie biting into my wrists—in my mind's eye, my hands now looked like the Hamburger Helper mascot.

I could stretch another twelve inches. If I was lucky.

Deep breath.

Stretch that leg three inches.

Nothing.

Another three inches.

Nothing.

That sob again, escaping before I could capture it.

CHAPTER FIFTY-TWO

One more deep breath. One more reach.

It was all I had left in me. One shot.

My boot touched something.

Now I *held* my breath, as if a puff would move the something away.

I probed with the boot. Whatever it was, it was firmer than a garden hose.

I risked an experimental kick, a soft one.

I heard a sound that, despite it all, despite where I was and how I felt and what I'd fallen for and what was likely happening to Kenny, made me smile.

It was a sound I knew well.

It was the sound of a toolbox.

A heavy, well-stocked toolbox.

Sweat dripped from my eyebrows as I raised my left boot and felt for a plastic handle that could make the difference between getting out of here and drowning in my own blood.

Not there . . .

Not yet . . .

There.

That sob, a third time, but packed with relief now. My weight was jangling on my overworked right foot, and my hands were bulging like something from a Warner Brothers cartoon, but I had that mother-fucking handle hooked and I wasn't going to give it up.

I pulled with the left boot.

Got an inch of scraping movement. Then a slip.

I wasn't quitting now. Shifted that boot, hooked that handle, pulled.

Again.

Again.

Then the steel box, that beautiful box, was squarely beneath me.

I stood on it with both feet.

The pressure release on toes and wrists and armpits was instant and beautiful.

And short-lived. Now it was *really* time to work, numb wrists and cartoon hands and all.

My ray of hope, the thing I'd spotted on the opposite wall, was an iron ring in a bottom-of-the-line anchor, not something stouter like an expansion-shield anchor or a knurled drop-in anchor.

The anchor I'd seen was just force-fit into a hole drilled in the block.

People use them because they're easy to install, and they work fine.

For a while.

Then time passes. Things cool. Things heat. Cinder blocks degrade. Chinese pot metal degrades.

A line from Randall popped into my head. *Things fall apart; the center cannot hold.*

I never asked, but assumed it was from a song or a book. He would say it in his Randall way, always at the perfect time, never explaining exactly what the line meant but never needing to.

You could use a little Randall right now.

Too bad you ditched him. He thinks you're in Marlborough. If he even cares.

You idiot.

All this passing through my head in a lot less time than it takes to explain.

Base assumption: The ring holding me would be attached the same way as the other.

It'd damn well better be.

So: How do you reverse a force-fit?

Force, of course.

A horse, of course.

I laughed a laugh that ended in another sob. It scared me some. I was losing my shit, if you want the truth. Maybe I was anticipating how much this next part was going to hurt my wrists and hands.

Tough. Time to go. Time to live.

I squared up. I rocked back and forth on the toolbox to make sure the platform was steady.

It was.

I glanced at my little ray of light. It steadied me somehow.

Then I turned my head and looked straight ahead.

I stared into blackness.

I pictured that iron ring opposite me.

I set my rear end against cold cinder block. I was a lever. My ass was the fulcrum.

Breathe. Once, then again, then again . . .

And pull pull pull. Yank that goddamn ring right out of its cheapo anchor. Imagine cinder block degrading year by year, pot metal going porous, and pull goddammit pull pull pull.

Nothing.

The ring didn't move.

Didn't budge.

Didn't offer a sliver of a fraction of hope that it ever would.

And I'd tried so hard.

Had put everything I had into the effort.

I collapsed. Even with the toolbox, which had stood up well, my weight sagged, lighting a new fire in hands and wrists and armpits.

I sobbed.

As before, I sobbed only once.

More than that would have been the give-up. The tearing of the muscles around the armpits, the fainting, the lungs filling.

No. I sobbed only once.

I wondered what I'd done wrong.

It came to me.

I'd worked with my arms, had worked from shoulders up.

Compared to the legs and ass, the shoulders and arms are weak.

So try again.

A corner of my head wondered how long I'd been here.

It felt like a month.

Stop. Control what you can control.

I experimented with my weight. Got my rear end planted hard against the wall, pushed outward with my feet—as if I were trying to slide the toolbox toward the wall opposite.

Which would kill me, of course, but I had to know how much friction I could count on.

Plenty, I decided. Between the rough concrete floor, the scratched paintless steel of the toolbox's underside, and my weight, the toolbox wasn't going anywhere.

Now it was time to go for real.

Rear end against the wall. Breathe once, twice, and . . .

I pushed from my feet, pushed with everything I had left. The image was of me driving my ass straight through cinder block. Whatever happened with the iron ring was an afterthought—an effect, not a cause.

Drive drive drive.

Push the toolbox through the floor, push your ass through the wall, drive drive drive drive drive . . .

CHAPTER FIFTY-THREE

It happened all at once. There was no slip, no hint, no warning of impending failure.

The ring and anchor popped from the wall without making a sound.

I spent half a second flying through blackness.

I got my elbows down to break my fall. Hurt my elbows bad, but the alternative was a busted nose and most likely a knockout.

I lay there for a long moment, cheek on floor, forearms in a sort of praying-mantis position beneath me.

A long moment: that was all I allowed myself.

No time to gloat, no time to feel good. A back room in my head had already planned my next moves, had set priorities.

What I truly needed was my wrists freed.

For that I needed light.

For *that* I needed another lever.

And that lever was close by.

I elbow-and-kneed dead ahead until I touched the side of the bed that Lobo Soto had used.

I liked the way my head was working now. With the worst of it, the make-or-break, over, I was regaining efficiency.

There would be no more sobbing.

About time.

From here on out, I just had to do the work.

Work meant, for starters, kicking the mattress and box spring from the bed frame.

The frame was one you've seen all your life: black angle iron, nuts and bolts at the corners so the unit folds into a parallelogram. Easy to deliver, easy to store.

Working without sight but with a clear picture in my head, I found two corners, ran the nuts off the bolts, yanked free one long side of the frame.

I stood.

Even though I had to fumble the length of iron between my near-useless hands and my blown-up rib cage—the pain there had gone into a Never-Never Land of pulsing agony—I smiled.

Three steps took me to the ray of light at the bottom of the roll-up door. I dropped to my knees and used a whole bunch of body parts— crotch, stomach, thigh, knees—to force my lever through the crack. I got eighteen inches outside, leaving me the rest to work with.

It was tight. Even with the weather-rotted seal, the door's pressure held the lever firmly against the floor.

Which meant I had to ask my wrists for help one more time.

I moved quickly, not giving myself a chance to dread the pain.

I rose, got in a squatting position, and duckwalked backward to the end of the lever.

Then I shoved my palms along the floor, making sure the ziptie slid between lever and concrete. Now the ziptie was the strap I would use to lift.

This is gonna hurt like holy screaming hell.

Shut up.

Then I reminded myself to use my legs again, as I had at the wall.

I rose.

It hurt so bad I actually saw stars.

I ignored the pain, ignored the part of me wondering if my hands would ever work right again.

And I rose. Drove through my heels, through my calves and thighs, through my rear end.

Unlike the ring in the wall, the door gave gradually, with a slow and stubborn sound.

It bent.

That bending brought light.

Honest daylight.

Which damn near had a *taste* it was so welcome.

I stopped straining when I'd torqued a U-shaped tunnel near the door's center. Not much of a tunnel—it wasn't a foot and a half at its highest point—but a tunnel.

It'd be a squeeze, but I thought I could get through.

Not yet, though.

Blinking over and over against sudden light, I turned and spotted my savior: that plain-Jane beat-up toolbox. It was black, as I'd pictured it. It was a Sears toolbox no different than ten million others, but it had saved my life.

I dived at the box, fumbled loose the catch, and flipped it open. Would it save me one more time?

No.

I saw hammers and a plane, box wrenches and sockets.

I saw no knife, no blade, no snips, no wire cutters.

I stopped breathing. It wasn't fair. It wasn't fair to get this far and not find a blade in the box.

Don't be a baby. It's black, *for Chrissake, and it's a typical messy toolbox. Check again.*

I knocked the thing over, spilling its contents onto the floor, then riffled the pile with my past-numb hands.

There it was.

A Stanley utility knife, the kind everybody's got in a kitchen drawer or on a basement bench. You know the tool. Press the little tab on top and out slides a triangular bit of blade. Presto.

Except there's no such thing as presto when your hands haven't seen blood flow for fifteen minutes. I wrestled with the knife, ended up using a combo of floor and knees to extend its blade.

Actually cutting the zipties wasn't any easier. Again I used a knee to pin the knife, lying on its side now, to the floor. Got my wrists positioned more or less where they needed to be.

I couldn't feel a damn thing, and I couldn't see so great either.

There was a chance I was going to go through all this and slice an artery.

Wouldn't that be something.

Tough. Go.

I sawed.

It took longer than it should have.

I heard, or maybe felt, a tiny pop.

My left wrist was free.

Pain flooded.

I ignored it.

I flipped myself around and went through the same sawing to free my right hand.

That ziptie popped.

I held up my hands.

They didn't look or feel like they had anything to do with me.

Except for the pain.

Which started heavy and got worse.

"Go," I said out loud.

I knee-walked to the light at the door's bottom, not trusting my hands to help me crawl.

I lay flat, extended my arms through the hole, and made like a worm.

When my head cleared the opening I shut my eyes tight, knowing they'd be useless in sunlight.

I shimmied and wriggled and made myself as flat and small as I could. I got stuck a couple times, but I had a head of steam by then, and I even forced my hands to help me claw out, and no corrugated door was going to hold me.

Then I was out.

And standing.

And alive.

And ready to kill Lobo Soto. Ready to kill him a dozen times over if I had to.

And Tricia Kollar to boot.

Today, everybody would pay for my friend Eudora Spoon's death.

I won't say I'm proud of what I did next, but I won't say I'm embarrassed either.

I spread my feet wide and opened my eyes wide and beat on my chest with both flaming fists. Over and over, for thirty seconds at least.

For every one of those thirty seconds, I made a yell you would've sworn came straight out of a Tarzan movie.

I guess I hoped Lobo Soto was still across the road at Kenny's place.

I guess I hoped he heard me.

I guess I hoped he knew I was coming down the hill to kill him.

CHAPTER FIFTY-FOUR

Warm crisp day, leafless trees.

It was easy to spot Tricia's Infiniti parked in front of Eudora's house.

No more than a couple hundred yards away. As the crow flies.

Right now it felt like a hundred miles. Because whatever they were doing in there—and I had a pretty good idea what it was—they wouldn't be long. Kenny must be putting up a hell of a fight, or they would've been ten miles down the road already.

I fetched the gun from the truck. Then I began to run down the drive, splashing through little runoff rivers.

You'll never mistake my Red Wing boots for track shoes, but once I get a rhythm going, their chunky weight actually carries me along pretty good. Especially downhill.

I ran.

Did I ever.

When the world slows for your head, when you're operating where I was operating, you'd be amazed at the things you notice, even the things that don't matter.

I ran.

An old-school pull-tab from an aluminum can, glinting at the side of the driveway, washed clean by sand and snowmelt. It stuck in my mind because when did they stop making those things—thirty-five years ago?

I ran.

A Staples delivery truck passing on 142 from my right to my left, headed east, its diesel engine needing a tune-up.

I ran.

A tiny cardinal, red as a strawberry, fresh out of the nest and learning to fly. It paralleled me as I leaned into one of the driveway's tight curves, only thirty yards from the road now.

I ran.

As I pounded toward 142, peripheral vision telling me the coast was clear, I caught sounds from Eudora's place: car doors slamming, not quite in unison, *slam*-slam. Then a car starting.

I ran.

Into shade: Eudora's driveway, unlike Harmon's, was surrounded by trees. Facing an uphill slope now, I lost momentum, the weight of my boots no longer helping.

The drive had one kink to it, a right-hand turn from my perspective. I heard Tricia's car accelerating before she and Soto rounded the corner, so I guess I had an edge there.

If a man on foot facing down a thirty-two-hundred-pound car *can* have an edge.

Soto was driving. When he spotted me, he flinched. The car's left-side tires caught one of the few remaining patches of ice, and he damn near lost it.

Which would have been one hell of a break.

Instead:

The Infiniti lurched right, but Soto and the car's computers pulled it back into line. He made the curve, already deep into the gas as the car straightened out.

He came at me with the throttle buried.

Yet I felt like I had all the time in the world. My brain had slowed the world, and my senses were grabbing up everything.

Everything:

Tricia's wide eyes in the passenger seat. Mascara tear-tracks on her cheeks. She wore the look of a woman who'd been somewhere awful. No, who *was* in an awful place, and wasn't sure how she got there or how to come back.

I tried to muster up some sympathy for her.

I failed.

Tricia clutching a seat belt in her right hand. As if she'd automatically set out to snap it shut but had forgotten about it.

Lobo Soto: dead eyes, the eyes of a pro. He wasn't wasting energy wondering what'd gone wrong with his storage-unit plan. That plan was blown. I was right here in front of him. Those were the facts as they stood. He was running time-speed-distance measurements in his head, wanting only to put me out of the picture and get gone.

He wasn't the only one planning, though.

I stopped running and stood still, legs apart, knees loose. I'd been running with the gun in my right hand. Now I extended it in both.

I wasn't ready for the pain in my hands, which were finally flooding with blood. Think back to the worst pins and needles you ever felt when your foot woke up. Then multiply by a hundred. While you're at it, swap those pins and needles for daggers and pickaxes.

But I hung on to that gun.

Soto was closing fast and hard.

He wanted to nail me with the Infiniti's left headlight, but I had a hole card: He couldn't risk driving into a tree.

Instinct told me to dive for the trees as he neared me. I reminded myself that despite all the noise and adrenaline, the car couldn't be going much more than twenty—there just wasn't room in the drive for it to have built a lot of speed.

I'm not much good with a gun, so I had to let them close the distance.

Wait . . . wait . . . wait . . .

When the car looked huge, and I was pretty sure I could hit the driver's side of its windshield, I let loose three times.

CHAPTER FIFTY-FIVE

I got the windshield at least twice.

It cobwebbed.

The car swerved. The car slowed.

But it kept coming.

I stepped aside like a bullfighter.

Soto rolled the steering wheel right just a hair, to avoid shooting off the driveway, and matted the gas.

As he ripped past, I felt the Infiniti's fender brush my jeans, felt the edge of the left front tire whisper across my boot.

Then I crashed my gun, my hand, and my arm through Soto's window.

What else could I do?

The Infiniti's B pillar, the one at the rear edge of the door, hooked me. Damn near separated my shoulder. Or maybe it did, who could tell by then?

The impact made me drop the gun. It fell inside the car because that's where my hand was.

Then I was hanging on while Soto flew toward the road.

I tried to stop that car.

I swear to you I tried. Never wanted anything more in my life.

Soundtrack: the Infiniti's smooth six, pulling hard.

Tricia's screams. "Stop let him go stop let him go!"

She said it over and over, always with that rhythm.

"Stop let him go stop let him go!"

But Soto wasn't letting me go.

And I wasn't letting him go.

I ran alongside the car in a way that would've looked funny in an old silent movie, bicycling my legs in exaggerated motions, trying to keep my feet from being dragged under.

Because if they were, the rest of me would follow.

While he drove and I ran, Soto and I struggled. With my right arm jammed between seat and B pillar, keeping me attached—for the moment—to the Infiniti, I clawed at his throat, his eyes, and the steering wheel with my left.

Soto used his right hand on the wheel and fought me off with his left, slapping my hand, ducking, weaving.

I looked ahead long enough to see that time was his ally, not mine: At the base of Eudora's driveway stood a pair of pillars, five feet tall, built by Andy Spoon of stones from the property.

Eudora'd never liked the pillars—they forced her to inch farther into the road than she liked in order to find an opening in traffic.

I'd talked her out of pulling them down. Mostly because I had a feeling it'd be me did the pulling.

Right now, that didn't look like the best decision I'd ever made.

Because Soto had the Infiniti up to twenty-five or so, and in a few seconds he was going to pound me against one of those pillars, turn up the radio, and cruise all the way to the border.

I had one chance left.

The Stanley utility knife.

It was in my left pants pocket.

I reached for it, pinwheeling my legs like Charlie Chaplin, ignoring Tricia's screams, ignoring the pain in my right shoulder.

I wriggled the knife out of the pocket.

But when my thumb reached for the tab to slide out that nice little triangular sliver of blade . . .

The blade I would pull across Lobo Soto's neck . . .

The blade that would bleed him out the way he'd bled Eudora . . .

My damaged hand couldn't do the job.

It just couldn't.

Popping that blade, a simple thing I'd done ten thousand times, was like trying to thread a needle with ski mittens on.

The knife dropped away, skipping once on the driveway.

Involuntarily, my gaze followed it.

I lost concentration.

My left boot bounced off the car's rocker panel.

I fell away from the Infiniti in an ugly heap, hitting tarmac and stones and tree roots and who the hell knew what else.

The Infiniti bounce-skidded into Route 142, sliding to a semicontrolled stop.

Lying there with half a concussion, I heard something that didn't fit, wasn't right, but I couldn't ID it.

What I did ID was Lobo Soto's wordless roar of triumph as he punched the gas, spun his front tires a little, and drove west.

CHAPTER FIFTY-SIX

Gone.

Gone gone gone.

Gone baby gone.

Long gone, hard to find, like the baseball announcer used to say about home runs.

I dragged myself from the driveway.

I arranged myself into something that was standing.

I hurt everywhere.

In all ways.

I panted.

I had no phone. Tricia had taken it. I couldn't dial 911, or Venezia, or Randall.

So I made for Eudora's house, dreading what I'd find.

The first dozen steps or so, I thought I would just plain fall down. My knees weren't working well, and the ankle that'd been clipped by Tricia's car was swelling inside my boot, and my right shoulder made a Rice Krispies sound when I swung my arm to walk.

"Tough," I said out loud after those first dozen steps didn't kill me. "Kenny."

Then I ran.

Inside, the greyhounds were click-clicking around on the hardwood floors, the way they do when they're unsettled. They were so relieved to see a familiar face that Dandy's wagging tail knocked a photo off a table and Cha Cha piddled.

I made for Eudora's room, now Kenny's room I guessed.

A new sound: sirens.

Good.

Kenny was faceup on the neatly made bed, snoring an ugly snore. Beside him on the flower-pattern quilt: an open laptop computer.

Bedside table: three pill bottles and a near-empty pint of White Horse Scotch.

Now I knew why Soto and Tricia had taken so long down here: They'd decided to make it look like suicide.

Why suicide, with what they figured as a pair of dead bodies— Harmon's and mine—across the road? Who the hell knew? They'd made a bunch of dumb decisions ever since I hauled Kenny out of Van Nuys. Maybe they figured a Kenny suicide would make Tricia next in line for Eudora's dough.

Kenny was in rough shape.

I knew what to do.

Had done it before. More than once.

I stepped to the bed. Flipped Kenny so he faced away from me. Lifted him like a rag doll, clasped my hands beneath his belly, jerked my fists toward me in a half-assed Heimlich.

He made a deep groan in his throat, but that was all.

I jerked my fists again. Adrenaline-jacked, I heard one of his ribs crack. Winced.

Nothing.

Sirens. Loud loud loud now.

One more jerk.

Nothing.

Hell.

Staying put, leaving my right hand where it was, I stuck three fingers from my left into Kenny's mouth. Jammed them as far as I could, then used my right arm to jerk one more time.

It worked.

And how.

One, two, three blurts of puke shot across the room, the quilt, the headboard, you name it.

Kenny Spoon dropped to his knees at the side of the bed like a little kid about to pray.

He sucked oxygen and wheezed and cried and shook.

Through dumb luck, he hadn't puked on the laptop. The shaking of the bed had popped loose its screensaver, and I saw a short Word document. Guessed Soto had plunked out a suicide note by hand. Jeez, the guy thought of everything. Maybe he'd tried forcing Kenny to write one but hadn't had any luck.

Kenny's eyes were showing signs of life. He said, "Wha?"

He said, "Yuh?"

He said, "Tricia. Oh, Tricia."

Me: impatient. The sirens had shut down, which meant the cops must be at Harmon's place. I had to get over there and tell them about Soto and Tricia and the Infiniti.

Not trying to be rough but not really caring one way or the other, I grabbed Kenny's collar and set him on his feet. "Walk," I said. "Don't sit. Walk. Someone'll get you. Hear me?"

"Wuh—walk where?"

"Walk to Harmon's. I need to go now. Just walk. Don't sit, don't stop, don't sleep."

"I can't! I . . ."

But I was done listening.

I ran.

CHAPTER FIFTY-SEVEN

As I ran—staggered, truth be told—to the top of Harmon's driveway, the sun was dropping fast behind me. The shadows were a reminder that even in a freak winter of whipsaw heat waves, February is February.

I began to shiver. I dropped to a knee near a Ford Explorer decked out in the state cops' gray and blue. There were three other cop cars, plus a Bryar Fire and Rescue ambulance, its drivers joking with one another.

"Hey," said a young state trooper, the first to notice me. "Hey! Freeze! Right there!"

I just about laughed at the word "freeze." A couple of snappy action-hero comebacks passed through my head, but all I could do was kneel on the driveway and shiver.

I wasn't running anywhere.

Not anymore.

Not today.

The young cop's hollering must have caused others to spot me, because the next voice I heard was Randall's. "Jesus Christ, help him out!"

Man, was I happy to hear that voice.

Even happier when he dropped to a knee beside me.

I grabbed Randall's jacket with both hands, partly to let him know how important this was and partly to keep from falling over. "Soto and Tricia," I said. "Westbound on 142 in Tricia's Infiniti. Not long ago, less than thirty minutes. Got it?"

He made a sharp nod. "I'll tell Venezia."

"Windshield's busted. They'll need to switch cars soon."

He nodded again and ran uphill, paralleling the row of storage units.

Then one of the EMTs was wrapping a thin aluminum blanket around my shoulders.

"D-d-down . . . there!" I said, chattering and pointing, to the EMT. "He took pills. He's coming this way. Huh-help him out."

I made sure the EMTs got the message, got their ambulance headed downhill.

Then I did a pretty fair imitation of a man having a breakdown.

Randall sprinted back. He helped me into my borrowed truck, hopped in himself, keyed it, and blasted the heat. I could see staties going wild with the crime scene. They were using bolt cutters to open every unit, throwing doors up, rushing in until somebody hollered "Clear!" I caught a glimpse of Venezia supervising it all.

Randall followed my gaze. "Venezia radioed about the Infiniti. They'll get them."

"Unit D-8," I said.

"What about it?"

"Harmon's body."

He looked at me maybe five seconds, then hopped out, ran up the hill again to Venezia, and said something. She paused, nodded, and spoke to her guys. They moved farther uphill, out of my line of sight.

Randall came back holding a man's jacket and maybe the finest thing I'd seen all day: a steaming Dunkin' Donuts medium.

I didn't ask who he took the coffee from. Just sipped, slipped the jacket on, and let the heater warm me.

Randall was quiet.

Me too.

"Sorry," I finally said.

He knew what I meant.

He shrugged. "Probably best this way."

"How'd you end up here?"

"When you ditched me in Marlborough," he said, "I walked back to Route 20. Then I walked west."

"You were supposed to go east," I said. "Home."

"I walked west. Soon a state trooper passed me, clipping right along, lights but no siren. Five minutes later, *another* trooper went flying past." He shrugged. "All this had to be your doing. So I commandeered a vehicle at a stoplight and followed sirens to that awful safe house."

I stared at him. "You commandeered a vehicle."

"I did. And there will be fallout. But the important thing is I found Venezia, who turned out to be in the second car that whipped past."

It made sense. I'd left her that voice mail. She likely thought it a bogus tip, but had a trooper check it out just in case. The trooper had found the evil Brazilian and told Venezia to get there on the double.

"Once I convinced Venezia I was somebody worth talking to," Randall said, "we powwowed. You weren't answering your cell—"

"They took it away."

"This was the logical place to come next. One look at Unit A-2 told Venezia this was a crime scene. She started doing what they do."

Around us, the urgency ratcheted. Troopers ran up and down the hill. Distant sirens told me more ambulances had been called.

"They found him," I said. "D-8."

"I told you my story," Randall said. "Your turn. How'd you know about this Unit D-8? And who took your cell?"

I told it.

I told it all.

It took a while.

When I finished, it was full-bore night. A half-dozen young-looking staties, cadets maybe, here for grunt-work help, were setting up banks of sodium lights. Techs in white booties and bosses in suits milled around.

"Jesus," Randall said, squeezing my shoulder. "You did all right by Eudora, amigo. They'll catch Soto and Tricia. How can they not? You did all right."

"She was a Barnburner," I said.

"Uh-oh," he said, looking past me as a ring rapped my window. "I have a feeling you're about to tell your story all over again."

The ring belonged to Venezia.

CHAPTER FIFTY-EIGHT

I sure did have to tell it again.

More than once.

Nearly two hours later, Venezia found a cadet to drive Randall home. She told him he'd be hearing more about that afternoon's carjacking.

"I commandeered it," Randall said as the cadet walked him down the drive, now lit by a moon it seemed you could reach up and grab like a peach.

I thought I saw half a smile on Venezia's face.

She was okay. She was pretty cool.

The cruisers and K-9 units and techs and bosses had cleared out, as had the Channel 7 news van. Some investigative reporter, a pretty gal, had come striding up the drive. Venezia had told her to scram. The reporter had said Venezia would be hearing from her. Venezia had said she didn't doubt it.

Right now, it was just the two of us and that peach of a moon.

"What's the word on Kenny?" I asked.

"They took him to Milford," she said, meaning the hospital there. "He'll be all right."

"You haven't caught Soto and Tricia," I said. "Or you would've told me."

Long pause. "We found the car in a Stop & Shop lot in Grafton."

"Near the Pike."

"That's the one."

"They could be in Albany by now."

"Could be. But we'll get them."

We were quiet.

"I don't think you will," I said. "No offense. That Soto. He was something."

"If he was as big a something as he thinks he is," Venezia said, "you and Kenny would be dead."

I shook my head. "But as far as self-preservation goes, he's something. Trust me."

We were quiet.

"I gotta ask," Venezia said after a while. "All this because you and Ms. Spoon were in the same AA group?"

"It's a hell of a group."

"Must be," she said. "What's your next move?"

I nodded toward Eudora's house across the road. "Feed and pee a couple of greyhounds."

"That's it?"

"That'll do for now."

"Want a lift down?"

"No," I said, surprising myself. "I believe I'll walk."

It surprised her, too. "Sure about that?"

I shrugged. "You all fed me and coffee'd me and warmed me up. I'm okay now."

"Okay, then."

Venezia climbed into her Explorer, leaving the door open while she buckled up. "Maybe I'll see you around, then."

"Maybe." I tried to smile. Not sure how well that worked out.

She closed her door and started the truck and rolled away.

I stood there. Still as could be, warm in the jacket Randall had found for me.

I stood there because of something.

Something connected to something.

A noise.

I stood still, needing to catch it before it went away.

What noise could it be?

I rewound.

A noise from when Soto shook me off Tricia's Infiniti. I'd wiped out something fierce. I lay in a heap at the edge of Eudora's driveway. The car had bounced and slid and squalled into the road.

You heard something.

Something that didn't fit.

Then you were running for Kenny, and all hell broke loose, and you didn't get a chance to think it through.

Something had lit off that memory.

The something was Venezia closing the door of her cop Explorer.

You heard a car door.

The Infiniti bounced and squalled into 142. Then it took off westbound, spinning its tires just a hair. Between the squalling and the spinning, there was another sound: the sound of a car door thunking shut.

I stood still.

I looked at the moon.

Then I walked.

I walked up the rise of the drive, passing Unit A-2 and a bunch of others.

I walked past the litter the staties had left when they shut down their crime-scene circus.

I walked to the spot where, a million years ago, a river that was now Route 142 had taken a gentle curve.

I walked to the first *E* in WOLVERINE BROS. FREIGHT & STORAGE.

CHAPTER FIFTY-NINE

She was there, of course.
     She sat cross-legged on the E's top horizontal.
The one she'd made love on.
With Harmon.
With me.
I climbed the pipe ladder.
Her back was to me.
Her legs dangled.
She shivered uncontrollably.
I took off the jacket, set it on her shoulders.
"This is Harmon's," Tricia said.
"I guess," I said. "Zip up."
She zipped. "*Was* Harmon's."
"Soto shoved you out of the car, huh?"
"You knew he would."
"Yes."
We were quiet for a while.
"I don't even have the guts to kill myself properly," Tricia said.
"It's a hard thing to do."

"You've tried?"

"In slow motion," I said. "For twenty years."

"That's different. I wanted to sail to my death on Route 142, between Harmon's house and Eudora's. It seemed poetic."

I said nothing.

"You're forcing my hand," Tricia said after a while.

I said, "Nah," and took a short step toward her. Wished like hell for a stanchion or railing up here, something that'd bear my weight.

And hers.

But there was nothing. Just weather-rough plywood.

"The alternative," Tricia said, "is the trial of the century. I can't do that, Conway. I don't deserve that. I deserve . . . I deserve the splat. Don't you want me to splat?"

"No."

"Not even after Eudora? And Harmon? After the lies? After today in A-2?"

"You need to pay," I said. "But there's more than one way to do it."

"Everybody pays. You've said it ad nauseam."

"Soto, too. It may take a while, but he'll pay."

As I spoke, I lay on my belly beside her and felt around with my boot. Found one of the screws that had backed out an inch as the plywood creased and buckled.

It wasn't much.

It wasn't much at all.

It was all I had.

"Quite a moon," I said.

We were quiet again.

"How do things get where they get?" Tricia finally asked. "Plans and intentions. They start in one place, and they end up somewhere completely different."

"They sure do."

"I just wanted . . . I deserved something. *Something*."

I said nothing.

"And then needing to do this leads to needing to do *that* leads to needing to do the other."

I said nothing.

"And before you know it, you're jamming a butter knife in your brother-in-law's mouth so a Mexican gangster can dump pills down his throat." Her voice broke as she said it.

"Kenny's going to be okay," I said.

"That's nice," Tricia said.

I tensed. I stretched. I made sure my boot was hooked on the rusty screw.

"Good old Kenny," Tricia said. "That's nice."

She pushed off.

She would have gotten her wish on Route 142 below.

Except that Harmon's jacket had a hood.

I grabbed it.

By God I grabbed it.

Tricia swung.

Tricia keened.

Tricia bicycled her legs.

When Tricia realized I had her, she quit bucking and thrashing. "How *dare* you!" she hollered. "How *can* you? You . . . *can't!*"

Yes I could.

I got a second hand on the jacket, this time under an armpit.

I felt like I'd separated my ankle—it was the one I'd caught beneath the car a few hours ago, and it was bearing my weight and hers—but I hung on.

Tricia Kollar went limp in my grasp, swaying side to side as I organized myself to heft her. "How *can* you?" she asked again. "Why *would* you?"

I didn't have an answer for that.

So I said nothing.

I just pulled.

I pulled with all my might.